12 . 21 . 12

A NOVEL BY

Killian McRae

OMNIFIC PUBLISHING
DALLAS

Omnific Publishing
P.O. Box 793871, Dallas, TX 75379
www.omnificpublishing.com

First Omnific eBook edition, December 2010
First Omnific trade paperback edition, December 2010

The characters and events in this book are fictitious.
Any similarity to real persons, living or dead,
is coincidental and not intended by the author.

Library of Congress Cataloguing-in-Publication Data

McRae, Killian.
    12.21.12 / Killian McRae – 1st ed.
    ISBN 978-1-936305-53-7
    1. Egyptian —Fiction. 2. Mayan —Fiction.
    3. Cleopatra —Fiction. 4. End of the World—Fiction. I. Title

10 9 8 7 6 5 4 3 2 1

Cover Design and Interior Book Design by Coreen Montagna

Printed in the United States of America

*To Mary Ellen, who serves as a model of how much one person,
when acting with compassion, determination and faith,
can benefit the lives of many.*

DISCLAIMER

The author would like to advise readers that, while many of the historical elements of this book are factual, some measure of artistic liberty has been taken with some minor details.

07.01.09

Prologue

The damned sand got everywhere. In her shoes, in her hair, in her mouth.

Even in her... Well, even in her you-know-what.

Christine Smyth despised Egypt. She hated heat. She hated the desert. She hated nargeelas and kebabs and overcrowded Cairo city buses.

But she especially hated sand.

"Hey, Chrissie. Everything okay down there?"

But above all that, she loved Sheppard.

Christine craned her head back and looked up through the almost blinding portal of light. Shep's head was silhouetted against the late morning sun radiating unyielding rays from above. It almost looked like a halo, she thought, like he was a celestial being. Not that there was anything particularly divine about her husband of two years. He was a kind and compassionate soul, of course, and he loved her with an intensity she never could have dreamed of, but he was not without vices.

One particular vice, the one, in fact, that was the reason she was currently sitting in an excavated chamber in July in the Sahara, attempting to decipher two-thousand-year-old hieroglyphs, was Shep's sense of dogged determination—some might have used the word "stubbornness"—to prove his theory right. Never mind that his whole historic apostasy was based on one tiny fragment of papyrus. It had been found shoved into the leaves of a Coptic Bible in the back of an Ethiopian church. It was nothing of great import, just the records of visits paid by visiting luminaries and guests to one of the minor rulers of the area around the year 30 BCE. This specific entry had recorded the arrival of three children, two boys and a girl, and their female guardian. They were seeking asylum after, the entry claimed, "the Pharaoh, their mother, was killed for daring to war against Rome."

The researcher who made the discovery hadn't thought much of it. A quick internet search had pointed him to Sheppard Smyth's profile on the Harvard website, where he had waxed poetical for his love and professional dedication to Cleopatra VII. He sent Shep an email with a picture, and Shep flew to Addis Ababa the very next morning to verify and retrieve it. After running the necessary test to confirm its age, Shep put forth his theory to the world, the one that would assure his place in history along with the greats of his field. He had no doubt of the children's identity. No doubt, given the nature of the glyphs, the identity of the Pharaoh in question. He had no doubt in his hypotheses. The forces of history had somehow managed to pull off the greatest cover-up of all time: the murder of Cleopatra.

His colleagues had laughed him out of the professional community. Since, Shep had been hell-bent on finding proof. He knew it was true, deep down in his gut. It was almost…instinctive.

Which was why Christine was currently staring at some of the last hieroglyphs ever etched by the ancient Egyptian scribes. Shep believed it, and she believed in him. Besides, she reminded herself, it was Shep's supposed fool's errand that had brought them together.

Christine looked down at her etchings on the crinkly sketch paper. She had traced out all the lines of the carvings in front of her, but hadn't added to them the hint of color still visible in this particular relief. There were missing sections in the stonework, sections that made deciphering the words difficult. Shep was more versed in the ancient tongues than she, and she was sure he wouldn't have such a hard time later. Be as easy as reading the *New York Times* for him. There were a few characters in particular with which she was unfamiliar, ones she couldn't remember having seen before.

"Um, I've got the basics, but I left my pastels in the Jeep," she called up to Shep. "Would you…" Her eyes focused enough to catch Shep's smile.

"Of course, I'll go get them. It's my job, right? To bring color to your life?"

"Yeah, and some water wouldn't hurt!" she shouted back as his head disappeared beyond the edge of the hole. She heard his voice trail off in response, but couldn't quite make out the words.

She leaned back and closed her eyes. For a moment, the breeze above blew at just enough of a downward draft to swirl about in the chamber. Her sense of relief as it caressed her face was short lived; in her relaxed posture she had neglected to hold down the sheaths of paper on her lap. The breeze spread them about the chamber like a child blowing on a dandelion.

"God damn it!" she exclaimed as she leapt off her stool to catch them. Not that they could really go anywhere. Still, she was determined not to have to crawl around in that sand any longer than necessary.

Swatting down her hand, she stopped several sheets from swirling. The top page had been flexing in the breeze, and she cursed aloud when she saw how it now bore a crease down the middle.

And right down the confusing glyphs, bisecting them.

Christine could hardly believe her eyes. She hadn't been able to decipher the glyphs because they were written both forward and backward, one the mirror image of the other, making it difficult to recognize them for what they were.

They were, in fact, Shep's proof.

Above, Shep heard Christine scream his name as he rummaged through the supply bag in the back of the Jeep, and he ran. It wasn't that far of a distance, maybe two hundred meters, but it seemed so far as she shrieked louder and louder. She was saying more than just his name, however. As he got closer, he was starting to make out her repeated phrase.

"Beside us!" he thought he heard her scream. "Shep, it's beside us!"

"Hold on, Chrissie. I'm almost there! I'm c—"

Shaking unlike anything he'd ever felt threw him to the ground. It vibrated his whole person; even his insides seemed to be trembling.

With unbelieving eyes, Shep watched as the entry to the chamber began to loosen around the edges. The cave-in took only seconds. The earthquake wasn't intense—later he would learn it was a mere 5.9—but it was enough to crumble the ancient earthen walls, now dried out and weakened from exposure.

It took two days to dig out Christine's body.

12.15.12

Chapter 1

With a sigh, he threw the greenbacks and one more meaningless night down on the bar.

His cash was gone. He wasn't sure if he was still in possession of his keys. He could only vaguely remember where he'd parked the car when he'd gone for "just a drink or two" several hours before.

Last call had come and gone. But, despite his best efforts, the memories remained. He should have known better; Christine's face was burned too far down in his soul for the alcohol to reach so deeply.

The best Shep could hope for on these occasions was achieving numbness. He measured his success against his current situation. A guy sitting down the bar was eying him with repulsion like Shep was some vagabond off the street. Shep didn't give a damn. He hadn't showered in five days, and even he noticed his own smell was less than pleasant. Who the hell cared? On the TV, some reporter was gabbing on and on about the Mayan calendar and the end of…yada, yada, yada.

Numbness achieved. Whooptie-fricking-doo.

He rose and stared blankly at the barstool, trying to subdue the recollection of her eyes and sienna lips. Christine's eyes—so unique. Hazel irises, but with a rim of amber around the edges. For the past year, he had borne her memory like a shield against living, wore it like a cloak against happiness.

The barman cast him a concerned expression. "Need us to call you a cab, doc?"

He hated being called "doc." It made him feel old. He was only thirty-seven, damn it. Maybe not a young man any more, but hardly prepping his application for the AARP. That's why he always had the students call him "Professor Smyth," or even better, just Shep.

He returned the barman's glance, and answered, only slightly slurred, "No, Nick, I'll be fine."

The cold December air as he stepped from the pub brought him a tinge of sobriety. Enough to get him home safely, anyway. The keys had been in his inside jacket pocket, just like usual. The car had been parked in front of Lillie's Flower Shop, just like usual. Twenty minutes later, he stumbled into his one-bedroom townhome on Boston's South End, feeling empty and alone. Just like usual.

Shep surrendered his body to the couch, not even bothering to remove his clothes or his coat. One shoe made it off, but then the other didn't seem worth the time and effort. He wanted to sleep and quickly. The last thing he wanted to be conscious of was how crushingly lonely the house was, not to mention the upstairs bedroom.

He couldn't have slept an hour when the phone echoed through the nighttime hallways. The answering machine no longer worked; it still lay in pieces in a box on the counter, smashed the first time he had heard Christine's voice posthumously answer a call. He hoped the caller would give up, but no such luck. After the tenth ring, Shep rolled over and rose reluctantly. Pulling the old-fashioned desk rotary phone receiver off its base, he fought back an alcohol-induced belch.

"Hello?"

Only silence. He waited.

"Hello?" he beckoned again, this time with an edge of annoyance.

"Shep? Sheppard Smyth?"

The south-of-the-border voice was vaguely familiar, but he couldn't place it exactly.

With his free hand, he rubbed his sleep-laden eyes. "Yes, this is Professor Smyth, though I'm not accustomed to taking phone calls at," he focused on the grandfather clock in the corner, "three-thirty a.m."

"I am sorry, but this couldn't wait until morning," the caller continued, and the faint image of an olive-skinned man with a healthy black beard began to formulate in Shep's mind. "I don't know if you remember me? This is Hector Gonzalez. We attended Cambridge together."

As soon as he heard the name, he knew the person. Hector Gonzalez had obtained as much notoriety in the archaeology of Mesoamerican cultures as Shep had in Ptolemaic Egypt. They were both at the forefront of their fields. But whereas Shep counted himself fortunate to have the tenacity of tenure that academia granted to fall back on, Hector had recently gone the "clay for pay" route and ventured into the world of corporate-funded digs. Or so Shep had heard.

In truth, Shep hadn't heard anything directly from Hector Gonzalez in many a year. There had been a short email of condolences when Christine died, but he had never replied to it. Why, then, was he calling out of the blue, and in the middle of the night?

"Hector? Of course. How have you been?"

He chuckled softly. "Fine, thank you. Shep, look, I know it's very late, so I'll get to the point. I find myself in need of an expert in your particular area who can fly down and verify an artifact's authenticity, and I was wondering if you could assist me. I mean, when we found Cleo's statue, I knew I had to call you first."

He warily rubbed the sleep from his eyes. "Cleo? Well, there's nothing too unique about that. And I just finished teaching this term and was looking forward to—" *being left alone to wallow in my own self-pity* "—getting a little down time to—"

"Wait!" Hector exclaimed, and despite himself Sheppard flinched a bit. "Understand first that this is an undisturbed site dating circa 1100 AD. We also found some Arab and Norse artifacts in the same layer."

Sheppard sighed. He was beginning to grow tired of the intrusion. "Very interesting, but still I don't see—"

"Ask me where we found them," Hector interjected.

The fragments of the find and the mystery they induced were beginning to form in Shep's booze-hazed mind. Hector was an Olmec expert. Why would he be doing an excavation in the old world?

Shep bit. "Okay, where?"

Silence for a moment, then a single paradigm-shattering word. "Mexico."

Sheppard took a gulp of air as his heart raced. "I'll be on the first flight in the morning."

Socks, underwear, aftershave, Levi's, toothbrush, Passport abused beyond recognition. Everything was tossed haphazardly into the suitcase lying open on his bed. Would he need a coat? It was early winter in Boston, and old Jack Frost hadn't waited to stretch his arms. It was easily hovering around twenty degrees outside his townhouse, but he *was* on his way to Mexico.

Shep glanced down at his watch. Already 5:30 a.m. He had burned off his drunk, running around like a headless chicken with a vendetta for the past two hours, but he wasn't exactly sober either. The taxi had been arranged for a six o'clock pick up.

With no time to ponder, Shep tossed the leather jacket over the other random objects collected from the smash-and-grab through his drawers and closet. Almost as if from a scene from an old Marx Brothers film, Shep pulled the bag's other half closed, and found it was too stuffed to zip. Heaving it to floor, he sat down on the lid as he slid his hands over the edges. He hadn't known metal could groan, but groan the zipper did as he forced it into submission, sealing the bag closed.

Each stair was smacked on his way down as he heaved his luggage with him. Setting the bag by the door, Shep wandered into the kitchen. A swig of cranberry juice straight from the jug both turned his stomach and awakened his senses. As he closed the refrigerator door, he found himself staring into the most loving, tender pair of big hazel eyes he had ever seen.

Christine's photo was all over the townhouse, but that didn't mean he looked at her anymore. He couldn't. He was too ashamed, feeling like he had somehow let her down. If he had managed to move a little quicker or not looked through her bag for the missing jade-colored pastel, he could have gotten to her in time to save her. And since her death, what had he done to honor her memory? Found the evidence to show his theory right, the theory *she* died in trying to prove? No, he hadn't even tried to re-excavate the site after the rescue crew pulled her body from the sinkhole.

Maybe this was his chance. Maybe whatever Hector found in Mexico could finally give him the closure he needed and her memory deserved. And maybe, just maybe, he'd find a way to move on.

With a deep sigh, Shep's gaze moved to the countertop where lay the remnants of the couple's answering machine. Well, if he had any hope of moving on, best to start slow. He had actually bought a replacement machine a year ago, but just couldn't bring himself to pull away the collection of small bits left from the other. Even if it didn't work, Christine had touched it…

So, what? he suddenly thought. She touched the coffee pot too, but that hadn't kept him from buying a Krups when it'd broken. Right, time to move on.

Shep had just finished setting the time on the new machine when his door bell rang. He looked at his watch again. 6:03 a.m. Taxi was ready.

Switching the answering function on, he made his way out to the door, grunted as he yanked his bag to his side, and locked up.

And, of course, that was when the phone rang.

Shep's shoulders fell as he let out a slow, long breath and looked over his shoulder at the cabby.

"I can wait if you want," he declared in a thick Boston accent, "but meter's running."

Shep pressed his ear to the glass, trying to hear the caller's message if any. It came across garbled.

"Mr. Smyth…Katherine…calling from…at the request of…to invite you   "

Damn telemarketers.

He shook his head as a slightly-amused smile crossed his face. "My first answering machine in three years, and somehow *they* know to call right away."

Chapter 2

The first direct flight out of Boston to Mexico City departed at 9:43 a.m. From there, he would transfer to smaller plane to Veracruz. The dig site was ten kilometers southwest of San Lorenzo.

This wild goose chase was likely career suicide. Shep knew that with striking clarity despite his in-flight hangover. However, few questioned his tenacity as a serious academic anymore. Once, yes, he had boasted a reputation of worth. After finishing his PhD at Cambridge a decade earlier, he had risen to the top of his field and risen fast. Harvard had snatched him away from a two-year stay with Imperial College. By the time he was thirty, Sheppard was a tenure track professor at one of the world's most prominent universities and could claim digs on three continents. By his early thirties, he had met, fallen in love with, and wed one of his junior research associates, Christine Cezanne. By thirty-four, he had begun to show up on the occasional History Channel or PBS special, right next to good old Zahi Hawass himself.

When Ethiopia happened, the email about the discovery of the papyrus fragment found wedged between the pages of an eight-hundred-year-old Bible had seemed a godsend. Every great archaeologist needed a discovery that rocked man's conceptions about the past to earn his own place in history. Howard Carter had King Tut's tomb, and Sheppard Smyth would have Cleopatra's murder. He had always been a fan of Cleo's, ever since he caught the Elizabeth Taylor flick in high school. Learning the truth beyond the fiction of Hollywood had ignited an obsession in him with the last Queen of the Egyptian Empire. He probably knew more about Cleo than he knew about many of his closest relatives. And if there was one thing he knew about Cleo, it was how self-centered and self-aggrandizing she was. She seduced two titans of Rome just to secure her power. To Shep, that didn't seem like someone who was suicidal. She was murdered; it was the only thing that seemed plausible to him. He only had to find out by whom and why to claim his place in history. Most of his colleagues thought he was crazy; the accusations of insanity from his unorthodox hypothesis tarnishing the bright star he had become.

Christine, however, had stood firmly at his side.

Since her death, Shep had devoted all his non-teaching time to researching the last tendrils of hope for their theory. When he wasn't drunk, anyway. Devoted study of the effects of Jameson on the test subject hadn't resulted in any greater clarity, and the university was demanding more traditional research and more credible results. He'd refused, declaring that if he gave up the hunt for Cleo's killer, Christine would have died in vain. He needed to do it, he argued, for both of them. Unspoken, however, was a sense that he owed the revelation of the truth to Cleo as well.

The plane touched down in Veracruz in the late afternoon. Hector couldn't leave the dig site, he had said, but would send his assistant, Vick, to retrieve Shep from the airport. Shep waited patiently for Vick to arrive at the baggage claim. He glanced about the smoky room filled with aging tourists, a wide spectrum of the local specimens, and the occasional member of the clergy. After forty-five minutes, the angle of the sun sinking in the sky, he became annoyed at Vick's absence and approached the information desk to ask in his broken Spanish for hotel information, when he heard a woman's voice call out his name across the way.

"Dr. Sheppard Smyth?"

He turned with a grimace, assuming—yet again—that someone had recognized him from TV. It happened. Sheppard reached into his pocket to pull out the ever-ready pen to sign an autograph, when he saw her.

Olive skin was perfectly framed over a delicate twist of hip. She wore a knee-length white skirt and sleeveless top, a wide-brimmed hat topping off the ensemble. She wasn't excessively tall, but stood a few inches shorter than Shep, and he realized that this was an illusion; she wore three-inch heels to enhance her stature. No make-up, yet her cheek bones seemed to shimmer and her lips were an entrancing pale pink. Her hair fell in alternating honey brown and amber blond curls over her shoulders, down nearly the full length of her back.

The corner of her mouth rose when a speechless Shep finally succeeded in smiling.

"I'm sorry I'm late, professor," she subtly apologized in a tone that suggested, playfully, that she wasn't sorry at all.

"I'm sorry, do I..." He couldn't quite place her, though somehow he felt the oddest sense of familiarity with her. "Do I know you?"

"I believe you're expecting me? I'm Dr. Gonzalez's assistant, Victoria Kent."

"*You're* Vick Kent?" Praise be to unisex names. She nodded, her cheeks blushing a bit. "Well, hello, *Vick*. Yes, I'm Dr. Smyth. Um, *Shep*, if you don't mind."

Shep extended his hand and shuddered as Victoria wrapped hers around his.

"A pleasure to finally meet you, Shep."

She had a glimmer in her eye that seemed out of place, matched by an oddly bubbly smile. If he didn't know better, he would say she was...star-struck? Or, perhaps, proud?

A scuffle in the corner of the baggage claim area drew the attention of both of them. A scrubby man in dirty, brown clothes held a sign in front of him covered in sloppily painted letters. Security obviously didn't care for his presence as they tried to coax him out. With a threatening glance, the man stood his ground, yelling, screaming, trying to make eye contact with whomever would meet his gaze. At this moment, it was Shep. Across the expanse of the room, he mouthed something to Shep, his eyes almost pleading. Shep almost felt as though he should get closer, hear him out, but the *policia* had had enough. They belted the man in the stomach, forcing him to double over as another officer handcuffed him from behind.

"Shep, we should go." Victoria's voice brought him out of his gawking.

"Do you speak Spanish?" he asked her.

"He wasn't speaking Spanish; he was speaking Yucatec."

Damn. "I don't suppose you speak Mayan?"

"'Beware the end of the world,'" she returned without pause as she turned from the scene. "The people in these parts of Mexico are still close to their traditions. The Mayan calendar says the world is supposed to end in a week. Maybe you've heard of it, 12.21.12?"

Of course, he remembered. It was this decade's Y2K, a passing fad that gave cable TV something to hype on slow news days.

Which meant it was total bunk.

Victoria continued. "I'm afraid there are some superstitious types who believe that mumbo jumbo. This way, Shep. We should try to get back to camp before the rain sets in."

Victoria—Vick—led him to a rugged, mud-strewn 4x4 in the small parking lot outside the Veracruz airport. Without asking, the gently-curved, probable runway model took his heavily loaded luggage and tossed it effortlessly into the back of the Jeep. She blushed slightly when she caught the dumbstruck look on Shep's face.

"Oh, don't let these little ladies fool you," she offered as she ran one hand over the bicep of her opposite arm. "The digs bulk up a girl. I'm just lucky to have some genetics in my favor that keep me from going all Red Sonja."

Shep laughed despite himself. "Red Sonja?" he chuckled. "You're a little young to know anything about Brigitte Nielsen, aren't you?"

Victoria leaned over to pull her high-heeled shoes off and tossed them on the floor of the back bed, next to Shep's bag. She glanced up at him with a wry half-smile.

"Maybe. How old do I look?"

He shrugged. He always hated when women asked that question. Christine had thought it was an unfair position to put a man in. Guess too high, and the woman would be insulted. Guess too low, and the woman would think you were patronizing.

He eyed up Victoria's face for a moment. Her skin was smooth and silken, no laugh lines at the corners of her mouth. But her body was that of a fully mature woman, and she was the assistant to a prominent archaeologist. She was probably an advanced grad student or a postdoc.

"Twenty-five?"

She gave a quick nod. "Sounds about right."

Shep gasped next when Victoria pivoted the top half of her body and started pulling down the zipper of her skirt where it clung suggestively to her hip.

Again, she blushed. "Sorry, Shep, didn't mean to take you off guard. It's just…"

The flaps of fabric fell left and right, and she quickly shimmied the skirt down over her hips and past her thighs. Underneath she wore traditional field clothes; Shep saw that a very thin layer of khaki had been rolled up and secured with safety pins. Victoria opened the hinges and rolled the pants down, the material covering her legs to mid-calf. She followed suit by taking off her refined white top to reveal a somewhat dirt-touched undershirt beneath. The discarded clothing was tucked into a small duffle bag, and it too was laid on the floor of the Jeep's storage area.

"…I had a meeting that ran late in town before I came to the airport, and field gear was hardly appropriate."

Shep bobbed his head and cleared his throat. He hated to admit that the image of her undressing (despite the less than stimulating clothing underneath) had temporarily diverted his attention from matters at hand.

They drove away from the Veracruz Airport in silence; the whipping of the wind past their ears made conversation impossible. Shep felt anxious at the opportunity to examine Hector's discovery. He wondered if there had been any developments since his conversation less than twenty-four hours ago with his old colleague.

"Tell me, Miss Kent," he at last asked when they had reached more rural roads where the trees were becoming as thick as the humid air he was attempting to breathe, "where did Hector find you?"

"I'm not at liberty to say."

Her tone wasn't at all rude, but it was most definitely firm. Shep cocked his head to the side.

"Sworn to secrecy?" he joked.

Victoria didn't crack a smile. "Something like that. Our underwriter has us under strict guidelines for sharing any information about the dig or ourselves. I'm not permitted to tell you anything beyond my name unless you've signed a non-disclosure agreement, and anything further only if you meet our security protocols. Sorry, Shep," she pointed at the radio of the Jeep, and to a small blinking red light on the FM dial, "but our protocols are fiercely enforced."

Shep was confused. "Underwriter?"

"Kronastia," Victoria returned with a smirk.

Shep rubbed his weary eyes.

Kronastia? *Dmitri* Kronastia? Why was an infamous Russian investor/mafia boss financing a dig of Mayas ruins on the Yucatan peninsula?

What had Shep gotten himself into?

"Is he…um, Kronastia, is he…here?"

She laughed and shook her head, pulling an errant strand of hair from her eyes. "No, he hasn't gotten too involved on the ground level." Shep relaxed into his seat too soon. "He has henchmen here to do it for him."

Chapter 3

Shep had only been to Mexico once before. It was in college, spring break, junior year. He didn't remember much beyond landing at the airport and riding with his two friends in the taxi to the beachside cantina. Still, he was certain he had been less at risk of personal harm and/or death on that trip of drunken debauchery than he was as they approached the mafia-funded archaeological dig.

Victoria navigated through a series of ever more rugged roads. The paved surface gave way to gravel and gravel to mud. At the point they were now, he didn't know exactly how to describe the surface the Jeep was barely sliding over. Mud would have been a welcomed improvement.

Finally as the engine groaned, making its way up a slight pitch after a sharp left turn, Shep could make out the outline of work tents and several other equally utilitarian and rugged vehicles parked near an encampment. Even a quarter mile away, he could see the bustling of workers running around the camp as though they were practicing a fire drill. The work tents were much smaller than those his teams usually used in Egypt or Israel or Turkey. But this was the jungle, he reminded himself. The trees here were not so closely collected as to disallow any shelter, but instead just required the use of smaller tents.

Victoria steered cautiously back down the slope and parked between two large, thick-trunked trees. Shep noticed as the roar of the engine died away that the red light on the radio dial continued to blink steadily. He wasn't surprised, then, to also hear the low buzz of gears turning, a sound he knew well from multiple visits to secured facilities in Egypt. It was the distinctive hum of a camera lens pivoting and zooming in. Only, where the camera was, he didn't know.

"*Dios mio*, if it isn't the great Sheppard Smyth!"

The voice was undeniably Hector's. As Shep pulled his body from the seat of the car, using the roll bar for leverage, he turned and saw his former classmate's distinctive beard-bearing visage smiling from across camp. Shep grinned despite his usual unease with most people on any social level, and the fact that his fatigue from not having slept in the last thirty-six hours—several of those hours spent in a drunken state—was beginning to gain on him. When at last Hector stood shoulder-to-shoulder with him, he accepted the hug with only a slight twinge of discomfort.

"Good flight?" Hector asked as he pulled away and placed his hand on Shep's shoulder.

Shep grunted. "Decent enough to Mexico City. I have to admit, though, I get a little nervous when the pilot has to get out on the Tarmac and start the propeller turning. That second flight scared the living day-lights out of me."

Hector gave him a warm-hearted smile. "Still, good of you to come so quickly. And good timing, too. We just got dispatch from our lab up north that Hurricane Helene has shifted and is heading our way. You wouldn't have been able to fly in if you had waited any longer. We're trying to secure camp and get upland before she hits."

Shep groaned at the thought of the sleep he so desperately needed and now was almost certain to be denied. Behind him, he heard a plop as Victoria pulled his bag from the back bed of the Jeep. She quickly picked it up, along with her own, and stood behind Hector, awaiting movement or command.

Hector continued. "Luckily, you got here before we've finished prep-ping the main site for the storm." He leaned in closely as Shep turned and studied Victoria's patient stance, crooked, knowing smile, and twinkling eyes, and whispered teasingly, "Do you want to have a little peek at her?"

Redness filled his cheek as he turned quickly from Victoria's gaze, and tried to play innocent. "Who?"

"Cleopatra, of course."

He breathed a sigh of relief. "Um, yeah, sure."

Shep took in the scene as Hector led him down a mild, well-trodden slope. Little seemed out of the ordinary. After all, while the landscape might vary, Shep was no stranger to digs. He had been the primary di-rector of eight to date, and had served on the crews of countless others through high school, college, and grad school. Nothing here was out of place: the scrambling bodies going about to and fro, the makeshift tents, the scattering of the personal belongings of the crew. Even the occasional religious iconography seemed right at home.

The only thing that really seemed out of place was Victoria. It wasn't that archaeology students and professionals were stereotypically unattractive. On the contrary, Shep thought Christine had been one of the most beautiful women in all of creation. Oddly, it occurred to him that Victoria and Christine were a little alike in that regard. Victoria's beauty set against khakis and jungle seemed wrong somehow. He could picture her in a floor-length mink coat and a fine silvery gown.

Much to his shame, he could also picture her out of one.

Victoria did not belong here, an archaeological version of "one of these things is not like the other." Women as alluring as her were often reluctant to subject themselves to the rigors of a profession that required constant exposure to the elements and sometimes meant living for days at a time without a shower or modern plumbing.

As she outpaced them, Shep took in the lines of her figure from behind. He would have thought that when she changed out of her original attire—more suited for Venice than Veracruz—it would have muted the instantaneous physical attraction he felt for her. It did no such thing. As he watched her long, slender legs work over the terrain with his luggage weighing her down to one side, he felt a stirring of something...corporeal. It puzzled him, made him cognizant of the stupor in which he had lived much of the last few years. He hadn't felt that way since Christine. After a moment's pause to admire how the bottom fold of her khakis rubbed the back of her calves as she walked, he dismissed it. Widower or no, he was still a man, and subject to a man's yearnings.

Victoria pulled ahead of Hector and turned off to the left, up an embankment, and toward what looked like a collection of heavy-duty tool sheds.

"Hurricane shelters," Hector answered without being asked. "We've spent all day loading the technical gear and cots in them. Shouldn't have to wait it out too long. We'll only be catching the outer rim of the storm. A couple of hours, tops, and at night, no less."

Shep took advantage of the private moment with Hector. "Where'd you find her?" he asked with a gesture of his head in Victoria's direction.

Hector gave a wry smile as he saw Shep's eyes tracking his assistant.

"She found me, actually," he answered as they reached a sealed door that connected to a small building with a sharply slanted roof. Shep understood it was the covering of a stairway leading to the primary dig site. What he didn't understand was why Hector needed to punch in a string of numbers, and have both a fingerprint and retinal scan before the door opened. "She wrote me an email about three months back. Said she had been given an internship from Plaxis Corp. and my project was one of those offered in their schedule. Sent me her resume. Very impressive. Not widely studied, but apprenticed with a legend."

Shep raised an eyebrow. "A legend?" he chuckled softly. "Not many of those any more. Just who is this legend?"

Hector opened the door further and gestured Shep inside. He entered without hesitation, then felt all the oxygen exit his lungs when he heard Hector say somewhat smugly, "Anathea Hermapolous."

Shep's eyes quickly tracked to Hector's, looking there for some indication of jest. "Anathea Hermapolous?" he gasped. Hector's smile was plastered ear to ear as he nodded. "Impossible. *The* Anathea Hermapolous?"

"Talked to her myself to verify it," Hector reassured.

Shep was clearly incredulous. "*You* talked to Anathea? How? She's a recluse. She hasn't talked directly with anyone in thirty years."

Not to mention, she's ancient, thought Shep, though his gentlemanly upbringing told him such should go unsaid. As the story went, Anathea Hermapolous had been all of ten years of age when she and her father had been invited to visit a friend, Howard Carter, at his dig site in Egypt. Anathea was the only living person who had witnessed the discovery of King Tut's tomb. The event had sprouted a fascination with Egypt in her, and by the time the Second World War rolled around twenty years later, she was already a prominent member of the archaeological community.

Like countless others, Shep had spent years trying to meet her. After the war, she had gone on to discover several more no-less thrilling, if not as prominent, sites in the Middle East. In 1953, she abruptly stopped her work. Few had had the privilege of speaking to her since, even though she would occasionally publish or agree to author a preface to a book or special issue journal.

Shep wondered how Victoria had managed to worm her way into Anathea's good graces and company where so many through the years had failed. Including Shep, who—in a fit of desperation after Christine's death—had slept outside the gates of her Cairo mansion for three days in a last-ditch attempt to see her. Yeah, didn't work.

"I was only able to make contact with her through Plaxis," Hector added. "Don't be too jealous, Shep. It was a thirty-second conversation, and the line was full of static. Could barely make out a word."

That statement brought Shep back to the moment.

"Plaxis?" he asked. "You do realize Plaxis is a front for—"

"—the Russian mafia," Hector finished for him. "I'm well aware. Even then, they were reluctant to establish contact. The man who finally provided me the number only did so with my promise not to tell anyone it was him who gave it to me. And, further, Victoria came from Plaxis, so you see why else I thought hiring her was a good idea, regardless of her connection to Anathea."

Shep nodded and looked to the iridescent light of any number of bulbs strung haphazardly over the path before him. With a deep breath, he started his way down the stairs and into the pit.

The smell of semi-saturated soil told him at least parts of the site were only recently excavated. Or, alternatively, digging was still going on. As he reflected on the firm-looking state of the earthen walls and descended the stairs, Shep found himself a little jealous of Hector's work environment. No doubt the criss-crossing of the roots of the trees and other plants of the rain forest above made the ground around them self-supportive. It was the opposite of digging in Egypt, where damned sand got into every nook and cranny, some nooks that Shep, prior to working in Egypt, had been blissfully unaware he even had.

Shep reached the bottom of the stairs, Hector at his back, and turned up a make-shift passage only to come face to face with the largest, gun-bearing Ché Guevara impersonator he had ever seen. The titan eyed him with instant disdain and scowled instead of spoke. It proved a very effective form of communication for him, the international language of *Grr*…

Hector came around Shep's side and huffed. "José, *por favor!*"

Hector pushed the guard aside and strode up the passageway. The guard, none too happy at being so readily dismissed, grumbled something in Spanish. Shep didn't understand Spanish, but could pick out *la politica de Plaxis* and *no entrada* with ease. He wasn't supposed to be here, and Hector had to have known it.

Hector yelled something back in a clearly affronted tone. Shep looked over his shoulder as El Hulk-o burbled some more highly accented statements and took a cell—or maybe a satellite phone way out here?—out of his pocket as he turned to ascend the stairs. Hector waved his hand dismissively at Shep's worried expression. Shep continued to follow his friend down the passageway against his better judgment.

"If my being here is going to cause some kind of problem, Hector…" Shep trailed off.

"Pfft! Plaxis and Kronastia like to think they're in charge of this dig," he scoffed. "Just because they pay the bills doesn't mean they can keep me from getting your consultation. Their screening process can take weeks. I need confirmations now. If this is authentic, we have a whole other thing going on here beside a Mesoamerican settlement."

"Just because you happen to find one Cleo statue doesn't mean there's not a logical explanation. Could be something as simple as a Nazi escapee cubbyhole for stolen treasure. They're all over Central and South America."

Not that that seemed likely, nor could Shep particularly think of what other logical explanation there would be. Still, he was a professional and an academic. He knew that one oddly placed artifact did not a paradigm shift make. It could, however, inspire a Time-Life series or cult following.

They reached a chain-link fenced security gate. Hector fished a set of keys from his pocket and selected a small silver one to shove into the lock. With a wince from the sound of the door accordion-folding as Hector pushed it and taking two steps beyond the barrier, Shep felt his breath catch in the back of his throat.

No, one artifact did not a paradigm shift make.

But eleven certainly did.

Jaw dropping didn't seem an apt description, but full cranial detonation? That seemed about right.

First, Shep's eyes focused acutely in on the object of his piqued interest: Cleo. It was a small statuette, only about ten inches high, clearly carved of alabaster. She stood erect, her head held high, her shoulders back, her arms stationed serenely and languidly at her side. The statue represented her with tight braids and the traditional crown of the pharaohs. This was his Cleo, of that he had no doubt. He knew her face better than any other woman in his life, better even than Christine's perhaps. Christine had sometimes been jealous of Shep's obsession with Cleopatra VII, but mused afterward that of all the mistresses her husband could choose, probably the least threatening to their marriage was an Egyptian queen who had died nearly two thousand years before Christine was even born.

"Yep, this is legit. Small statuettes like these were often kept in temples on the far edges of the empires, so the Pharaoh could be worshiped along with the other gods. What did you do for dating?" Shep asked as he ran his fingers ever so slightly over Cleo's cheek, a chill racking him upon making contact with the smooth stone.

"Optical, but we're also running labs using some other methods to confirm."

Shep began eying the other objects on the work table as well. *None* of them made sense.

"Didn't the Olmec civilization die out before the birth of Christ?"

Even Cleo's death in 30 BCE preceded that event by two decades. Shep's grin faltered when he realized the discredit to the discovery even dating it would give. There was unlikely, and then there was impossible. An Egyptian artifact in a pre-Columbian site was, frankly, impossible. The first European civilizations didn't arrive into this part of Mexico until the sixteenth century. If this had been a Maya or Aztec site, the improbable object would be just as curious, but not chronologically impossible; both later cultures of the region suffered from the West's encroachments. The Olmec, however, predated European arrival by twelve hundred years, so Eurasian artifacts in their era just didn't compute.

Hector gave a chuckle. "Around 300 BCE, but this cache was found in a dug out home. This soil layer dates from around 500 BCE. Definitely Olmec, and several secondary dig sites nearby confirm it. But this site specifically where the cache was found? It dates later, around 1100 CE. We've found evidence to suggest that there was also a small Mayan settlement on this site around that time. But the placement at the center of the Olmec site so precisely, and the depth to which the home was dug? It seems unlikely that it's coincidence."

"And then there's these," Shep added, motioning with his hands to the objects on the table. "Have you had any luck in determining their source?"

Hector pointed at a small golden object some two inches tall and an inch across, similar to a fleur-de-lis in shape with several gems mounted on its surface. "This appears to be Mamluk in origin. Some sort of pendant. And this one over here…" He pointed this time at a small green container, a little bowl with a fitted lid. "This is carved jade, and the markings on the bottom place it in the Tang Dynasty, circa 730 CE. The ring over there, we've determined that's Visigoth. And the—"

"Hector, wait a minute." A fever was coming over Shep as he eyed the objects and tried to determine his role in the current situation. "Visigoth, Mamluk, Chinese…If it was just Cleo, I'd get why I'm here. But with all these other artifacts present?" He exhaled and ran his fingers through his hair. "Why me?"

"Because," Hector answered plainly, "I need you to read the scroll."

"What scroll?"

Hector only grinned in response.

"That little jade box?" He motioned again at the object. "Inside was a small papyrus scroll, Egyptian hieroglyphs, and some sort of amulet. The lid was sealed with resin. Whoever put it there meant for it to survive. We've sent the amulet to a Plaxis lab in Mexico City for testing just this morning; we couldn't figure out what type of stone it was. The scroll we've already relocated to one of the shelters up hill."

Shep was nearly spluttering now. "What does it say?"

"We were kind of hoping you would tell us."

Shep looked back at the collection before him. His mind was struggling to comprehend its significance. True, it could all turn out to be fraud; only he didn't expect someone of Hector's caliber to become involved in such a fiasco. The scientist in him was screaming that this couldn't be real—the explanation may be hard to grasp, yet it had to be there—but the little boy who had dug up arrow heads in his Oklahoma backyard was bristling with anticipation.

Hector broke into his train of thought. "You do understand what this means, Shep?"

He nodded his acknowledgement. "I think so," he said as he rubbed his eyes, becoming aware in the process of the greasy film on his face and the grime only international travel seems to induce. "I just—I can't—I mean, finding a collection like this in Europe or Asia? That alone would be monumental. But this? Here? In the New World?"

At this, Hector clicked his tongue and shook his head disapprovingly.

"You Eurasian archaeologists and your arrogance about time!" he retorted. "The civilizations in this so called 'New World' can be traced back nearly as far as any on the Tigris and Euphrates. Some of them were even more civilized and sophisticated than their contemporaries in your 'Old World.' What it means, though, Shep, is—"

"—somebody crossed the ocean almost four hundred years before Columbus," Shep cut off Hector.

Again, Hector looked disappointed. "We already knew that," he grumbled. Shep may have simply been too tired to scramble for the name;

the lack of sleep and jet lag were about to destroy him. "Leif Ericson, Shep. He made it to the east coast of modern-day Canada in roughly 1000 CE."

"Yeah, but—" Shep coughed. "I mean, seriously, Hector? It's one thing to say someone made it here over the ocean. But are you suggesting someone trekked thousands of miles over the North American continent? Doesn't that seem…impossible?"

Hector pinched the bridge of his nose. Shep was on a roll in letting down his old friend. "You're missing the biggest mind fuck of them all, here, Shep." The cursing seemed unlike him, perhaps a side effect of being financed by Russian mafiosi. "Whoever brought these things here—it's like they were bringing mementos back. These are souvenirs, Shep."

Then, the shock set in. Not only did this mean that someone in pre-Columbian times had toured Europe, Asia, and Africa. It meant someone had gathered these items to bring back.

Which meant that the traveler had *originated* in the New World.

"Holy shit!" Shep exclaimed.

But it wasn't the insight that he had just had that caused these words to tumble out of Shep's mouth.

It was the realization that a gun was pointing squarely at his head.

Chapter 4

Shep would like to have been able to say that it was the first time in his life a gun had been drawn and pointed at him. It wasn't. This marked occasion number three. A little devilish voice in the back of his head snickered. *Third time's the charm.*

Perhaps as the result of being well trained by a childhood of watching *Miami Vice* and *MacGyver*, Shep instinctively put his hands out to the side, both as a show that he was unarmed and that he would oblige whatever command the cold-eyed José would give him. He kept his eyes downcast, looking up only enough to be able to see if José would try making any further assault upon him.

Hector had probably never watched *MacGyver* or even heard of *Miami Vice*. Shep looked on with a mixture of dread and awe as Hector wheeled around and began spouting Spanish obscenities quick enough to disprove—or was that, confirm?—Einstein's Theory of Relativity. José, however, matched his rebuffs tit for tat. After several tense moments, each with Shep wondering if indeed it was his last, José lowered the gun and Hector motioned nonchalantly for Shep to follow him aboveground.

Shep took one last look at the table of artifacts before complying, trying to fix each in his memory. With a sigh, he eyed Cleo. There was nothing particularly unique about the statuette itself, save for its point of discovery. Now, Shep was more anticipatory of seeing the scroll from the little jade box that Hector had mentioned, and hoped the storm about to hit didn't put off that blessed union for too long.

They couldn't have been underground in the site for more than ten or fifteen minutes, yet Shep was surprised at the change in the quality of the air above in so little a time. Even for the rain forest, it was moist with humidity. Hector looked up in the sky and grimaced.

"Looks like Helene is coming in a bit earlier than we expected."

Shep rolled his eyes and resisted the urge to let all his pent up anxiety manifest into grabbing Hector's shirt and shaking the shit out of him. "The weather? You're going to stand there and make comments on the weather? What the hell just happened down there?"

"Security protocols," Hector answered briefly. Shep's demanding stare forced him to continue. "Plaxis policy is that no one is allowed to enter the main site without first getting their background screened and approved by the corporate overseer. Because I'm the site director, José had to listen to me and allow you in. But he followed protocol, called Plaxis, and went over my head to report the event."

"You knew!" Shep spit out with sudden realization. Hector seemed to ignore his venom. "You knew that he was going to pull a trick like that."

A nonchalant shrug nearly drove Shep mad. "Fifty-fifty, leaning toward ninety-ten," Hector admitted. "But it's done. The site was secure, your picture and file's been sent to Plaxis for follow up, no doubt with a little more speed due to it now, and José will handle the lockdown during the hurricane." He reached out a hand, as though trying to sense the presence of rain drops penetrating the sparse forest canopy. "Best get to the shelters. You could probably do with a nap after that, anyhow."

Yeah, Shep thought, *and a stiff drink and a lottery ticket to match my dumb luck wouldn't hurt.*

"You'll be in that one over there," Hector continued and pointed to the far ridge to their right lined with green boxy structures about the size of a garbage dumpster. "Two to each. You'll be with Vick."

Shep smirked as he walked over to his sleeping quarters. Make that two lottery tickets.

Once he was inside, the door closed behind him and was sealed. It wouldn't be inoperable in the case of an emergency; that Shep knew. If either he or Victoria needed (or wanted) to get out, they only had to take a few simple steps to undo the locks.

Shep looked at his cot to the right, and then to Victoria's—and at Victoria herself—on the left. Under the cots and in every other conceivable nook and cranny in the small enclosure were storage boxes likely filled with official equipment, personal effects, and emergency supplies. Victoria was lying flat on her cot, her fingers interlaced and her hands resting across her stomach, her eyes closed. She appeared to be asleep, and the weariness of travel was catching up with Shep like an insistent grad student at office hours. He was thankful for the opportunity to let his mind rest, and further thankful that he wouldn't feel the need to sit up awhile and make small talk. Or, if he were to be honest, he knew if she was up, he wouldn't be able to resist the urge to interrogate her on all she knew about Anathea.

He took off his shoes and placed them on the floor beside the cot, the toes pointing toward the door in case a quick escape was needed. He saw Victoria had done the same, and knew then that she had a good head about her to always plan for contingencies. He was never surprised at how often a small set of simple survival skills like these had saved his tail. In Arabia and Egypt, you never knew when an earthquake might strike or a military coup would take you by surprise. Thinking ahead was keeping your head.

Shep used a small wash basin and a bit of water from one of the recycled milk jugs to clean up a bit. He felt a little uneasy as he took off his shirt and set it aside. If Victoria awoke and found him bare-chested, would she think it indecent?

Too tired to contemplate decency at the moment, however, he looked over his naked shoulder to see if she had stirred from the sound of his movements. She hadn't, but she had turned onto her side, and the lapel of her shirt, top two unbuttons unused, fell slightly, giving Shep an intriguing glance at her cleavage. His breath caught as she gave a monstrous yawn, causing her chest to heave.

Nope, he didn't like the direction his mind was tracking one bit. Rather, he liked it a little too much, and he knew it was both ill-advised and, frankly, a little creepy. After all, she was at least fifteen years his junior. It had too much of a *Don't-Stand-So-Close-To-Me* feel. Shep decided it was time to lie down and put his mind and body to rest before the presence of the praline-haired beauty led him to distractions he knew better than to indulge in.

A good deal of time had passed when Shep awoke to the distinctive sound of a ballpoint pen scratching over a sheet of paper. The wind was howling outside and the machine gun-like cadence of gust-driven rain was pounding the wall. The hurricane had moved over their location. Shep rolled over slowly, making sure to keep the thin blanket covering as much of his bare chest as possible.

Victoria had awoken and was sitting up, notebook on lap, and scribbling with nearly superhuman speed. Every so often, she would trace her fingers over the margin of a book that lay open on the cot next to her. It looked like she was comparing notes between the two objects of her focus.

Shep decided that it was rude to spy and that he should make his attention known.

"Hey, there, Vick," he said. She jolted at the sound of his voice. "Whatcha working on?"

"Dr. Smyth!" she exclaimed, her hand still clamped around the pen as it fluttered up to the delicate curvature of her neck. Yes, Shep noticed that neck. "You gave me a fright."

Shep smiled his apologies. "Not intended, I assure you."

She beamed back at him, her eyes twinkling. It was then that Shep took a moment to really look at her eyes in detail. He couldn't remember seeing eyes that exact shade of green before, almost feline-like in their hue.

"Of course, not. I'm, um, translating something. Some of these runes, however... I haven't seen them used in Mayan writing before, so I'm trying to reference them against some variant dialects."

Her eyes narrowed on Shep, and he realized that she noticed his partial nakedness. Feeling a blush come over him as if he were a sixteen-year-old school girl, he sat up and grabbed his shirt from the foot of his cot.

"Too bad it's not Egyptian," Shep commented as he slid the tee over his torso. "I maybe could help you on that."

Victoria chuckled. "Not to try to show you up, Dr. Smyth, but if it was Egyptian, I wouldn't need your help."

"Cocky, aren't we?" God, had he actually just licked his lips? What was wrong with him? "Why are we back to *Dr. Smyth* again? I told you, you can call me Shep."

Victoria smirked and leaned over her notepad toward him. "Some call it cocky; I call it confidence. And I've decided that Dr. Smyth is the appropriate nomenclature. It appears, after all, that you are my senior, both in terms of age and experience. It would be good of us both to keep in that in mind."

She looked away abashedly. Could she possibly be feeling this same, odd draw to him as well? Was that why she was trying to form this wall of formality between them?

"Well, I guess Hect—um, *Dr. Gonzalez* would approve of that decision," Shep conceded.

She nodded. "Yes, and it's the way I was taught as well by my mentors."

"Oh, that's right!" Shep exclaimed as he woke up completely and remembered his conversation with Hector. "You studied with Anathea."

She grinned and continued her penning. "Dr. Gonzalez told you, huh?"

"How did you manage that?"

Victoria sighed in her frustration, folded her notebook, and set it aside. "She's kind of related to me."

That didn't make sense to Shep. He knew Anathea had been an only child and that she had neither married nor had children.

"Distantly," Victoria added, answering almost directly on cue to his unspoken question. "You have to go back more than a few generations to make the connection, but still. And yes, you could say I know everything she knows, and then some."

"Confident in that, are you?" Shep asked.

"No," Victoria boasted through her smile, "cocky. I could tell you, for example, what's on that scroll that they found in the jade box." She sniggered lowly again. "But then I'd have to kill you."

What a lovely carrot to dangle. "You've seen the scroll?" She nodded. "And you could read it?" She nodded again. "But, then, why would Hector say he needed me to translate it if you already did?"

Victoria rolled her eyes and mocked innocence. "Let's just say, he doesn't exactly know that I've seen it. Besides, he assumes that because I seem so young, I couldn't possibly have a grasp on Ptolemaic-era script well enough to be able to decode it. He's a bit of an ageist, you know?"

"So…" Shep waited impatiently for her to continue, and nearly screamed despite himself when she didn't. "Damn it, Victoria, what does it say?"

He felt himself actually getting angry at her when she refused.

"That knowledge seems such a petty thing to die for, doesn't it?" Her eyes were mischievous, not letting him know if she was serious or jesting. She continued, "It's one thing for someone like me to have read it, Dr. Smyth, but another to share classified Plaxis information."

"Duly noted," Shep answered with an acknowledging nod. Not that he was about to accept that. "Of course, I understand. After all, I can imagine how embarrassing it would be for you if later, when I read it, your translation turned out to be wrong. Not to mention, that would support Hector's opinions of your age vis-à-vis your ability. It's probably better to just let me think you know."

Her head shot up. "You think I can't read it?"

He smirked. "Like you said, you're so young, and the language, so very, very old."

"It won't work."

"What?"

Victoria sighed, throwing her legs over the side of the bed and arching her back to stretch. "I'm not going to tell you what it says." Shep mocked disappointment. Sometimes appearing to give up was the best way to lure an adversary into the open.

But Victoria only smirked in response and turned back to her work. Shep stood and stretched, deciding to visit the topic again later. He found his cell in the pocket of his carry-on bag and checked the time: 9:14 p.m. A glance out the small window of the shelter didn't yield much. All he could see was the rain pounding against the book-sized glass.

"So, is *that* one anything you can share with me?"

Victoria sighed. Obviously, she wasn't in a chatty mood, and quite frankly seemed a little annoyed with Shep's inquiry. Perhaps that was why when Victoria did give him a response, it was anything but conversational.

"Not really, but I'll tell you this: Anathea thinks you're right," she declared. Shep only looked at her blankly. "About Cleopatra."

He nearly spit his own tongue from his mouth. "Sh-she…she said that?" he stuttered.

"She's quite a fan of yours. Thinks you've got a good head on your shoulders."

It was like a lowly Catholic priest receiving accolades from the Pope himself. Pride and vanity surged through him. He couldn't resist inquiring. He may never meet Anathea himself, but Victoria seemed to be close enough to her to give him some sort of friendship-by-association buzz.

"Does she—has she—said anything else about me?"

"Yeah, she passed me a note in homeroom that said you're really cute and wants to know if you'll go steady," Victoria returned sarcastically.

Shep chuckled just to amuse her. "Sorry. Not trying to, um, pry. I know she's a very private person."

"No problem, I understand." She took in a deep breath and exhaled slowly. "She was very upset when Christine died."

Shep felt himself go instinctively numb at the mere mention of her name. It was better to be without any emotion than to again be consumed by rage. "Me, too" was all he could respond.

A tense silence hung between them for several moments. They both found different spots on the floor to study. It was an annoying state to be in; Shep was rested enough that the need to sleep wasn't pressing on him, and yet the time of day and his current locale made working impractical. He figured, since there was nothing better to do, he'd take advantage of the company of the beautiful woman sitting across from him.

"Seems unfair that you seem to know so much about me, and I know so little about you," he said. "Tell me a little?"

Victoria shifted around uncomfortably, tucking her hands under her legs. "Well, not much I can tell you, Dr. Smyth. I'm actually from not too far from here. I come back from time to time, but I've spent much of my life abroad. I was getting a little homesick and was really happy when I found the opportunity with Plaxis on the Olmec dig."

"And how did you become interested in the Olmec? You were trained in Egyptology, no?"

"True enough. But my interests have always varied. And, being from these parts, the Olmec are part of my heritage."

"Yes, you must be one of the Veracruz Kents," Shep laughed. "Not a very Latin-sounding name, Kent. How did your family end up down here?"

"Keep a secret, Dr. Smyth?" She leaned over, a conspiratorial look meeting his. Shep mirrored her movements, bringing his face within inches of hers. She licked her lips...*her* lips...and he couldn't help but wonder if they were as soft as they looked. "Victoria Kent isn't really my name."

Shep couldn't make out from her half-smirk and taunting eyes if she was jesting or sincere. Nor could he bring himself to shift away from her, though he knew that he was inappropriately close.

He couldn't explain it. Sure, finding her attractive made sense; she was young, intelligent, beautiful to a near goddess-like level. Still, why this overpowering sense of...lust and familiarity? He was drawn to her somehow. It wasn't anything emotional, of that he was certain. His heart had always belonged to Christine, and it always would. But there were desires bordering on need, and they hadn't been met in quite some time. He needed to close the distance, needed to kiss her. Victoria bit her bottom lip and, as her eyes fluttered closed, Shep felt his pulse spiral out of control. He inched forward tentatively.

"You feel it too, don't you?" Shep whispered, his eyes closing as he awaited the gravitational force between them to bring him crashing into her.

"I shouldn't, but I do," she admitted. "Sheppard, you don't know how long I've—"

But the moment passed as she drew back instead. Her mood had seemed to change as well, as she became almost regretful in her expression.

"I'm sorry," Shep found himself barking out before he could even fathom what he had to be sorry for.

She shook her head violently. "No, no. I'm—I'm sorry, I didn't mean to get so close. I didn't…That would have been very wrong of me."

Shep was at a loss for words. Wouldn't he have been the one taking advantage of her? He was the senior member of the pair—relatively speaking, of course—and she the young, impressionable one.

He parted his lips to speak, to assure her that she had nothing to apologize for, and that the near slip had been his fault, but was stopped short by Victoria jumping to her foot as she stuffed her book into a leather satchel and threw it over her shoulder in such haste that she didn't notice one loose leaf of paper flutter down to the floor.

"I have to go."

It was so impossible a statement with a hurricane raging outside and at night that, for a moment, he thought she was making some sort of bad joke. But he was hardly laughing as he watched her undo both pressure locks on the door and open it.

"Victoria, if I said or did something to…I'm sorry."

She gave him the briefest, most intriguing of smiles. "It wasn't you, Shep," she answered simply. "It's always been me."

And with a swish of her coat and hair falling behind her frame as she exited, she was gone.

Shep was left perplexed. He couldn't figure out what just happened. And what didn't. Would it have been so wrong to kiss her? Had she not wanted to? Sure, he wasn't a college kid anymore, but was he so repulsive to her young eyes?

Bending over, he scooped up the paper and looked at it. Several pictorial lines were scrawled at various angles, most in glyphs he didn't recognize. *Mayan,* he assumed, though underneath each were various words in English. As he looked at a scrawling of letters in the center, his heart nearly stopped. He couldn't say exactly why he knew at that moment that Victoria had been lying, but he understood nevertheless.

Anathea fears Shep will suspect what really happened to the queen.

He barely slept the rest of the night, lapsing between slumber and consciousness with every roll of thunder or cadence of rainfall. In the dimming light of morning, he finally found rest as the rain lessened into a gentle tap-tap-tap on the window that was nearly hypnotic.

Much later in the morning, the rain and wind had stopped. Shep rolled over, and was only slightly surprised that Victoria was not in her cot. He wondered where she had gone, and why. He replayed the evening in his head. He couldn't make heads or tails of it. What had she thought she'd done that required her to leave in the middle of a tempest?

One thing he knew for sure: he had to talk to her, pronto. He considered telling Hector about Victoria's little admonition, but decided against it considering how seriously Plaxis took their security *protocols*. No doubt there was a reason she didn't want Hector to know she had seen the scroll, and he couldn't see how outing her would get him the answers to his questions any quicker.

Shep was broken from his thoughts by the unhinging of the locks from outside and the crashing open of the door. Hector's quivering frame filled the space, his face whiter than Shep thought possible for a man of his complexion.

"Gone," he said in a disbelieving voice.

"I know," Shep said stoically as he rolled up on one elbow. "She took off about nine-thirty. Any idea where I can find her?"

"Not just Vick," Hector gasped. He stumbled into the room as though in a trance. "Everything. The jade box. The scroll. Even Cleo, Shep. It's all gone."

Chapter 5

Victoria Kent was a lot of things, but stupid she was *not*. Self-serving, manipulative, coy, arrogant, and deceptive she would cop to. In proper company, she'd even admit that she wasn't even human. Well, not totally human. Half-human had to count for something.

Hell, even the Guardian didn't know about her other half. *He* arrogantly presumed that all her abilities—the telekinesis, the empathetic manipulation, the ability to teleport, etc.—was all his doing, the result of his Bonding on her. The Guardian was Altunai. *Full-blooded* Altunai. Although the members of the alien culture were, in essence, just humans in an advanced state of evolution, the difference between an iPad and a Commodore 64, they were enough removed from the remedial Earth versions of *Homo erectus* to consider themselves a different species. Victoria knew better. Despite their uppity self-importance, they were still mutts, only blended of higher pedigrees.

Which meant that Victoria Kent was the five-thousand-plus-year-old, bastard half-breed of the two. Sure, ancient humans had considered her as one of the Altunai, declared her a goddess, and worshipped her as divine as they did with the full-blooded. Some humans, The Order, worshipped her still, but she never had fit into either side of the equation. She was the balance, the necessary link between the two. For all the Altunais' greatness, their minds were too advanced to be able to work their mental magic voodoo directly in the humans' heads. They needed a conduit, a transformer. A damned metaphorical bridge over the River Kwai. And they need her for their little experiment to be carried out.

That was why she had no qualms about the risks involved with her little activities here on the Yucatan. It was against their rules, and the

Guardian would be uber-pissed once he found out about the stunt she was about to pull, but she was made safe by the fact that she was indispensible. From his perspective, anyhow.

Yeah, Victoria was *not* stupid.

And that's why she hadn't kissed Sheppard Smyth. She really had no designs on the man, but some part of her just had to know what his draw was. What was it about him that had captivated Christine so? Was he a secret Valentino with a talent for seduction? Could he recite Shakespeare at the drop of a hat? Could he, like Victoria herself, speak thirty-six languages, or any portion thereof? Really, she should know far more about the good doctor than she did, considering.

That he had felt some degree of attraction to her was to be expected. She was drop-dead gorgeous with full Helen-of-Troy potential, after all. But there seemed stronger forces at work there, almost like he was compelled by instinct to move in on her. That he might be drawn to her was a possibility that she had acknowledged, but gave it only as much credit as one accepts that someday the sun might explode or professional athletes would be infamous for their monogamy.

She cursed herself for allowing that *slight* possibility such short shrift as she fought through the rain, away from the hurricane shelter where, no doubt, Shep was nursing a bruised ego from her sudden departure. It was the best thing, she thought by way of rationalizing. It wasn't as though she could offer him anything; her heart was locked into its own dead-end, co-dependent relationship. She reminded herself that Shep had been Christine's husband. Even if there hadn't been another reason, she owed it to Christine's memory and service to keep a watchful eye on her widower, even if Christine had renounced her allegiance to Victoria and relinquished her place in The Order. Victoria had marked Christine as one of her own, even made her a proxy by sharing her blood with her, Bonding her as once she had been Bonded, giving Christine protection against sickness and disease and imbuing her with the powers of limited telepathy and empathetic intuition.

Becoming a proxy was a great honor, one most of the members of The Order dreamed about. Christine had abdicated her position when she fell for Shep and married him. It was the first time a proxy had left Victoria's service for any other reason than death.

There was no precedent for it. Bonding could be implemented in one of two ways: sharing of the blood, or sharing of the bed. Victoria had Bonded Christine by blood, and Christine had shadow Bonded Shep by the bed; that was the only thing that made sense. Like a copy of a copy, the Bond lacked clarity in Shep, but it was strong enough that when he met Victoria, his body had sung with the recognition that something in her was the same as something in him, and more still, the same as something in Christine.

Bonding, the ultimate STD.

Victoria Kent didn't bestow that honor on just anyone. In fact, through her pentamillenial lifespan, there had only been twelve. To make someone a proxy was to offer them a blessing and a curse, however. Sure, the perks were great, but when you became Bonded to Vick, you inherently became a target of the Guardian. Quite frankly, the Guardian was one bad-ass you didn't want to mess with if you didn't have to.

Not that he was evil, per se. He was purpose-driven, the yang to Victoria's particular yin. It was part of his gig, as far as he was concerned, to keep the existence of the Altunai on the down low. It was hard to Bond someone without them getting empirical evidence of the race's culture, together with a take home bag of alien DNA that could be isolated in a lab in the modern era. Too risky in the Guardian's view. He ran a tight ship. What humanity did remember had become part of folklore and mythology; the superhuman abilities and proclivities dismissed and incorporated into the tales of Mount Olympus, Valhalla, or, most famously, into the Egyptian Pantheon. Egypt, after all, was where the Altunais' activities and residency had been most prominent, and where the gate to their own world could open and close.

The Altunai had seeded human life on Earth in ancient times, their experiment to study the growth and evolution of civilizations in a self-serving attempt to better understand themselves. Of course, a proper experiment needed controls. It mustn't be tainted by the knowledge that annihilation was a possibility if humanity didn't track the way the Altunai approved of. Thus, whenever they seeded a new planet, they stayed only long enough to help the new breed get going, set up basic infrastructure, and disperse as much knowledge as was needed to thrive. Then, the Altunai removed themselves for thirteen baktun. On Earth's scale, that equaled roughly 5,125 years, though in the Altunai's world, only a handful of years passed in the same time frame. At the end of the thirteenth baktun, they returned to analyze and cast judgment on whether or not the experiment had been a success. That is, whether or not humanity should survive or be destroyed.

The thirteenth baktun was ending in seven freaking days, and Victoria hadn't even picked out which shoes to wear to the party.

She barely stifled a curse as she fell knee-down in the mud while making her way to the outlying shelter where the cache of artifacts had been secured from the storm. Speaking of the storm, really, what had she been thinking by manipulating the forces of nature and willing the hurricane as her cover-up? In her defense, she had been praying for just a really intense thunderstorm. Playing around with weather control—well, that was the whole thing. You couldn't *control* the weather; all you could do was nudge it in one direction or another. Still, she hated being wet, and she hated being dirty. Here she was, in the middle of the Yucatan rain forest, soaked, soiled, and sullied. You would think after so many lifetimes, she'd be a little better at this by now.

Luckily for her, Dmitri's hired goons had been wise enough to get out of the storm, it seemed. From the outside, the shelter appeared to be unguarded. Shielding her eyes with her hand, she punched a series of numbers into the keypad on the security door, and followed by pressing her thumb to the scanner. A beep, a click of the lock, and she was in.

Looking at José.

Of course, Mr. I'm-too-Sexy-for-Détente would be on watch, wouldn't he? A hurricane couldn't possibly be considered ample protection against thieves, robbers, and all-purpose swindlers, would it? Ha, but she was here, wasn't she? Only thing was, he probably had no idea why.

One of her mistakes when she'd arrived in San Lorenzo two months before was not hiding the fact that she spoke Spanish. The Plaxis hired guns were wild, trigger-happy testosterone factories, and Victoria was the pretty, young fresh meat that had wandered into their hunting territory. Of course, José was their alpha dog, and had warned the others fairly quickly that Victoria was his bitch to claim. If there had been a language barrier, she might have had an easier time fending off his advances. As it was, however, after two months of feigned gentleness and demure temper on her part, José was getting hungry for some action. She could hear it in his thoughts, whenever she got brave enough to peek in his head at the risk of having her stomach turn. He was planning on pinning her to a cot (or the ground or the wall—whatever was convenient when the opportunity arose) and claiming her properly at the first sign of weakness or subtle come-hitherocity. Quite frankly, Victoria was getting a little sick of his efforts. The last thing she needed right now was anyone's attentions, least of all the head of security's.

"*Mi corazon!*"

José leapt to his feet, turning away from the bank of monitors that were still streaming visuals in from all over the camp despite the heavy rain that made many of the screens look like modern hydro-art. From the corner of her eye, Victoria saw one screen that peeked into the interior of the shelter where Shep now reclined wearily on his cot. *Frickin' bastard was watching me undress and sleep*, Victoria thought with a grimace. Beyond disturbing, it was quite frankly low, even for a mafia-funded gun-for-hire.

"*Hola, Señor Montoya.*" She hoped an approach of formality would give her enough time to figure out the best tactic to both distract him from his conquest and find a way to get a hold of the objects that were padlocked in the air-tight crate behind him. Continuing with his Spanish, she said, "Did you draw the shortest straw, having to ride out the storm in the security shelter?"

"I volunteered for it, Victoria, to keep an eye on you." His eyes pitched toward the bank of screens, indicating the one showing where she had been moments before. "I don't trust this gringo. He looks at you with hunger."

It took every ounce of her self-discipline not to roll her eyes. "I'm more than capable of taking care of myself, Sr. Montoya."

She shivered in revulsion as he reached out and smoothed his callused hand over her long, multi-hued hair. "A real man takes care of a woman, Victoria, no matter how strong or weak she may be. He protects her honor, as much as his." For a moment, it looked as though he might try to claim a kiss from her as well, but Victoria shifted away just as he leaned in.

"Plaxis security protocols forbid co-team romance," she staunchly reminded him.

He cocked a devious smile at her. "I'm the chief of security. Who would it be reported to?" His hand reached out and stroked her cheek. "You are such a beautiful woman, Victoria. I'm not really surprised the *americano* is attracted to you, but you need someone worthy of your…assets, not some pansy-ass professor."

An ingenious little grin spread over her face as she realized she'd get up the stream faster if she was paddling with the current instead of against it.

"Are you worthy, José?" she cooed as she batted her eyelashes just the smallest bit. "Not really too many 'real men' for me way out here. At least," she leaned in closely and spoke into his lips, "none that have made me feel secure enough to trust yet, none that I could get…close to."

His tongue darted out and slicked his bottom lip. "Security is my specialty, *senorita*. You can get as close—" his hands reached out and grabbed her at the waist, pulling her relatively slender frame hard against his "—to me as you'd like."

He pressed his mouth to hers, his tongue jutting into her mouth without pause. Victoria mocked a moan and pulled at his shirt, leading him to think she wanted him closer, closer. Which she did, but not in the way he presumed.

Lust did things to men, and not just physically. It turned off certain switches in their heads, made their brains run at a slower, more primal pace. As blood was utilized for other purposes, the decrease of cognition of the higher brain functions made it easier for her to infiltrate the cerebral core and nudge things around. In short, letting him poke at her below, let her poke at him up top.

José's hands threaded her hair before landing on her shoulder and squeezing hard. Even with her above-normal muscular endowment, she flinched at the intensity. Alpha dogs tended to be sadistic, and she wasn't surprised when he manhandled her hips and came to attention against her midsection, all the while kissing her…frankly, quite well.

Okay, so the creep could kiss. She had a job to do. Victoria arched her back and tipped her head to the side, letting him trail his mouth down her neck. She closed her eyes, letting out a hiss as he bit at her ear, and began to extend her thoughts into his. The barriers of his mind were walls built of sand, and hers was a swell that knocked them down with ease. She knew the moment she had penetrated them, because his body froze solid in her arms.

"José?"

Just a dull, zombielike groan in response.

"Will you do something for me?"

As if she had to ask. "Anything."

She slithered out of his arms, and his eyes tracked her with a forlorn look, as though she were taking away his favorite toy.

"I need the items in this box," she said, tapping her hand over the security chest. "I know you have the code for it. I could ransack through your brain looking for it, or you could save me time by just opening the damned thing for me."

The puppy bounced around, happy to please its master. The mind-slave's emotions always broke near the surface, the every whim of the controller their reason for living from moment to moment. To have such an ability was addictive. Victoria couldn't deny that she'd abused the power more than once in the past, but she was fighting down the rush being the dominant gave her. She had to stay focused, had to stay vigilant.

The box's lid sprang open, and José stepped obediently out of the way, giving her unfettered access.

"Good, José, very good."

There they were. No fancy cover cloths or plastic bagging or anything really to protect them. The box they were stored in was lined with velvet which would no doubt help to soften any blows, but Victoria understood what she was looking at. These items had been packaged for immediate departure. Likely Hector had intended to ship out the discoveries to the lab in Mexico City for further study as soon as the hurricane cleared. Lucky for her, she'd gotten to them first.

Memories filled her as she reached down and ran her fingers over the objects before her. The dagger with the jewel-crested handle had belonged to Ahzim, a proxy of hers dating from the Abbasid Empire. The jade box was the prized possession of Ma Wu, who met her end at the Guardian's hand during the Tang Dynasty. Each of the eleven objects represented a proxy she held precious. Very precious, she thought, as her finger ghosted over the cheek of Cleo's statuette.

Of course, one proxy had been formed in the modern era, and for her there was no memento in this collection. Not unless she included the nearby Sheppard Smyth.

Victoria bit back the tears threatening to spill as regret and nostalgia battled for control. Biting her bottom lip, she swung the leather satchel she had been carrying on her back forward and began lowering the objects into it. She took up the jade box last and hinged it open, an exhale of relief issuing from her when she saw the scroll was still contained inside. Really, it should have upset her, given that papyrus as old as it was likely to come to quick damage once exposed to the elements, and even more so being that they *were* in a rain forest. Of course, Hector was a Mesoamerican expert, so the knowledge of how to properly preserve a piece of pilfered papyrus wasn't his particular predilection. Luckily the scroll also had inside it…

"The amulet!" Victoria shouted as she opened the scroll and searched through its folds. It had been there when the scroll went in the box, so…"Where the hell is the amulet?"

"Gone." José's deadpan only made her panic seem all the more overblown.

"Gone?" she repeated unbelievingly. "Gone where? Hector said he wasn't going to—"

"Plaxis lab," José murmured. "Mexico City, this morning."

The equivalent of "fuck me" in a tongue too old to be remembered by anyone else rang from her lips. She wanted to hit something, hard. Hard enough to knock it into next week. Remembering the purpose of the amulet, she laughed sarcastically at the sentiment.

Whatever. Fine, she did have seven whole days still before she *really* needed it. She'd just have to think of something later. For now, though, she was needed elsewhere and her time—and energy—was running out.

With a swing of her arm, Victoria hoisted the satchel over her shoulder and turned back to José, who stood with a blank look on his face and stared intently at nothing in particular. She pressed her body against his, and, with utmost delicacy, let a little bit of the control over his mind slip, just enough so that he was well aware that she was leaning into him. His desire for her body could be used as a weapon; with proper orders, she could harness that craving for the flesh and manipulate it into a wish to please her in any way she asked.

"Do you want to make me happy, José?" she coyly queried, taking his earlobe between her lips and sucking as he answered.

"Yes, *mi corazon*. I'd do anything."

"Anything?" She let her hand snake around his sides, running her fingers in circles over the lower part of his back. "Would you even betray Dmitri Kronastia for me?"

He grimaced. Even with most of his ability to think rationally contained, he was still a soldier. The human need to war—particularly in the male of the species—was almost instinctive, and loyalty to the commander was akin to the pack yielding to the alpha.

"I…would."

His resistance to commit quickly or completely told her that any manipulation she could plant in his brain for later use would have to be subtle in nature. She couldn't, for example, have him swipe the amulet outright and get it to her, but he could prove useful otherwise, a sort of insurance policy if all hell broke loose and she needed Dmitri sidetracked.

"José, I have to leave." She saw the shadow of sadness on his face. Muted emotions were often revealed only as passing expressions. "Don't worry; I'm sure we'll see each other again." He smiled. "When we do, José, it may be in a time where I am in need of help. If I ask for your help then, José, can I count on you? Even if it means betraying Kronastia, would you help me?"

"Always."

"Good, and for that, you deserve a reward."

She closed her eyes and let go of the hold of his thoughts, like throwing the tow line off a boat and letting it float away from the dock and into the current. José blinked a few times, trying to sharpen his gaze on the face and the situation in front on him. Confusion danced over his features, but in moment or two, he cast aside his reticence and threw his arms around her, drawing her closer.

"What did you say again?" he asked, a sly smirk on his face.

"I said, kiss me."

His lips curled into a grin. Without another thought, he bent down and pressed his lips to hers.

The contact was all she needed to see out the tail end of her impromptu escape plan. It was time for the getaway, before José caught on to what she was doing and before keeping the storm overhead took too much toll on her metaphorical batteries. She couldn't afford to leave the Plaxis chief of security dead; Dmitri was going to be pissed enough after the call he was sure to get in the morning from Hector once her swindle was discovered. At the same time, she didn't want to risk having José get all caveman-like and trying to keep her from going by force. If he could just…pass out for a while, it would provide the cover she needed and give her time to get out of Dodge before anyone was the wiser.

José felt a tingle when his lips moved over hers. *Damn, I knew she'd be a damned fine kisser,* he thought as the sizzling sensation spread out. Soon, though, it was replaced with an eerie iciness, like someone had just shot him in the back of his throat with Novocain. He tried to focus on the heat of the kiss, but his knees had turned to jelly, and the room was beginning to swirl and get…cold. Frigid. So amazingly cold.

But Victoria still felt warm, hot even. No, it was just him, just his hands shaking and his breath quickening. He pulled out of their kiss, and the coldness stopped spreading.

"What's wrong, José?" Victoria asked, lifting her hand to stroke his cheek.

The moment her fingers met his flesh, the ice entered his veins again. When she cupped his cheek, it was like she was a hot water bottle and his face was an ice pack.

José stumbled back as his knees buckled. It was Victoria. Whatever was happening to him was because of Victoria.

"What are you?" he begged of her, falling into a chair now as numbness spread around his body.

Victoria tracked him, never breaking the contact as he stumbled. She leaned in closely, feeling a rush as the sip of his life force she was consuming refueled her. "Just an old friend of Dmitri's. You let him know the Jaguar sends her greetings when you see him, okay?"

Recognition, betrayal, and perhaps even awe inked into his features before the muscles began to relax. It was evident in his eyes. Jose understood; he had been duped. Victoria *wasn't* Victoria. She was an impostor. More than that, she was a thief.

Victoria mussed his hair condescendingly. Taking his black beret off him, she slipped the cap onto her own head. She turned to leave, pausing at the door and looking back for just a moment to take in the view of her victory once more before departing.

"Look forward to working with you in the future," she said with a bow of her head. "And do me a favor? Keep your eyes on that so-called gringo. Make sure he keeps his hands out of things that shouldn't concern him, if you know what I mean."

12.16.12

Chapter 6

The passing edge of the hurricane hadn't damaged camp too badly. The jungle cover had served as a deterrent to the full force of both the rain and the winds. With the exception of a few shredded palm fronds or haphazard pieces of refuse, there was little evidence that anything out of the ordinary had happened. The damage evident on Hector's face was another story; that was monumental in its scope.

Hector immediately began accounting for every member of his team, trying to pinpoint an accomplice. After thirty minutes, it was determined that no one else was missing. Just Victoria.

And Cleo, Shep thought. He felt like he was mourning a family member with the statue's disappearance, and he was oddly suspicious that Victoria knew something about the unbefitting location of the Egyptian artifact perhaps even by way of Anathea Hermapolous.

José seemed oddly emotional over the events of the previous evening as well. To Shep, the security chief was as misplaced among his team this morning as a suntanned Swede. After some coaxing from his men, he ordered a sweep of the nearby jungle but found nothing. Hector couldn't quite figure out how Victoria had done it and disappeared without a trace, despite the lockdowns needed for the storm. José reported passing out at some point during the night in the security shelter, claiming he discovered the items gone when he awoke in the morning. Victoria hadn't taken any of the team's vehicles, which meant either she had escaped on foot or arranged a rendezvous somewhere nearby.

"She's a smart girl, I'll give her that," Shep mused as he sat with a frazzled Hector. Hector broke from his silent contemplation to crook an eyebrow at him. "Of course she didn't take any of your team's cars; they're all bugged. Come to think of it…"

Shep recalled the day before when he had been met at the airport by Vick.

"When she picked me up yesterday, she was late because she had been meeting with somebody, she said."

Hector's eyes widened. "José! *Uno momento, por favor.*"

The be-muscled minion approached and leaned down close. They conversed in rapid-fire Spanish, during which Hector pointed briefly to Shep and said Victoria's name. Understanding seemed to wash over José's face, and he barked something that sounded slightly wary and somewhat threatening at Hector. Hector was insulted, or so Shep guessed, as he all but leapt up from the table and began to pace around. José continued to plead his argument, and as Hector's shoulders slumped, Shep could see that somehow or other, Hector had conceded to something. José only nodded as Hector sat back down. The big guard left and returned only a few minutes later with a bulky-looking cell phone.

"So, what's up?" Shep asked, bemused at the exchange despite himself.

"We're going to see if we can get a trace report on where Victoria was driving yesterday before she collected you," he answered. "Only, to get that kind of information, we need to call our contact at Plaxis. The tracing information is all uploaded directly to their servers in Moscow each night. This…is going to hurt."

"Huh?"

Hector chuckled lowly. "This project is coded gold by Plaxis. Top priority. Gold project security reports and permission requests go directly to Kronastia's right-hand man. Which means Kronastia will know about it in minutes, if not sooner. This is going to bring hell down, and fast."

As Shep turned over that fact in his mind, he had another realization. If what Hector said was true, that meant that the evening before, it had been Kronastia's guy whom José had called about their trip down into the pit.

Shep wasn't sure what exactly it meant for him that a Russian mob boss was now familiar with his name. He suspected that it was nothing good.

Hector let out a hefty sigh as he looked down at what Shep now realized must be a satellite phone in his hands. In clear resignation, Hector coded in the number and raised the phone to his ear as though it was a fifty-pound dumbbell. Or a loaded gun. An association with Russian roulette seemed oddly appropriate, considering who would be at the other end of that phone call Hector was making. Hector's eyes pinched shut. Though he had near-native fluency in English, whenever he got overly excited or nervous, he began to babble like a third grader trying to explain Tolstoy. Shep recalled the way cool, collected Hector back in college could be reduced to monosyllabic chattering when the right coed was in company.

Finally, with a static-filled click, the other line picked up.

Kronastia never answered phone calls, it was said, unless he had specifically requested the call. One more security measure. All telecommunications went through an intermediary, usually his valet, Anton Sluga. Although Kronastia lived his life in the public eye—he was infamous in the Moscow clubbing scene—he still maintained a bubble around him into which only trusted individuals were permitted to enter. Attempts on his life were not unheard of. News of such events was used by some in Russia as an indicator that it was time to change the oil in their car.

"Da?"

Shep heard the voice come through the phone, and Hector jolted. Shep didn't know if Russian mobsters had voice mail, but no doubt Hector had been hoping so.

"Hector Gonzales calling from Project Bullfighter for Mr. Kronastia."

Now the words on the other end were more muffled, but there were a few unintelligible mumbles followed by a pause, and then another voice, this one a baritone as opposed to a tenor, spoke lowly.

Shep tried to decode from Hector's expression the direction of the discussion as he now took in the one-sided conversation.

"Mr. Kronastia, Hector Gonzales, verification code alpha-omega-six-epsilon. Sir, we've had a robbery on site." A few words from the other side, and Hector grimaced in his discomfort as he sucked in his bottom lip. "All of them, sir."

There was a long pause, and Shep swore he actually saw Hector tremble before Kronastia solicited another question.

"We're pretty certain we know who it was, sir, yes. She went missing last night the same time everything else did. We believe it was the intern from Plaxis, Victoria Kent. We think if we could get a trace on the vehicle she was driving yesterday..." A questioning phrase was returned to him. "I said Victoria Kent, the intern, sir," Hector repeated, raising the volume of his voice slightly and over accentuating each word.

Shep could have sworn he heard a wry laugh come from the other end before Kronastia spoke again. There was little he could glean, however, from Hector's next responses.

"Yes, sir…No, I wasn't aware of…Yes, Smyth is still…No? But then, how…Of course, not, sir. I'm sure you're right…Yes, of course…All of it?…Yes, sir, will do. Th-thank you, Mr. Kronastia."

With that, Hector lowered the phone and hit the end button. He sat stunned for a few moments, his face pale, all blood draining away.

"Hector, what's going on?"

As though he just realized there was another living being in his presence, Hector's eyes rolled to Shep's face. Now Shep was certain the man was absolutely shaking.

"He's coming."

"He…You mean, Kronastia?" Shep felt his own body begin to tremble.

Hector nodded slowly, the shock on his face still apparent. "But that's not all," he continued in a wavering tone. "Apparently, Plaxis doesn't have an internship program."

Chapter 7

Dmitri Kronastia considered himself a patient man. On occasion, he had even been called compassionate. He didn't like the term "Russian mobster"—didn't think it suited him. He thought of it as pigeon-holing. Like being called the pope. Sure, put on a pointy white hat and a matching souped-up bathrobe, but don't lose your temper or the masses would look at you like you grew two heads. He despised labels, and tried never to use them in reference to anything he had done or to the efforts of others.

But as he pressed the end button and nearly crushed the satellite phone into tiny pieces in the palm of his hand, he thought that one of the labels so often applied to him could be true: ruthless.

"Problems, sir?" Anton, his red-headed valet (for lack of a better term) asked with professional concern.

Dmitri slowly let out the breath he had been holding as he shook the pieces of the scapegoated electronic from his hand unto the table.

"How soon can we be in San Lorenzo?"

"Four hours, sir," Anton answered without pause, like he had already charted the course and was bringing the car around front as they spoke. "Shall I have your jet prepared?"

"Yes, Anton, please see to that. Also, call Moscow and have them forward me the profiles of all crew on Project Bullfighter, and whatever security data has uploaded for the past three days."

How fortunate that he happened to be in Miami at the time. Of course, with such an important project in the works, one with which he had such a deep personal interest, he had kept mostly to the Americas the last few months. Honestly, he would have liked to remain on site during the entirety of the excavation, but he wasn't sure exactly what was going to be unearthed at the site. Despite his reputation, Dmitri was not an indiscriminate killer. He never terminated without cause, and even then only as a last resort. If something in the excavation indicated...well, anything...he respected both Gonzalez and Smyth on a professional level too much to end such promising careers so needlessly.

When news had reached Dmitri of the telltale artifacts found by the Plaxis-funded team, namely the scroll and amulet, he had decided that a personal visit to the site was better arranged sooner rather than later. Unfortunately, he had a few obligations to see to stateside first. With the strict security procedures in place, he hadn't feared much about the safekeeping of the objects until his arrival. The call from José Montoya De La Plana alerting him to the presence of Sheppard Smyth had hardly been welcome news. Of all of the archaeologists in all the world that Hector Gonzalez would choose to call in, it would be Smyth, wouldn't it?

But Smyth wasn't too much of a concern. Even if he had managed to piece together anything from the smattering of evidence at the site, it was unlikely his human mind could wrap around the truth. Smyth was small potatoes.

When the next phone call had arrived, however, Dmitri knew they were in serious trouble. Only one person would have the gumption—or the capability—to pull off such a heist. She was also the only one who stood a chance of getting in the way of the ultimate goals of Project Bullfighter.

"And Anton?" Dmitri asked, calling his valet's attention back from his fervent keying on a laptop across the room. "Pull whatever strings you have to to get me the phone number for Anathea Hermapolous. Tell her it's time she and I had a little chat."

As estimated, four hours later found Dmitri's plane beginning a descent approaching Veracruz. Anton, of course, was accompanying him. He was nothing if not loyal. Dmitri knew he could count on Anton to do anything requested, even lay down his own life if that was necessary. But sometimes, Dmitri questioned the intent of his servant, the reason for his eager devotion. It could be the money; Plaxis did compensate him very generously. But Dmitri wondered if what kept Anton ever-ready was what other "benefits" being liked by Dmitri Kronastia was rumored to bring.

The chirp of Anton's cell drew Dmitri's attention away from the window. He looked at him expectantly as he conversed quickly in what Dmitri recognized as Greek, before handing the phone over to his master.

"Dr. Hermapolous, sir," he said as he presented the Blackberry.

Dmitri acknowledged him with a nod and pulled the phone to his ear. He didn't bother with small talk. What was the point with someone with whom he had so much history?

"I bet you think you're pretty sly."

He waited patiently for the other side to answer. He could hear her breathing, slow and steady, a clear indication that she was not surprised nor was she panicked. It was likely she had been expecting the call. Hell, she had probably sat down somewhere and just stared at the phone, willing it to ring so that she could get over with it.

With a long sigh, he continued. "You'll never get away with it, Anathea. 12.21 is less than a week away, my dear. What can you possibly achieve in a few days that you haven't been able to get away with all these years?"

"Weren't you the one who told me that I could achieve anything I set my mind to?" she finally stated rather amusedly.

He gave a wry chuckle. "I will admit, the intern angle was clever. Don't suppose you'll tell me whose arm in security you twisted to get the proper credentials?"

"You should know better, Dmitri. I never reveal my sources." She paused, then added in a sheepish voice, "Intentionally, anyway."

He returned to the more pressing issue. "What exactly do you intend to do with it all, I wonder?"

"Whatever the hell I want," she answered in a conceited tone. "Maybe I'll expose the truth to the world. You've managed this cover-up for far too long."

"No one will believe you."

She was silent for a moment before she answered in a voice lacking of all doubt, "I don't need everyone to believe me, just a few in particular. Don't doubt my abilities. I took my lessons from you well, and now, the student has become the master."

Curling his hand over the receiver to ensure that Anton heard nothing, Dmitri growled with a lusty lilt, "I still could teach you a lot, Anathea, if only you'd give me a chance."

"Please, I'm an old woman!" Her throaty, insincere dismissal rang in his ears. "One of the first things you taught me so long ago, Dmitri, was never to trust anything you say when you speak in that tone. Have a nice visit to San Lorenzo, Mr. Kronastia."

Two beeps, and the signal was lost. Dmitri handed the phone back to Anton and resumed his stare out the window, his mind traveling back across the years and to memories of driving a young woman half insane in his bed, using that tone of voice when he screamed out her name.

Chapter 8

Shep's eyes followed Hector as the latter approached the newly arrived black Humvee. Hector walked like a man to the execution block, and Shep wondered for a moment if, in fact, that was exactly the scene he was watching unfold before him. He ransacked his brain, trying to recall the little he did know or thought he had heard about Dmitri Kronastia.

Oddly enough, Kronastia was somewhat known in the archaeological field. It was rumored that he had started life as a classics student, but had been caught in the wrong place and the wrong time. As so often happened, being in the wrong place and the wrong time had been the right decision, as the conjunction of said time and place had opened the door of opportunity for Kronastia to start a slow but steady rise through the world of organized crime. Even back in his own undergrad and graduate days, years ago, Shep had heard cautionary tales about the new black market antiquities dealer making a name for himself. When Kronastia branched out to the more traditional mob activities of drug and arms trafficking, however, the threat to antiquities had seemed to be temporarily abated.

That is, of course, until Kronastia rose high enough in the ranks that *he* got to call the shots. Plaxis, a small time Moscow-based tool and die company, had been procured as a front for directing his international projects. They still produced tools and dies. The tools were any number of international criminal leaders. And the dies? Well, Shep really hoped they weren't about to be recruited into that allegedly vast, "discontinued" product line.

Hector looked like a shamed puppy who knew darn well he had destroyed half the house and peed on the silk rug when master was away. When alas the back door of the Humvee opened and a young, graceful man perhaps in his late twenties stepped out, an Armani suit despite the rugged locale, Shep wasn't quite sure just who they were looking at.

Hector's head bowed in submission as the finely dressed young man approached.

"Dr. Gonzalez," he said by way of greeting, his accent somewhat Kurgan, "wish I could say, 'happy to see you,' but, of course, not so much under these circumstances. Anton!"

From around the other side of the vehicle, the sound of another door opening and closing came. A moment later, a somewhat balding, thin stick of a figure rounded the front of the Humvee, approaching the first man with utter obeisance.

"Mr. Kronastia, sir?"

Once, then twice, Shep blinked in shock. Surely, this was a joke. How could it be?

Dmitri Kronastia was already taking down hits when Shep was still fulfilling liberal arts requirements, yet he didn't look a day over twenty-six. *There must be something in the water in Moscow,* Shep thought. *Perhaps schools of plastic sturgeon fish.* The mob boss was graced with shiny, black locks that John Edwards would have envied, and sparkling gray eyes bright for one who had no doubt led so stressful a life. More than being toned, he was even a little built, though the suit likely hid more defined musculature below.

Kronastia turned to whom Shep supposed was his butler. "Anton, have Dr. Gonzalez take you to the security server and pull up the relevant files. They should have been transferred by now, no? I want to see this supposed *intern* for myself. You remember my personal access code?"

"Of course, sir," Anton answered without hesitation and with a slight bow of his head.

Kiss ass, Shep thought. When Anton's gaze and attention turned to Hector, however, his tone was less cordial.

"If you don't mind, Dr. Gonzalez." He veritably scowled, showing clear disdain for the screw-up who had apparently slighted his master.

Hector looked back over his shoulder at Shep, who tried to return a sympathetic and reassuring smile. It faltered somewhat. Shep's eyes followed the pair as they turned and trudged off, noticing as Anton's jacket swayed with each sweep of his arms the presence of two holsters secured to his side. A shot of concern ran the length of him, but his stress turned inward when he felt the weight of a stare upon him and looked up to see a smirking Kronastia, quixotically beaming at him.

"Dr. Sheppard Antonius Smyth," he at last breathed, each syllable crisp and precise. "I cannot tell you what an honor it is finally to meet you."

"It is?"

The words of shock were out of Shep's mouth before he could stop them. Immediately sensing his faux pas, he coughed to clear his throat and tried to conjure an air of formality that he often reserved for meeting university donors or field luminaries.

"Indeed," Kronastia reassured him as he paced slowly over, holding out his hand.

Shep took it lightly when within reach, and was somewhat disheartened as the abnormally chilled flesh made contact with his palm. *Great genetics, but shitty circulation,* he assumed, thanking the gods that even when it came to Russian mob bosses, there was some justice in the world.

Kronastia grinned. "I can't tell you how long I've followed your work with great interest. I've been particularly fond of your efforts regarding Cleopatra VII. While I find your theory preposterous and far-fetched, I'll give you credit for thinking outside the box. Your wife's article on the subject a few years back *nearly* had me thinking twice. Speaking of which," he paused, his head turning and his eyes searching from side to side, "is she here as well?"

For the second time in so many days, Shep felt the stab of his sorrow as he was reminded yet again of the truth.

He shook his head meekly and replied in a small voice, "No, Christine passed a while ago."

To his credit, Kronastia looked believably ashamed and saddened. "My sympathies and apologies."

By default, Shep shrugged, a hefty sigh issuing from his lips.

"Well," Kronastia resumed, pulling his hand back and placing it casually in his pocket, "as delighted as I am to meet you, I wish it could have been under more...ideal circumstances. Still, now that you are involved, I suppose it's either recruit you to the project or kill you."

The tone had been indiscriminate, and Shep searched Kronastia's expression for clarification. No cracked smile, no break in his sincerity. Realizing that it wasn't a joke, he gave a sardonic chuckle and studied the native vegetation at his feet. "Well, sir, I've always considered myself a team player."

Kronastia smiled wryly. "Glad to hear it." He motioned his head to the side, indicating the same direction Hector and Anton had gone. "Walk with me, and tell me what you know. Please, don't leave anything out. I do so revere your work, and there's no reason for us to be enemies. Yet."

Shep noted that they were walking back in the direction of the hurricane shelters.

"Anytime you're ready to start, Dr. Smyth," the Russian stated suggestively after a few moments of silence.

Shep let out a sigh of resignation and began. "Two nights ago, I got a phone call from Hector telling me about the statue of Cleo that had been unearthed. I haven't talked much to him since we were grad students together, but his reputation has always been good, and I knew he wasn't pulling my leg. I hopped on the first flight. His assistant—the apparent thief—picked me up from the airport when I arrived yesterday."

"And did Hector show you the other objects as well?"

Lying could be a deadly choice if later the truth came out, so Shep didn't hold back. "Yes, but only briefly, and I didn't have a chance to examine the scroll before Victoria took it. *She* seemed to know what it said, though…"

Shep bit his tongue, remembering Vick's request not to share that smidgen of information. However, walking next to one of the most notorious underworld figures on the planet, he didn't think abiding by that agreement was suggested.

"Oh, *Victoria*, I'm sure, is more than aware of what the scroll said," Kronastia muttered, a slight chuckle to boot. "She didn't tell you anything about it, did she?"

By this time, they had reached one of the outlying buildings, this one somewhat larger than the one Shep had stayed in through the storm. He noted that this one was also equipped with a fingerprint scanner and had a relatively large antenna protruding from the roof. At a pressing of Kronastia's finger to the sensor, the locks clicked and the door swung open.

"Um, no, she joked—I think—that she'd have to kill me if she did." Shep paused, and added tentatively, "I *think* I may have seen one of the translations she was working on."

Kronastia stopped, his expression full of amusement. "Really? And what is that?"

"She dropped a piece of paper that mentioned Anathea fearing I might catch on to something about what really happened to Cleo." He knew it sounded crazy, and no doubt jumping to this conclusion only served to foster and fester his own widely discredited theory. "I think that the scroll tells of the death of Cleopatra."

At that, Kronastia gave a fully-bellied laugh, though he seemed to speak to himself. "Ah, glad to hear she still has that same old sense of humor. Any luck with the video, Anton?"

The valet's ears perked up as they entered, and both he and Hector turned to take in the newly arrived pair. Shep breathed a sigh of relief at seeing his friend seemingly unharmed. For now, anyway.

"Yes, sir, we've just isolated some of the footage from her arrival to camp yesterday."

As they entered the shelter, Shep was somewhat surprised at the bank of screens, buttons, gadgets, and otherwise technical gizmos, and on a book-sized screen, a looping video of Victoria and himself pulling up in the Jeep. He marveled again at her grace as she jumped from behind the wheel, landing lithely on the ground, and the ease with which she hoisted his rather large bag from the back. Hector shrunk back in a corner and was still clearly writhing in his unease of his fate. Kronastia's eyes narrowed on the screen. Slowly, his hand rose when the image stilled, locking Victoria in frame. His fingers traced over the outline of her face, and Shep was struck with a sudden sense of unsubstantiated suspicion.

Kronastia nodded. "Just as I suspected; she managed to kill the upfeed link, but she didn't realize that there was a local back up as well. Good, that works out well for us. What about the vehicle trace?"

Anton leaned over and punched some combination of letters and numbers into the keyboard. In a moment, one of the monitors brought up a map of the Veracruz area. Shep spotted immediately the airport, and the red line that ran adjacent to it on the overlay indicated the path the vehicle had taken. Tracing the route with his eyes, he saw the line meander through the streets of downtown Veracruz.

"Just a moment, sir," Anton requested as he keyed in another set of commands. A flashing dot indicated a location on the east side of the city. "She made a few routine stops: a market, a coffee shop. Hmm, an outdoor supplier. But, here," he pointed at the dot, "this is the Hotel del Mar, and the data feed says she was there for about two hours."

Kronastia took it all in calmly, his chin resting in his fisted hand. "If I didn't know her better, I'd say an illicit affair. But Victoria would never let a lover off the hook with just two hours of his time."

Shep couldn't help himself. "Speak from experience?"

His stomach dropped when he recalled that his life at the moment depended on the very good humor of a seemingly humorless man.

"I'll see if I can grab an image," Anton added, again keying.

And, there she was. Her hair was strewn about her face in a haphazard fashion. The wind batted it about like a flag as she drove. There was no sound to the grainy video, but she was obviously singing along to the radio. Her expressions were wild and carefree and, yeah, sexy. At one point, she turned to the camera—clearly she was aware she'd been filmed the whole time—and winked. Anton froze the image.

The air was thick with tension as the three other men beheld the Russian's momentary regret-filled gaze. Immediately, however, the moment passed, and Dmitri's teeth gnashed as subdued rage overtook him.

His eyes remain focused on Victoria's image as he ground out, "Anton, a moment, please. I need to speak with Dr. Gonzalez and Dr. Smyth privately."

Anton reacted as though someone had told him to leave the party when it was just getting fun. To say "clearly put out" would be an understatement. Anton looked, well, pissed. However, with an indignant huff, he nodded his compliance and took his leave.

"Close the door behind you," Kronastia further ordered, "and be certain that we are not disturbed."

Hector gulped so loudly that it almost sounded comical and cartoonish, like Bugs Bunny had just emerged from his hole to find Elmer Fudd's gun aimed between his eyes. Shep was thinking along the same lines. Clearly, they had seen something they weren't supposed to, and they were about to be "whacked." Whatever it was, it must have been something very, very critical, because surely most whacking rights were delegated to the made men, Shep thought. It must take some measure of importance to be whacked by the head honcho.

Well, if you're going to go, go big.

When Kronastia reached into his pocket, neither man was really surprised. They passed a quick glance to each other, saying in unspoken words that, for whatever it was worth, at least they were with a friend in the end.

So when instead of a revolver, Kronastia pulled out a photograph and held it to the screen instead, both Shep and Hector were at a loss for words. Death by Polaroid? Just didn't seem possible. They looked at the photo, of course, and were surprised to see that it was clearly Victoria, only dressed in what appeared to be fatigues. Not the sexy attire like Shep had first met her in, nor the standard-issue khakis and tees in which Hector quite often saw her. No, in this photo she wore camouflage, head to toe.

Her caramel hair was pulled back tight, and strapped to her side was a fully-loaded ammo belt and a gun that would make a grown man cry.

"They called her Yonina Berkmalov when this was taken," Kronastia stated rather stoically. "But don't get hung up on that. She changes her identity like some women change shoes, and she's got a collection that would have put Imelda Marcos to shame. Recently, however, she has one moniker that seems to follow her about: Jaguar."

Hector nearly spit up a lung, he was scoffing with disbelief. "Jaguar!" he exclaimed. "Vick is Jaguar? *Our* Victoria? No, that can't be. I mean, Jaguar's a…a man, right?"

Kronastia tucked the photo back inside his jacket pocket. "She likes people to believe that. So few ever assume that one of the most notorious black market antiques dealers of the current era is a woman. The assumption proves very useful for her, allows her to use her 'feminine wiles' to an even greater extent. All play, though; she never follows through." He smiled devilishly. "Well, *hardly* ever."

Shep shifted uncomfortably in his place, recalling the near kiss the night before. As though Kronastia sensed Shep's unease, he turned, a corner of his mouth raised.

"Something you'd care to share, Dr. Smyth?"

Shep thought back. It had been so unexpected, so unprompted. Was she trying to charm him? Had she thought he might be of some use to her? Newly arrived to the excavation, the only thing Shep could offer was his expertise. Victoria had studied under Anathea Hermapolous, however, so what could she possibly learn from him that she couldn't get from the grandmaster guru?

Despite his instincts telling him to sing like a canary about anything he was asked, Shep decided to keep this one to himself. He lowered his eyes and shook his head.

But, if indeed she was Jaguar, he now understood why she had kept the scroll's details secret. No doubt such an item on the black market would net her a tiny fortune. Even reputable museums might pay a hefty fee for such a document. And Shep didn't deny that, if he could somehow track down the item and retrieve it from her first, he would be looking at more than just material wealth from nabbing it. His reputation would be saved. Of course, he had to survive today.

Kronastia still smirked but didn't pursue further.

"She's expert in her field," Kronastia continued. "She knows how to work the system, *any* system, and manipulate the right people, how to get in and get out with little suspicion and unhindered by obstacles. I have to admit, though, this intern scheme of hers is quite impressive, even for her. Didn't you wonder, Dr. Gonzalez, why Plaxis would make an exemption to its 'no women on Project Bullfighter' policy for someone as lowly as an intern?"

Shep's head snapped in Hector's direction as he quickly scanned through his few memories of camp since arriving. In a stark *well, what do you know?* moment, he realized only in reflection that other than Victoria, he had in fact seen no other women about.

Hector shrugged. "She came bearing all the necessary credentials, and having been instructed by Anathea Hermapolous, I couldn't—"

Kronastia cut him off. "I get it, doctor. As I said, she's very adept at what she does; though had you followed my edict, this might never have happened. She knows what she needs to do to work her way in, and she knows which projects will be the most rewarding for her. She's been a thorn in my side for quite some time, but I never thought she'd be so bold as to try to get access to this site. Then again, this project is somewhat personal for her, so maybe I assumed too much."

As though he'd had a sudden realization of the way to get back into his patron's good graces, Hector leapt up from the corner. "Mr. Kronastia, surely she couldn't have gotten too far, and the items are so unique she won't have an easy time finding a buyer too quickly. Perhaps even if we contacted the Mexican authorities, reported the items stolen..."

Kronastia clicked his tongue. "I simply cannot do that, doctor. You may or may not believe this for a man of my particular...*profession*, but I do not believe in lying. You see, Victoria didn't really steal anything." He paused and leaned in, both the archaeologists doing the same, as though the walls themselves might overhear something they shouldn't be privy to. "All of the objects you found actually belong to her."

Chapter 9

"And will you be checking any bags today, Miss Kent?"

Reflexively, her hand smoothed over the surface of the canvas tote, weighing heavy at her side. She was still surprised that she had been able to get it through security so easily. Putting the "Made in China" and mock price tags on the bottom of each artifact had seemed sufficient to substantiate her story to the customs agent that they were merely trinkets she had picked up while on an extensive multi-destination holiday. She hadn't actually suspected Alex's idea would work, though. The plunging neckline of her dress, no doubt, had helped to distract the agent just enough for her to pull off the con, however.

"No, my bags have already been taken by my...friend." Victoria smiled, remembering her brief rendezvous with Alex in Veracruz.

In a fortunate twist, the arrival of Shep Smyth had provided her a convenient excuse to make the rendezvous with her most favored acolyte. Even more convenient, she was able to drop him off for his outgoing flight just as Shep was arriving. Talk about winning the logistics lotto.

Not that anything had happened during their meet up, per se, but it wasn't because of her lack of appreciation for the human. Oh, she would never have actually done anything with him. Even though she occasionally gave herself leave to mess around a bit if someone caught her fancy, she never did so with a member of The Order. Too many political complications and group dynamics to contend with if she did. For Alexander Cezanne, however, she might have made an exception.

"There's just this one I'll keep with me," Victoria added, rubbing the sack like it was Aladdin's lamp. The gate agent's eyes tracked down to the piece as she nodded. Her attention then turned back to the screen as her fingers began a cha-cha across the keyboard. After a few more moments, she smiled and looked back up at Victoria.

"Yes, Miss Kent, I think we can accommodate your request for an upgrade." She beamed. "We have one seat available in our first class section for this flight. Oh, but…I'm sorry. The additional fare will be well over five thous—"

"Price is not a problem," Victoria said by way of cutting her off. Already, her hand was reaching for her wallet and for the magical plastic card inside it. Credit cards had seemed such a novelty to her at first, but in recent years she had grown to love them. How convenient in this modern era, she had thought, to have nearly all your expenses quickly put aside with the sway of a rectangular piece of hardened polymers and authorize a single bank transfer monthly to handle the bill. It was an efficiency, and she had always been a fan of efficiency.

The agent took the card with the same tissue-box smile. She ran it through the reader and presented it back to Victoria along with the charge slip and new boarding pass. Victoria signed accordingly.

"I wonder, now that I have upgraded, might you tell me if there is a business lounge I could have access to? I need to make a few calls prior to the flight, and I would appreciate some privacy."

A map of the terminal was laid flat on the counter as the agent circled the first class lounge and motioned to the left with her hand. Victoria thanked her, pulled her tote close to her side, and fished her cell out of her pocket. As she walked, she keyed in the text message and the secret phrase they had agreed on:

Honey, mother's coming. When will you be home?

The answer was actually to be an indication of when it was safe to call, but only she and her contact would know that. Approximately thirty seconds later, the cell vibrated. She looked down.

Detained for now, dear.

The key word was *now*. For some reason, he was alone at this exact moment.

Victoria looked up from the phone and was happy to see that she had arrived at the lounge reception counter. She presented her newly printed, first class boarding pass and her passport, and a few minutes later found herself in a private room equipped with a computer, a printer, TV, and an arm chair that could be reclined as a bed. Without hesitation, she locked the door behind her and placed the bag gently on the floor. She punched the numbers into her cell with lightning speed and waited impatiently for the other line to pick up. The receiving click was quickly followed by the answering party's concerned voice.

"Are you outbound yet?"

Victoria put her ear briefly to the door to be certain no one was on the other side. There was only silence. "Shortly. I was able to get in on a London flight. Just to be safe, I'll travel land and sea routes to Cairo after I address The Order. Shouldn't take me but a day or two."

"I would prefer you let The Order assist you. Traveling alone so close to the end of the baktun isn't—"

She abruptly cut him off. "Bite your tongue, Priest. I've been preparing for this for far longer than you or anyone in The Order, and I know well what is required and what is best."

"Of course, milady. It wasn't my intention…" His voice, a mixture of apology and humility, trailed off. "In any case, if you should require anything of us—"

"—then I know whom to contact. I assure you, I'll be fine. Just keep a close eye on things on your end, and if either Gonzalez or Smyth start to add up anything, let me know. In the end, though, if I can keep clear of Kronastia, and if you can obtain the amulet, everything should be fine." She found her mind drifting for a moment as the image of Dmitri Kronastia seeped into her consciousness. In a voice far smaller than her experience, she asked, "How…how is he? Dmitri, I mean."

She could almost hear Priest's teeth gnash in frustration. If there was one thing he did not understand, it was her complex history with, and lingering attachment to, Dmitri Kronastia. They had discussed it many times. It made no sense to him. Dmitri and Victoria were legendary adversaries, were they not? How was it that at the same time they worked at opposite ends in their pursuits, they both seemed to yearn for the other in the in-between?

"He is well enough," Priest answered stoically, though a little sigh of frustration passed in his pausing. "A little peeved that you were able to make off with all the goods, though. Milady, I hope I'm not being too improper, but how long has it been since the two of you—"

"Long enough that I have clarity about why it can't work, Priest, and don't inquire further. You are the Priest, and you serve me. The nature of my relationship with Dmitri—or *anyone* else, for that matter—is none of your concern."

She looked at the clock on the wall; it would be time to board soon.

"I need to go," she announced. "Alex will be meeting me in London. Don't be late. I can't afford to linger."

"Of course, milady. The Order—and I—live to serve."

"Thank you, Priest. I hope only that your service proves worthy of its sacrifice in the end."

She closed the phone with a click and stared at it for a moment until the display went into sleep mode. Despite the bravado with Priest, she couldn't explain her nerves or the butterflies in her stomach. It had never been her intention when she started this life to end up as an international smuggler of antiquities and treasures. But, as it turned out, it was good work for those with the tenacity and talent. She possessed both in spades, as well as certain other…skills, which only added to her superiority at her accidental trade.

But this was different. This time wasn't for practice or thrills or revenge or even money. It wasn't just about her or a client with deep pockets and low morals. It wasn't even for the sake of evidence, as she led the members of The Order to believe. This time, it was for survival.

Of all the concerns she had ever had, survival had never been one of them. In a first for her, Victoria contemplated the possibility of meeting her own death. As yet, she hadn't decided whether or not it would be a welcome fate.

Breaking from her reverie, Victoria ran her fingers through her hair before placing the cell on the table top next to the monitor. Swiftly, she raised her right hand as she held the object in place with the other. Her palm alighted toward the target, destroying it—and cracking the table—beyond any reasonable measure of repair or reclamation. As much as possible, it was necessary that she leave behind little evidence. The escape was crucial. Using stationary provided by the airline lounge, Victoria crumpled up several sheets of paper and covered over the fragments of electronic strudel she had thrown in the waste bin.

A quick, determined pace through the terminal brought her to her gate. Her tote, of course, stayed strapped to her side as she took her first class seat. A flight attendant was soon at hand offering both hospitality and champagne. Victoria refused both, instead choosing to take out her notebook from the side pocket of her bag. The A4 folio fell open on her tray table, and she pulled from it, handling very delicately, a parchment made not of paper but papyrus. It had been folded twice in half, once by width and once by length. Gingerly, she opened it and splayed it flat, the glistening of red and blue pigments reflecting the blaring LED-reading light shining down from over head.

"That's some fancy calligraphy."

The voice had caught her off guard. She looked to her side to see a finely attired businessman—no doubt his suit was designer—looking at the flattened scroll. She gave a polite nod to acknowledge his comment before resuming its study.

"Sort of looks like something out of an Indiana Jones movie."

The final coach class passengers were filing past her. A little brown-headed girl, perhaps no more than seven, caught Victoria's eye as they exchanged smiles.

"It's Egyptian," Victoria added without turning toward him. The little girl passed along at the insistence of her mother, though Victoria would have preferred for her to linger and talk a space. "New Kingdom hieroglyphs, though it wasn't written until years later."

"Can you read it?" he further inquired.

Victoria smirked smugly. Turning her head, she could almost have sworn she saw him quiver when she answered frankly, "Can I read it? Of course, I can. I wrote it, after all."

The Brit nearly gagged on the champagne he had been sipping at that moment. "You...wrote it?"

He eyed her warily, as though trying to size her up merely based on a visual exam for mental disease. Victoria leaned in over the divide between them, looking him squarely in the eye.

"Yup." He looked anxiously back, but when her lips curled into a smile, then a laugh, he relaxed. "What I mean is, I actually copied it from the original which was written in roughly 25 BCE. This copy is...substantially newer."

Victoria was adept at learning a lot about people just from their appearance. She took in this inquisitive being with a wayward glance. Thirty, thirty-five perhaps? Old enough to have done well enough for himself, but his roughened knuckles suggested that he had performed some form of manual labor in his short life. Or, perhaps, he just had a hobby of working with his hands. His skin was fair, and his accent placed him in upper class South England. Still, he had an air of informality about him; he had been educated in the States, maybe Canada. No, Harvard—the class ring he wore gave him away as an MBA.

No wedding ring.

Her eyes twinkled, and the corners of her mouth rose. He loosened his blue-striped tie a little, perhaps unconsciously even.

"Hieroglyphs?" he asked. "Doesn't look like the kind you see in museums and such. Seems—"

She completed his sentence. "Simpler?" He nodded. "Well, most of the hieroglyphs you see in museums were the possessions of the affluent or royalty. Image is all the thing when you're trying to preserve your reputation for posterity or make a bold statement to your contemporaries. This kind, however, is a sort of shorthand. These types of glyphs are more about content than character, if you'll forgive the pun."

It peeved her that reading minds on an airplane proved so difficult. Not impossible, but it required extreme concentration, sending her into an almost trancelike state that often alerted those around her and drew unwanted attention. There was just something about the navigational equipment, some sort of low-frequency buzzing that she felt around it that always caused her havoc.

But she was fluent in body language. So when he smiled back at her, she knew she was reeling him in. A highly placed businessman had a lot to offer her at the moment: a secure, comfortable place to stay where she had no previous ties, which if nothing else, would serve as a place to hide out between the few hours of landing at Heathrow and meeting Alex.

His finger reached over and traced along the edge of the scroll. She faked a tremor.

"Can you tell me what *that* says?"

His voice was low, husky. She had succeeded in the first step of any seduction: letting him think he was in control.

The papyrus cracked in the echoes of its age as she delicately traced her fingers over the characters. The plane had pulled away from the gate.

"It starts, 'I killed her.'"

"Please note, the nearest exit may be behind you..."

Victoria found herself competing with the sound of the flight crew's safety instructions.

He leaned in even further, though his attention was wholly focused now on the parchment. "It's a...murder confession?"

Victoria nodded.

"In the event of a water landing..."

She moved her finger to indicate the next set of glyphs. "But, it continues, 'It was not my intent, and in that I can claim innocence of wrong. May Isis judge me fairly when I stand before her once more.'"

"...use caution as items may shift during takeoff..."

"'Could that I give my life to replace hers, it would be done. But I wish only to say, I loved her, and my regrets will flow as long as the Nile. I vow as my penance, her blood under my crest shall shelter find.' That's it; that's all it says, except..."

"...sit back and enjoy your..."

A crooked grin spread across his face. "There's more there than what you're reading, isn't there?"

Her finger pointed at a specific glyph at the top, its pictorial representation slightly more elaborate than those surrounding it, highlighted with golden-hued accents.

"She, they, her...meaningless. No pronouns in this particular dialect. This is the name of the victim, and *this*," she moved to a different glyph, one traced over in red, "this is the name of the murderer."

He sat back in his seat and crossed his arms over his chest as the plane reached the end of its taxi. They both heard the engines begin to rev in preparation for takeoff.

"How about that?" he mused. "An ancient signed murder confession. Wonder how long a sentence he got?"

Victoria scoffed. "*He?* So certain it was a man?"

He seemed very certain of himself as they both were pressed somewhat back in their seats, the force of the speeding jetliner forcing both of them to submit.

"'I loved her'?" he repeated back. "Clear case of a guy offing the woman he loves because he can't have her. Kings may fall and nations may rise, but some things remain the same."

So like the rich to indulge in their arrogance, Victoria thought to herself. Out of the corner of her eye, she could see the land miniaturizing underneath them, and she breathed a sigh of relief, feeling she might actually have managed a clean get away.

But she said only, "I suppose," as she maneuvered their conversation to other topics.

She learned his name was Terrance, and he had been in Mexico working on behalf of a British oil firm. He was thirty-three, lived alone in a West Side flat, and drove a Bentley. A used Bentley. At each piece of information he revealed, she feigned interest and even awe.

They sat in silence as the movie started, though Victoria assured the *accidental* touch of their hands several times during the epically long picture. When dinner was served, she made sure that the fork was pulled alluringly from her mouth with each tiny, symbolic bite. The feel of the food on her tongue nearly broke her concentration. She couldn't recall the last time she had been forced to consume so much for appearance's sake. She shuddered when she considered how much "food" was seated around her, and how she hadn't fed properly in a few days. Sure, she had gotten a small sip off of José the night before, but she had never been a big fan of Mexican food.

Finally, some hour or so before their scheduled arrival, Terrance turned his interest to her. Victoria presented herself as a graduate student in ancient civilizations at Cambridge. It was not wholly a lie; she had been once. The difference was only the tense of the verb, and that hardly qualified as lying. Terrance asked what had brought an Egyptologist-in-training to Mexico.

"Why, the pyramids, silly," she giggled back, her fingers traipsing over his wrist and her eyelashes batting just enough to be effective. "I was engaging in some interdisciplinary studies."

He smiled coyly at her, returning the feather-light movement by tracing the contours of her wrist. "You came *from* Egypt to see pyramids? Isn't that like being in Paris and going to China to eat brioche?"

"Common misconception," she answered. "Actually, the pyramids in the so-called New World rival those in Egypt in size and age. Some would even argue, depending how you measure, that it was the Aztec who built the largest pyramids, out-scaling Giza easily."

"Is that so?"

She practically beamed as she allowed him to believe she was flattered by his interest. *Yes, continue to let him think he's in control.*

"Indeed. Not only that, but the pyramids in Caral, Peru, predate the oldest in Egypt by nearly a century," she added.

But now, he had clearly had enough of the topic. "Where are you bound in London?"

She smiled, glad he had finally broached the subject. "Well, we land early in the a.m., and I have a meeting later in the evening, so I was planning on just hanging out at the airport for a few hours."

"Perhaps I can buy you breakfast or an early lunch?"

Snagged.

"I would en—"

"Ladies and gentlemen, this is your captain speaking…"

The voice over the announcement system frustrated her. Once she had the rhythm of a con or seduction established, she hated being interrupted. Trying not to let her aggravation outwardly show, she let out a tempered sigh and fell back against her seat.

The voice over continued. *"Just to keep you in the loop, folks, I wanted to let you know that we are experiencing some temporary malfunction of some of our onboard navigation systems."* A muffled gasp arose from the passengers, but Victoria only rolled her eyes. *"Not to worry. We've got eyes on the ground watching out for us, and our secondary systems are coming online as we speak. Just as a precaution, you may see off either side of the aircraft in the next few minutes two military craft. Please know that this is no reason to become concerned; they're just walking us home."*

"Son of a bitch!" Victoria burst out, and not less than a few heads turned her way in frustration. She ignored them and undid her seatbelt, rising unceremoniously just as the ping from above indicated that all passengers should buckle up.

The first class flight attendant stepped forward to intercede. "Miss, I'll need you to remain in your—where are you going?"

Victoria was at the pilot's door in a moment. The flight attendant found it useless to pull her back; despite her feminine frame, Victoria proved too strong to budge.

Burying fingers into the stewardess' chest, she pushed her firmly against the wall of the galley.

"Listen, sweetie, this can happen in one of two ways. Either you can tell the captain to open up these doors nicely and go back to your job, pretending nothing has happened, or I can break the door down and start mass panic."

The flight attendant's voice broke with fear, though she at least tried to appear confident in her warning. "Under international law, you are now disobeying the direct order of cabin crew and will be arrested upon our arrival to—"

"Can it!" Victoria shouted. "Do you know something, Freida Flighty? Navigation equipment screws up no matter what flight I'm on. Call it a gift. This is the first flight, however, where that results in fighter jets being scrambled, and don't think I don't know why. Now if you—"

Terrance was the last person she expected to see come to the stewardess' aid.

"Now, now," he almost cooed, his hands held out in the international sign for *calm down*. "Ms. Kent, I think you're taking things a little too harshly. You're scaring the people here and back in coach. Why don't you just come sit back in your seat, and we can talk this out."

His tone was completely changed from before. Whereas he had been coy and flirtatious with her just a few minutes ago, now he was cool and professional.

Something was off. Something was terribly, phenomenally off with this picture.

"What's it to you?" Victoria's voice was soft, but her tone was oh-so-snippy.

Terrance cracked a smile and pulled back his jacket. The barrel of a gun flashed as it was revealed in the light, matching perfectly the authoritarian badge pinned on his suspenders.

"As I was saying, Ms. Kent, why not just come sit back down? And it's more than merely a suggestion."

"Would you like to cuff me, then?" Victoria held her wrists together and presented them out. Terrance said nothing, but his smirk was all the affirmative she needed. Rather than the old fashioned metallic manacles, two plastic stripes were covertly threaded around her wrists. "You know who I am?"

"Victoria Kent, archaeology student," he answered, playing along. "I'd love to know your real name, Jaguar. Perhaps your prints when we get you processed will finally solve that."

Victoria said nothing, only allowed herself to be more-than-suggestively led to her seat. This time, Terrance shoved her in first so she was against the window as he claimed her aisle seat. With a laugh, he bent over and picked the sack that had slipped from Victoria's lap when she had jumped up to accost the flight attendant. Undoing the drawstring, he began to fish items out from the inside. The jade box and statuette he eyed with only amusement before returning them, but when he found the knife with the jewel-encrusted handle, he turned it over in his hand again and again.

"You knew it was me the whole time," Victoria stated. Terrance didn't try to deny it. "Who tipped you off?"

"Come now, Ms. Kent, you must know I can't divulge that information."

"An anonymous call?" she asked. Again, no answer.

Fine, if he was going to be so reluctant...

Victoria relaxed her consciousness and let her own mind expand outward, bumping first into the air that surrounded them, before honing in on Terrance's mind. Even feeling the heavy stares on her as, no doubt, her eyes rolled, she began looking for the truths he was holding back so near the surface.

"Ah!" she exclaimed as she threw off the effects of the hypnotic state. "A tip from the Plaxis corporation." Terrance's eyes narrowed, letting her know she had hit the nail right on the head. "More to it than that, isn't there? A little quid pro quo, it seems. Are you guys so easily bought off these days? Dmitri Kronastia gets a tip on Jaguar leaving out of Mexico City on a morning flight to London, and in exchange, MI-6 gives him a free pass through immigration when he flies in following us?"

"What the *hell?*"

Truth like water flowed from his mind, and Victoria was drinking it all down.

"Terrance, or should I say *Christopher.*" It was the name he kept thinking as an automatic correction whenever she said his cover's caller. "Let me give you some props. Yeah, I'm a little surprised I didn't see this coming. Congratulations. It's not often someone sneaks up on me the way you did. Probably my own vanity's more to blame than anything you did, but whatever. Point is, you did it. But, hate to tell you, it ain't going to work."

"Save it for the hearing," he muttered, his mouth turning down at the insult. Victoria smirked slightly. That was what she wanted, to get under his skin.

Victoria continued as though he had said nothing. "Of course, being on a plane, it will be harder to get away from you. Dmitri would think of that, wouldn't he? Oh, I'm sure he could have had some of his goons waiting for me at Heathrow, but this way makes it difficult for me *not* to cause a scene."

The agent leaned in and whispered in her ear, "Face it, puddy tat, you're caught. Now just simmer down until we get to London, okay? Nice knife, by the way. Concealed weapon without a permit on an international flight? That should tack another ten years on to your triple life sentence."

With a chuckle, he threw the knife back into the sack and put the bag over her hands, concealing her bound condition from the other passengers.

A few in nearby seats had started taking in the occasional sideways glance at them, and she could see that it was making him nervous.

"Christopher, I understand you're just doing your job. But I'm really sorry about this," she apologized, though her tone hardly seemed remorseful. "You do seem like a really nice guy."

He shivered when he felt Victoria's fingertips bend around his wrist. "What the—"

He looked down at the joining of their hands in confusion, watching the blood drain out and the skin grow paler. Was it shock? Was she squeezing so hard that she was actually forcing the blood from his hand?

Then the feeling of ice began to flow up his arms, slowly snaking its way toward his chest. Trying to reclaim his hand, he found it useless. She had him pinned, and he could not negotiate his release. Instead, he looked at her with a confused expression.

"Teleportation is a difficult thing, takes lots of energy," she said simply. "I'm so sorry that you have to die, but *I'm* just doing *my* job."

The ice climbed up his jugular, finally hitting the base of his brain. As he felt the first seizures overcome him, he was vaguely aware of a great flash of light. His body was practically stone now, every ounce of heat exported into the mass of fire before him. With his last living thought, he only wondered how she had done it.

The flight attendant screamed.

A man was dead, and a woman had just dissolved into a flash of light before her eyes.

12.17.12

Chapter 10

His eyes cracked open from the sting of sunlight beaming across the cabin, landing on his face. His mouth tasted like a hangover, and his muscles ached from the unorthodox sleeping position.

"Feeling better, doctor?"

The tempting bare legs of a woman came into focus as his eyes adjusted. It was the flight attendant—if that's what you called them on a private jet—leaning over slightly and literally presenting relief to Shep on a golden platter. Shep shifted and pivoted, pulling himself up as his hands massaged his pounding temple before moving down to rub the sleep from his eyes. He graciously took the ibuprofen and glass of water offered. He would admit to boozing up the night before, but the surrender to an alcohol-induced unconsciousness was the only way he knew to deal effectively with the overwhelming and, frankly, unbelievable story the Russian had presented to Hector and him.

Shep looked across the galley of the small private jet to see Kronastia's eyes trained on him, a slightly amused smirk on his face. Shep downed the pills before turning to his insistent host.

"Are you sure there's no more alcohol aboard?"

Kronastia chuckled. "Sorry, I don't partake of it myself. It makes me a rude host, I suppose. Then again, I don't often have guests aboard. I apologize. But we should be landing soon. No doubt there'll be plenty of alcohol in London in a few more hours."

That took Shep aback. He wasn't sure exactly when they had left the Veracruz airport, but he guessed midnight. The sun was definitely shining brightly now, and it seemed to him as if they should have been in Jolly Ole England some time ago.

As though reading the very question in Shep's mind, Kronastia added, "We had to make a quick stop over. Dr. Gonzalez needed to retrieve something for me."

Shep's eyes searched out Hector and saw him sitting at the back of the cabin, silent, his gaze fixed unwaveringly out the window. No doubt he was trying to rationalize—no, trying to decide whether or not to rationalize—the explanation they had been offered. While Shep's comfort to confusion was usually 60-proof, Hector's involved utter silence and introspection.

And, it seemed, induced the sniffles. As Shep's eyes focused, he saw that Hector had prepared himself a cocoon. He sat staring out the window, swathed in a cotton blanket.

"What's wrong with him?"

Kronastia gave a passing glance to Hector, then shrugged. "Stress induces cold-like symptoms in some people, I've heard. Air travel doesn't seem to agree with him, either. He threw up both times we took off."

"What did we make a stop for?" Shep couldn't imagine what would have been deemed worthy of a delay. The patchy memories he had, before the alcohol had made everything blissfully irrelevant, told him they had left the excavation in quite a rush. Kronastia had been hell-bent on getting to London, seeming to know inexplicably where Victoria was bound. "The amulet," he said suddenly in realization. Kronastia gave an acknowledging nod. "That figures into this whole wild goose chase just how?"

Kronastia's only response was to smirk slyly. Almost as if he had timed it exactly to coincide with a question Shep was actually quite eager to have answered, his cell rang. He held out one finger to Shep and opened his cell. "Excuse me a moment, Dr. Smyth."

What followed was a rapid fire conversation in impressively elegant Arabic, though Kronastia's dialect seemed old and refined to Shep's ear, accustomed to the crude vernacular of manual laborers in the Egyptian sands. Shep had spent enough time in the Middle East to have a basic working knowledge of the tongue, but Kronastia spoke with the grace and fluidity of an upper class native. So much fluidity, in fact, that Shep found it difficult to follow. He was getting some sort of news, and whatever he was hearing wasn't pleasant, judging by the frankly pissed look on his face.

"Problem?"

Hector stretched his arms and legs out long as he too took notice of the odd tension and air of frustration now radiating off Kronastia.

The Russian nodded. "They found out which plane she was on," he answered as he closed down his phone. "*Was,* that is. We've confirmed from security cameras that she did indeed board in Mexico City, but unfortunately, they failed to apprehend her. It seems she was no longer *on* the plane when it landed."

That didn't make any sense to Shep. Not that much had made sense to him for about the last twenty-four hours or so. He hadn't expected anything involving the cast of characters he had encountered since arriving in Mexico to be humdrum, but he had expected it to be…possible.

In the sobering light of day, he recalled what had transpired the night before. Dmitri had looked both grim and amused when he'd told them, "All of the objects you found actually belong to her."

Despite the fact that the man before them could easily end their lives with a simple phone call or, hell, probably with any number of firearms within a twenty-foot vicinity, they had scoffed. More than scoffed, Hector and Shep had barked with disbelief.

In an odd sort of way, Shep was relieved to see Hector's body relax as his laughter overtook him. "Ay, *por favor.* These items have been buried underground for at least a thousand years. The site was undisturbed. How would someone as young and inexperienced as Victoria Kent be able to pull off such a hoax?"

Kronastia's face flickered into a half grin. "She's not as nearly young as she looks, and by no classification is she…inexperienced."

Shep picked up on a bit of disdain and, perhaps, regret in the way Kronastia described Victoria. As though he had the very experiences with her that told him just how *un*-inexperienced she was.

But still, he didn't get it. "Okay, some women look really good for their age, and perhaps Jaguar is in the habit of using plastic surgeons to stay incognito. But those legs. I've never seen legs like that on anyone over the age of thirty."

Kronastia smirked again, like he was the exclusive party to an inside joke. "Until now."

Shep's smile evaporated. Kronastia wasn't joking. He may well have been crazy, but his tone was sincere. Shep decided to play along to see just how far off his rocker the Russian was. And to stall his own probable and impending death. "Okay, just how old is she?"

"That, dear doctor, is classified. But let's just say: she's been around. And those objects she stashed here? That's just the beginning of her cache.

She's got little treasures buried in every nook and cranny from Tunisia to Timbuktu, though I daresay none so precious to her as these. It's almost accurate to call her a hoarder, though in her case, it's not really her fault. More of her programming, really. Anyway, I always suspected that she would have taken those specific things back home to store if she caught on to news of the excavation. Like a damned cat bringing its kill back to its master."

Now it was Hector who was beginning to realize that Dmitri Kronastia was not joking. At least, whatever insane thing he was saying, he himself fervently believed it. "Wait a minute. You actually believe that Victoria—what? She buried those things here herself?" He swallowed his nerves in one hard gulp. "In... 1100 CE?"

Kronastia mused and nodded vaguely. "Give or take a lifetime or two, but yes." He clearly sensed the learned men's skepticism of his statement. "I have no proof to offer you specifically about the Olmec site. I know you are both men of science, and scientists always want undeniable proof. But I trust you are both familiar with the statistical concept of an outlier?"

They nodded. Of course they were. Outliers were data points that were simply too far from the generated cluster of other data points to be considered a valid part of an analysis. In short, anomalies. That didn't make them, however, necessarily false. They were just different.

Kronastia continued, "Well, Victoria Kent is the outlieriest of outliers. You might have to look outside your current conceptions to see her, but I assure you, gentlemen, she's worth the journey."

Giving a nervous chuckle, Shep crossed his arms over his chest. "Okay, let me review. First, you're saying that our little intern, Victoria Kent, is actually the international black market trader, Jaguar. All right, if you say so. I'm sure odder things have happened. But now, on top of that, you want us to believe she's a thousand years old and buried a stash of objects she collected from ancient Europe, Asia, and Africa before the advent of transoceanic travel, in a Mayan settlement, because she felt it was safest that they be stored at home? In the Mayan Empire? A thousand years ago? When she was alive?"

Every one of his repeated questions was steeped further in a tone of accusation, evidence against Kronastia's grand delusions.

But the Russian simply shook his head and laughed wryly. "No, professor, the Mayan Empire wasn't her home." Shep felt a momentary sense of relief and a certain air of I-told-you-so before Kronastia slashed it away. "She's an Olmec."

A scoffing laugh degraded into a coughing fit for Hector. As Hector gained control of himself and Shep finally met his friend's eyes, he could see that they were on the same page. Whereas they had been scared of Dmitri before, now he just seemed a pitiable, insane fool.

"Mr. Kronastia," Hector objected, "where to begin? First, she's way too tall. Second, she's too pale. And, third and most important, she's alive."

Kronastia was not deterred. "There are reasons for those…discrepancies. As I said, outlier."

But Shep sided with his friend. "Frankly, Mr. Kronastia, I think you're just abusing the fact that we're afraid for our lives in your presence to get a good laugh because of us. You want us to readily agree with you in hopes that you'll spare us because we're sympathetic. Well, I'd rather die with my integrity intact."

Hector nodded in agreement, but crossed himself the next moment when Kronastia grinned and slid his hand into the recesses of his jacket. Shep and Hector both tensed and grew silent, fearing that the Russian was finding what might later be labeled—if they were lucky enough to have their bodies discovered—"Exhibit A."

Kronastia read the fear on their faces and grinned in amusement as he withdrew not a pistol, but an alligator-skin wallet from inside his jacket. "Relax, gentlemen, it isn't deadly. Not even in my hands."

He pulled a black and white photo from one of the wallet's flaps and handed it to Shep. Hector came to sit by him and examine it.

"Marilyn Monroe?" Shep asked.

It was a simple picture of the famous bombshell seated at some club, dressed to the nines, a martini in one hand and a smile on her face. But then he looked more closely, and saw another familiar face, partially obscured by a cascade of light brown hair, seated to her right.

Victoria.

Hector scoffed at it. "Photo manipulation. Half the fifth graders in America could do that."

Kronastia nodded but seemed no less confident. He pulled another photo from another fold of the wallet and presented it. This one made Shep gasp.

Here was another's face, one far more familiar to him than that of Marilyn Monroe, and far more dear. Yes, Victoria's smiling gaze was in this photo too, though her hair was tied playfully in ponytails this time, giving her a slightly more youthful demeanor. She wore a University of Michigan T-shirt, and had an arm draped over a beautiful brunette with sparkling blue-green eyes as they posed in front of the Delta Sigma Theta sorority.

Yes, the other woman had been younger and she wouldn't become such a meaningful part of his life until long after this photo was taken, but this was his sweetheart, his Christine.

"Victoria knew…Christine?" he muttered in disbelief. "How is this…You didn't even know I was coming until…There's no way you would have had…"

Shep's pulse echoed in his ears. Passing out was one option his brain was considering to stop him from going into an all-out nervous breakdown, and sweat glistened across his brow. Kronastia had tried to continue telling him the story, but frankly, Shep had heard little of it after that. Words clumped together like autumn leaves falling to the ground.

Ancient…warrior…traveler…goddess…Victoria…

Dangerous.

Just arbitrary mumbling to him, like someone had set the dictionary on random.

But nothing made sense after seeing Christine and Victoria together. Except the alcohol.

Now, sprawled out on Dmitri's jet, he couldn't rationalize or reason this. He had tried to find some modicum of sanity in the reality. Repeatedly, Shep reminded himself that Dmitri Kronastia was a rich, criminal mob boss. Surely if he wanted a photo manipulation of Perez Hilton French kissing Rush Limbaugh, it would just take a phone call, ten minutes, and wiring funds into the proper account. But Christine wasn't Perez Hilton or Rush Limbaugh or anyone famous—she was just…Christine. Nobody special. Well, nobody special to Dmitri Kronastia. So why did he have a picture of her, and why was she standing with…well, what evidence was suggesting was a…

He didn't know just *what* Victoria might be.

"You know what I think?" Hector suddenly piped up from the back of the cabin. "I think you're a sick bastard who's trying to mindfuck a couple of helpless innocents before you tire of the game and kill us both."

If Kronastia took offense to the accusation, he never showed it, only kept his gaze fixed on Shep, whom he seemed to have decided was the more open-minded of the two.

Working through a post-binge hangover wasn't Shep's specialty, but he was trying. "So, okay. She got on the plane in Mexico City. The plane landed in London, and she's not on it. So, logic tells us that one of two things explains the disconnect. Two possibilities. One, it might be that one of our assumed facts is wrong: either she never got on in Mexico or she did indeed get off in London. Maybe she slipped past security or had some way of changing her appearance on the plane. Or, she got off the plane somewhere in between the two and..." He searched for a scenario that would allow the second hypotheses to prove true, because, damn it, he needed *something* to make sense. "...parachuted into the Atlantic Ocean, apparently."

The Russian grimaced, as though he had been so proud of his child making excellent progress in understanding something, only to have him reach the same, ultimately wrong conclusion. "I wouldn't put it past her, but jumping out of a commercial 777 at forty thousand feet is hardly Tori's style. Besides, security was unusually tight when the plane landed, given the dead body she left behind and all."

"Not to mention that no human could survive the jump," Hector grumbled, drawing momentary glances from both the men, neither of which Hector chose to engage.

Shep turned a curious eye on his demanding host. "*Tori?*" He repeated the familiar clipped named as a question. Yes, he was curious why there was a dead body on the plane, but unless that body was Victoria's, he wanted to keep Kronastia talking as long as he could about Jaguar.

Kronastia knew the seemingly insignificant nickname had not slipped by unnoticed. In fact, he was glad he didn't have to explain *why* there was a dead body on the plane. He was certain they weren't quite ready for that yet.

"Victoria and I have...history together. Complex, not always friendly, but not always *unfriendly*." He looked off in the distance for a moment before refocusing. "Well, anyhow, Dr. Smyth, as it happens, I know precisely *how* she got off the plane. I just don't know exactly where she went."

Dmitri's brow furrowed in thought, but he didn't miss Shep start to roll his eyes before catching himself. He knew what the doctor was thinking, and in any other case he'd be exactly right. Because, really, in the middle of the Atlantic, where was there to go but down?

12.18.12

Chapter 11

"Holy *hell!*"

The currents nearly dragged her under before she got her bearings. No matter how she would steel herself in preparation, teleporting into water always shocked her. Victoria rolled on a demanding wave of December-cold river water washed over her, before determinedly kicking hard and breaking the surface once more. The view pleased her: she was in London, all right, having managed to land in the Thames. Still a few hours before daybreak, the water traffic was minimal. A deluge of rain was falling from the sky, creating a cloak for her to make her way to the banks unnoticed by the few water taxis and other ships within sight.

As she pulled herself out of the river in a relatively inconspicuous place, she turned her eyes skyward. The plane wouldn't arrive for an hour or so, and she knew that once it did, her face was likely to be plastered over every broadcast medium the BBC had. It was an inconvenience of the modern world; escaping attention was so difficult. It was for that very reason that she didn't use her abilities in public too often. Her particular lifestyle required that she stay as incognito as possible. She never would have pulled off so risky a procedure unless she was sure there wasn't any other way.

She had suspected that the flash of light caused by her transference would alert the pilots of the jets of her departure. No doubt their orchestrator would have advised them that engagement was pointless if there was such a display. Had Dmitri been purposefully trying to get her to draw attention to herself in so blatant a way, knowing that it would force her into the shadows, or had he actually been contemplating having the jets fire in an attempt to kill her?

"Well, that's stupid," Victoria mused to herself. "He knows I can't die that way. Bastard."

Glancing over her shoulder as water dripped from her saturated clothing, Victoria spotted Big Ben. *4:35 a.m.* Two hours, three tops, before she would have to stay out of public view. She hadn't been meant to meet her rendezvous until nightfall, but she realized now she had no choice but to call him to make speedier arrangements.

He picked up on precisely the tip of the third ring.

"Aren't in-flight calls sinfully expensive?"

"Wouldn't know," Victoria grumbled. "Sort of had to make a personal emergency landing. I'm in Westminster."

"Do I want to know?"

She smirked. He always played coy with her. "I'm guessing it will be all over the news before lunch. You might not have much of a choice in the matter. Look, I'm cold and I'm hungry and I'm wearing the Thames. Can you just come get me?"

"Hungry? You do plan on eating before I collect you, don't you?" he asked sarcastically. "I would hate to cut short our holiday together. And ultimately, I would like to remain alive."

"Tut tut, now, Alex. I haven't killed anyone for at least…Oh, God, I think disco was still in style."

She wasn't about to tell him about the corpse aboard an Air Mexico flight that would be landing just after dawn.

"And that's supposed to make me feel better *how?*" Alex teased.

"That fact that disco's no longer in style should, if nothing else." Victoria was getting a little annoyed with his banter. "Look, bell bottoms should bring a death sentence for anybody not a standing member of the navy. Are you coming to get me or not?"

"Promise me you'll eat first." Alex waited patiently, his silence enduring as she mulled the notion. "Victoria?"

"Fine. Fine. I'll just…find a bite and meet you in front of Parliament in, what, twenty minutes?"

"Make it thirty. I have…" Victoria heard a girlish giggle in the background. *Monique.* "…something to take care of first. But where are you going to find something to eat in Westminster at this hour?"

Just at the moment, a random Londoner passed her phone booth, clutching his trench coat tightly as he made haste to get out of the downpour.

Victoria gave him a hungry and approving gaze. Sucking life from someone never really made her happy, but she did enjoy tracking her prey nonetheless.

"Street vendor. Thirty, Alex. Don't be late."

"Never am."

She hung up the phone and picked her bag up off the floor of the phone booth. Making quick, light steps, she started off in the passerby's direction, determined to wet her whistle.

Chapter 12

"*Mon coeur*, who was on the phone?"

Alex set the cell on the side table and turned his body back to Monique, raising his hand to her face and gently tracing a finger down her jawline and over her red, swollen lips.

"An old friend," he answered simply, smirking at the joke that the French woman in his bed would never understand.

Monique, instead of giving in to his touch, crossed her arms over her naked chest, sat up, and stuck out her bottom lip in a classic pout. "It was a woman, I think. I could 'ear 'er voice. An old lover, *non?* You want 'er, not me."

"No," he agreed.

Monique looked dismayed. "No?"

But Alex was becoming confused. "Yes, it was a woman. No, not an old lover. And I only want you. Now, I don't have much time as it turns out, so if you want to—"

"Why? Where do you have to go?"

He could see the course of the pre-dawn rendezvous had definitely changed, and his unexpected phone call had spoiled the mood. With a huff, he rolled to his side of the bed, suspecting that he would be taking no pleasure from the few minutes he had left with his stopover lover.

Not that he wouldn't like her full time. Monique was impetuous, rich, and young, and didn't hold against him the fact that Alex had been an orphan with no family much of his life and held no social capital in the world from which she came. He delighted in her company, and had convinced her to move to London after his activities with The Order required him to stay in closer proximity to their safe house. Alex had never known a place he considered home. He had bounced around a dozen foster homes as a kid, though, and despite the system's general reputation, his placements had always seemed like golden tickets with wealthy, sympathetic families. He had no objection, therefore, when it had been *strongly suggested* that he move to England from the American Midwest, but he still felt guilty for asking Monique to give up her home. It was a miracle she'd said yes, even though, due to The Order's demand for secrecy, he couldn't tell her why he had chosen the West London flat as home. He hated keeping the biggest part of his life away from her, but sharing with those on the outside just wasn't allowed, and he owed *everything* to The Order.

Sometimes, he still had trouble believing it was all real. Alex remembered very little about his parents; they both had died when he was ten. His sister had been old enough to be declared an independent minor, but didn't think she was capable of taking care of her younger sibling. Eventually, at fourteen, Alex received an unsolicited acceptance letter addressed to one of the most prestigious boarding schools in Switzerland, the hefty tuition paid for by an anonymous benefactor. As a child, he had never questioned it. He knew well enough that the money hadn't come from his parents. They had been lower working class, one a history teacher, the other a librarian. It wasn't until news arrived of his sister's death a few years ago as he finished his Master's degree in Economics that Priest had approached him.

Explaining that the private "ecumenical" organization had provided funding for his schooling, Priest offered Alex an introduction to The Order. At first, meeting only casually with other members, he found their belief system old world and...bizarre. Goddess worship sounded like a cult to him, and he couldn't picture himself biting the head off of a chicken or being used for ritualistic sex. Just when he was about to make a respectful departure from the group, Priest had arranged one last meeting. Alex walked into the West End Coffee shop to find himself instantly entranced by the sand-hued woman with pecan-caramel hair and bright jade eyes. He had loved Victoria from the start. Not romantically, per se, but in a familial way, like the older sister he had barely known.

"Tell me, Monique, what are you doing for Christmas this year?" he said with a sigh, changing the topic as he snapped back to the reality of the moment.

Cleary perplexed by the shift in agenda, Monique slanted her head. "I go back to Paris every year for the 'olidays."

Alex reached down to the space between them and took her hand into his, raising it to his lips and kissing her fingers. "Don't. Stay with me."

She nodded meekly and shrugged. "I suppose I could. Why, Alex? We 'ardly see each other as it is. You travel so much, anymore. What's so special about—"

Leaning over and covering her mouth with his, he cut her off. As he pulled back, he licked his lips, still tasting the echo of the champagne they had drunk earlier.

"Life is so short, Monique, and we never know what tomorrow holds for us. For me, I'd like to think it holds you."

Twenty minutes later, Alex found himself alone in the emptiness of his car, repeating the words he had spoken. Looking in the rear view mirror, he ran his fingers through his spiked hair. He had a suit picked out that he had wanted to wear to their meeting in the evening. It was at the cleaners; he had hoped to pick it up after lunch. Nor had Alex Cezanne imagined arriving for his meeting with Victoria Kent—as she liked to be called these days—with sex hair. The emotional request to Monique had stirred her heart and ignited passion, allowing for a quick lover's dance before he had left her.

Still, better to show up in a barrel with straps and on time than properly attired and groomed but late.

He told himself that it likely didn't matter. Victoria had told him when she chose him from the Priest's acolytes to be one of her inner circle that she admired his non-conformist attitude. Showing up in a three-piece suit probably would have disappointed her more than the blue jeans and Rolling Stones tee he now sported.

"After all," she had joked then, "I certainly didn't get to where I did by following the path expected of me."

Even at this early hour, a few cars were beginning to weave their way around the streets of Westminster. He hoped the slowly upticking flow of traffic had not impeded her ability to find sustenance without detection. He further hoped that she hadn't been joking about her dietary requirements no longer resulting in manslaughter the way Priest had said it once had.

Alex spotted Victoria looking somewhat bored, arms crossed and leaning against a street lamp just a block away from Parliament. He noted the bag hanging at her side, the way the fabric was pulled taut from the weight of its contents. He had been too scared to ask on the phone if the heist had been successful and if she had deceived customs, or if instead he would have to find a way to acquire a Heathrow security guard uniform to sneak it somehow off the plane or out of customs' retention room.

The brakes squeaked as he slowed and then stopped alongside the curb. Victoria slipped into the passenger seat expressionlessly, setting the bag between her legs and slumping back into the seat with an air of distant resignation.

Her clothing was still damp, and her hair was a collection of knots and clumps gathered in random lumps over her shoulder and back.

"I hate flying."

Alex didn't respond; he wasn't sure what to say to her. Somehow, in her presence, he always found his overly abundant sense of self-confidence drained. "Want to talk about it?" was all he could offer her.

Her response was almost stoic. "Not really. Just suffice it to say, this is going to make things harder." Her body shifted as she stretched and yawned and straightened into a confident, commanding repose. "Do we have a time set?" she asked, her tone now much more professional and expectant.

"Per your request, milady."

Victoria rolled her eyes and clicked her tongue. "*Milady,*" she mocked. "Oh my goodness, this isn't Arthurian times anymore, Alex."

Alex shrugged. He realized suddenly he didn't know exactly to where he was driving, so he just kept making random turns that would take him generally westward. "Sorry, I just...never know what to call you...to your face. Goddess seems a little high-strung."

"You had no problems a few days ago in Mexico."

"No one else was around. It wasn't the same."

"So, we take you away from The Order's proximity, and you finally see me as a friend, not an authority. I can't tell you how pleased that makes me." Her smile proved it true. She nodded, and then added, "You can call me Victoria or Vick, Alex. No need for fancy titles."

"Yes, m'—Victoria. Do you, um, want to stop and get some dry clothes somewhere?"

From the corner of his eye, he saw Victoria smirk devilishly. "We could borrow some from your French lady, perhaps?"

A gasp revealed his surprise, and his mouth went dry. Alex hadn't told anybody in The Order about Monique. In his new line of work, he understood how dangerous it could be for her should their connection become publically known.

As a preventative measure, Alex hadn't been privy to Victoria's little hobby of mindreading. If he had been, he would be all too aware of the extent to which she knew of Monique: her hair color, her favorite designer, her preference of Barbera to Merlot, the noises she made when he got her overly excited.

"How did you kn—"

"That perfume," Victoria said, cutting him off, using the quickest excuse she could think of. "Mind you, I'm no expert, but by chance, I'm familiar with this blend. It's only sold at one particular shop in Paris where it is hand-blended by a Lebanese shopkeeper named Zeyneb. Very good taste, if I do say so myself. And also the champagne. She must have snuck it through customs the last time she came back from France, as I think that particular vintage and label would be quite difficult to get out of the country. Oh, she's sneaky, Alex. I like her."

"All that from scents?" Alex queried. He had been told by the Priest that Victoria's senses were heightened, but even this was beyond what he could have imagined. "Just from the way I smell, you know she's French?"

Victoria shook her head as she waved to the right, instructing him to turn. Perhaps it was unfair of her to keep the secret from him any longer. "Not really. All that is just supporting evidence. What really gives it away is how her voice sounds in your thoughts. That accent is unmistakable."

Alex was dumbfounded. That fact hadn't really been discussed in serving-the-goddess orientation. "You can...you can...hear me think?"

She almost laughed. "Priest hasn't told you?"

Alex grimaced, wondering now if she could pick up on the frustrated, four-lettered comments running through his mind. "Priest says all will be revealed when the time is right, that I'm too young to understand everything you can do."

"You're twenty-five, Alex. Two whole years older than I was when I learned the truth. Priest gets a little uppity sometimes, but yes, Alex, I can read thoughts, when I want to. I can even control your mind; give commands to your subconscious. In fact, it's one of my specialties, one which certain Altunai were very eager to use by..." she chuckled "...*proxy.*"

He turned left and gunned the gas as they finally broke out of the city. "You mean, they can't..." His voice trailed off.

"No, they can't hear humans. I'm the bridge. Through me they can hear and speak, control and manipulate."

"Control?" Alex repeated.

"Alex, Alex, Alex...Tsk tsk. Determining what a person thinks is the easiest way of controlling him. Leaders and warlords have been doing it for eons with fear-mongering and scare tactics. My method is simply more...direct."

"But, doesn't the person know you're, like, in their head?"

The most devious of smiles spread across Victoria's face. Twisting herself in an almost catlike fashion, she leaned over the center console and whispered in his ear, "Why do you think you're driving the direction you are now?"

Chapter 13

"The limo is waiting, Mr. Kronastia."

Dmitri acknowledged Anton's statement with a slight nod as he led their party with a determined stride through the customs terminal.

"This is never going to work," Hector grumbled as he pulled up the rear of their group.

Shep wondered if perhaps he was looking for a way to escape into the crowd by dragging behind and dashing off at the first opportunity. More than that, he looked...clammy. As Shep's old-world grandmother had been fond of saying, he looked wind-whipped, world-weary, and right-worn.

Kronastia gave one doubting chuckle. "Dear Dr. Gonzalez, have you so little faith in me?"

"If this were Russia or China or Yemen, I wouldn't doubt that you could get the passport agent to bow down and declare you a god. But in England? Not sure how you're planning to pull this off."

"I'll meet you on the other side, sir," Anton broke in before heading off in another direction.

Shep eyed him as he joined a queue for British nationals. Kronastia intercepted Shep's questioning glance.

"Anton was raised in Russia, but his mother was from Wales. He was born here, still carries a commonwealth passport."

Reaching into his pocket, Shep ran his fingers over the worn cover of his own US passport. In so many parts of the world, the document was like a golden ticket, and he doubted he would come to have any trouble when he was at the inspection counter. Kronastia was certain to have at least a handful of passports in the briefcase he took with him from his plane. But he worried about Hector. Not only was he without his passport when they left Mexico, but even with it he would have had to apply for a visa prior to travel. Indeed, Shep was just as curious as his colleague about how this would play out.

"No, not that one."

Preparing to queue in one of the several open lanes, Shep felt himself jerked back as Kronastia grabbed the shoulder of his coat and yanked him to the line at the far end of the terminal. None of the lines were particularly long, but Shep wondered if there was something specific about this one that drew the Russian's preference.

Ten minutes later, two world-renowned archaeologists felt like children watching their father approach the booth to buy them each a ticket to go on the merry-go-round and a cotton candy.

The agent was a young woman, perhaps late twenties, who appeared to be of Indian descent. She held her hand out expectantly as Kronastia gently deposited his passport du jour into her waiting grasp. Shep noticed how his fingertips brushed the woman's wrists as she took the booklet, and even swore he saw her shudder as her eyes raised to meet his. From their distance and hindered by Kronastia's decision to keep his voice low, neither Shep nor Hector could make out their words. But Shep was a college professor; he recognized blatant flirting when he saw it. He smirked with a good sense of humor. If Kronastia thought this little scheme was going to outwit a British—

"Gentlemen, are we ready?"

Kronastia motioned them with a quick jerk of his head. Shep turned to Hector to find the latter's jaw making a dive for the floor. The agent gave them a tempting smile as the two walked through the passport check, passports *unchecked*.

"How did you…What did you…"

The Russian smirked, but his steps remained constant, dragging them forward. "I have a certain way of charming young ladies, gentlemen. No need to worry. Ah, there's Anton."

The valet was waving from near the terminal exit door, outside of which sat a waiting limo. They all piled in with their sparse carry-ons and relaxed into the plush leather seats. Shep looked around wildly to see if he could find a wet bar, and was soon rewarded with the discovery of a single serve gin. He downed the poison without asking permission, without even looking around to see where they were headed.

As the warmth of the alcohol began to spread through him, he became observant of way too many media trucks staged on the edges of the parking lot around Heathrow. Just beyond that, more government cars and black vans than he had recalled seeing in quite some time anywhere.

Hector must have noticed the same, for a moment later he asked, "What's going on here? What's all the excitement? The queen fall down a flight of stairs?"

Anton leaned over to his master and whispered something in his ear. Kronastia nodded. "Yes, Anton, please do."

The valet leaned forward to a TV screen embedded in the front console of the passenger compartment. With a flick of his wrist, the screen lighted with the image of a middle-aged woman and an older, balding man sitting at a desk, the bottom halves of their bodies obscured.

Breaking news, flashed across the screen.

"…and I understand now that an image of the suspect is about to be released," the woman was saying, pushing a hidden earphone to clarify the message. "Yes, Scotland Yard is now identifying the suspect as none other than—believe it or not—Jaguar, the renowned underworld thief and black market antiques dealer. We have here an image taken of her as she boarded the flight in Mexico City yesterday and…"

Shep and Hector gasped as the familiar face of Victoria Kent flashed across the screen.

"I guess you weren't lying after all," Hector mumbled.

Kronastia only gave him a wry, told-you-so look in response. "Ah, see there?" He tapped his finger on the bag hanging from her side in the photo still, its image grainy and green-hued, definitely taken from a security camera. "That must be the bag of artifacts she made off with. Trust me, gentlemen, she won't let that bag leave her side unless it's into very trusted hands."

Shep was rapt with curiosity. "She'll find a buyer that quickly, you think? Even with all this heat on her?"

"Silly Dr. Smyth, she's not going to sell those. They're emotional prizes for her, completely personal. She's going to try to absorb herself in the grandeur of her past to defer having to think about the future. Not that I blame her. She knows exactly what's going to happen. She thinks she knows *exactly* what my role is, and what I'm preparing for."

Shep looked at him from the corner of his eye with great unease. "What?"

He gave an amused smile. "Why, what else? The end of the world."

"And are you?"

Dmitri gave no answer, only a mischievous smirk as response. Hector, who had been sitting rather quietly, even lethargically, jolted when Dmitri's phone chirped.

"Took you long enough," Dmitri spoke into the receiver, though his tone was almost playful. The other party conversed for a few minutes, and if Shep wasn't mistaken there was some screeching involved. "What can I say, Anathea, dear, I pulled in some callers. You didn't expect anything less dramatic of me, did you?"

"Anathea Hermapolous?" Shep mouthed. Dmitri nodded, but put his fingers in a hushing motion over his lips.

"Of course I didn't expect anything less, but you can't blame me for trying. And I wanted to see how far you'd go. You know me, always trying to get the best performance out of my prized creation. I'll have you know, though, arranging fighter jets on such short notice was no small feat, and secretly, to boot. I almost decided against it, but, as always, I let the temptation get to me. Now the dead body... That was more than I could do. Good thing Jaguar was there to blame, eh?"

An insincere smile spread across his face as Dmitri clicked his tongue in disapproval. "Well, if the opportunity should arise, I'll look forward to doing just that."

With that, Shep heard a resounding grunt of frustration and a click.

Shep spoke immediately after. "It probably shouldn't surprise me that you know Anathea Hermapolous as well, I guess."

"As well?" Dmitri repeated. He exchanged a knowing glance with Anton. "No, probably not, Dr. Smyth. Ana and I go back some ways, in fact."

Shep leaned forward, beckoning Anton nearer. The valet, a little surprised to be addressed directly, leaned across, wearing a confused expression.

"Is he always so damn cryptic?" Shep asked.

Anton was relieved at the jest. He smiled and gave a quick nod. "More so, usually."

Chapter 14

"You're nervous."

It wasn't a question but a firm conclusion. Alex and Victoria had been sitting in the driveway for the better part of two hours as twilight had descended around them. He knew better than to speak, to suggest that they should go inside finally. He was her servant after all, and it wasn't his place to tell her what to do. Still, they couldn't just sit out in the driveway in front of the mansion in the English countryside all night. No doubt there were some inside who had noticed their arrival, and must be wondering at what they were getting at. Alex may have been serving his own interests in engaging her in conversation. The last thing he wanted was to be saddled with throwing off the schedule. He had been assigned one task by Priest: get Victoria to the ritual on time.

"I'm not nervous," Victoria finally returned stoically. Then, she sighed deeply. "I'm scared."

"Scared?" The very idea was preposterous. "Of what?"

"These men." Victoria swept her hand to indicate the house. "They see me as something I'm not. Maybe it's my own fault. I've rarely sought out correcting anybody who called me goddess. Still, facts are facts. Fact is, I'm not a goddess. I'm nothing more than a half-breed tool of the Altunai. But everyone inside is expecting me to…to…"

For a moment, Victoria appeared to be overwhelmed. Perhaps realizing her own loss of control, however, she quickly reeled it in with one deep, cleansing breath.

"To save the world?" Alex completed her thought. She nodded, her expression tense and uncertain. "Listen, I may be new to The Order, and maybe I'm not quite embedded to the depth that some of the old fogies inside are." He paused when Victoria grinned. "But if even one-quarter of the stories I've heard about you are true, we don't have anything to fear."

"You haven't heard that many stories, it seems." Victoria shrugged. Then, her eyes narrowed and she looked at him inquisitively. "Just out of curiosity, what *do* you know?"

"You mean, what do I think I know?" She nodded. Fine. If she wanted to procrastinate, he would do his best to indulge her. After all, he was pretty certain that once they walked through those front doors and into the hall the ceremony, he would never have such unfettered access to her again. He would miss Victoria Kent, or whatever incarnation she was living under. Despite her lofty position—she *was* freaking immortal, after all—he thought of her as a friend.

Alex pondered a few moments, trying to select something unlikely to enhance her current anxiety. "Okay, so, your age? I've heard everything from a thousand years to a million."

"Neither, nor."

"Approximately?"

She mused for a moment. "Well, I was twenty-five when I Bonded to the Guardian, and two years passed before the start of the first baktun. I guess that would make me roughly five thousand, two hundred-ish. But, Jesus, Alex, not a million. Don't be so gullible."

"I didn't say I believed it," he chastised, his eyes twinkling at hers. "Give me a little credit, Victoria. I wasn't born yesterday, either. Hmm, 'Victoria.' I very much doubt that's actually your name."

"Well, I have so many."

"Such as?"

She smirked at him. "Of course, you know the most famous one."

Alex smirked right back. "Sekhmet. That's what The Order calls you. That's how they worship you. Any more you care to share with me?"

"I've always been partial to Hecate," Victoria answered matter-of-factly. "I thought that incarnation was a good representation of my true nature. But I'll tell you something, Alex, that none of those *old fogies* inside knows. My name, the one my mother gave me: Tlalli."

It was clearly an intimate moment, he could see by the warmth in her eyes. He could barely make out her face in the darkness now, but her eyes almost seemed to glow in the dimness. *Just like cat eyes*, he thought.

"Yeah, you're not the first one to think that," she said out of nowhere. "Why do you think they dubbed me 'Jaguar'?"

Alex shivered. "You were reading my mind again," he concluded.

"I have to. See what you know and what you think you know. You have to understand, Alex, you know things about me now the others don't. Certain entities might try to obtain you because of that. If you switch sides, or fall victim to their devices, I have to know what you might be able to tell them."

He took a pack of cigarettes from his pocket and tapped one out into his hand. Pursing it between his lips, he lit it, taking a long draw before slowly blowing the smoke out in one, long stream. "I would never switch sides."

"You'd be surprised. Take Priest, for…" Victoria's voice trailed off, leaving the thought incomplete. She grimaced as the smoke made contact with her nose. "It changes, by the way. The eye color, I mean. Depends on my mode."

"Your *mode?*"

Victoria grinned as she reached down between her legs to the floor and grasped the bag. "You may see soon enough. This is your first ritual ceremony. A lot will become clear inside. *Those* things will kill you, you know."

Nodding in an almost amused fashion, he stared at the smoldering end of the cigarette. "Don't imagine they'd kill you though, would they?"

She shifted uncomfortably in her seat. Victoria couldn't quite explain what it was about Alex that she found so comforting and novel, but she admired the way he was always so direct with her. Others groveled or ceded, but Alex always put the questions front and center. It reminded her so much of her beloved Cleo.

She looked at him with an air of slight hesitation, hardly believing her own ears when truths unspoken to any human began to fall from her lips.

"I cannot die by human hands," she began, "but I can get very weak, very sick, or very injured if I don't feed from a human's life force for too long."

"'Not by human hands'?" He let the phrase hang in the air.

She grimaced, as though recalling an unpleasant memory. "The Altunai can kill me," she admitted, and then the corners of her mouth twitched. "I stand a chance of killing one of them too, I think, but only if the Altunai ceded their life. And since that isn't likely to happen…" She glanced off into space before snapping her head back at him, her eyes again luminescent, "Well, enough chit chat."

"Are we going in, then?" He took the keys from the ignition and pushed them into his pocket.

"Now that it's dark, there's no point in sitting out here. Better get in the right mindset, though." She turned to Alex as she reached out and cupped his cheek. "Alex, remember that the ceremony is theate. I'm playing a role. It's not really me. If I seem cold or unfamiliar…Well, just remember, it's just a thing I have to do. Just go along with it, okay?"

"Got it, chief." Alex gave a mock salute to her. "Go along, get along. Be a good boy, drink the Kool-Aid."

Suddenly, Victoria's look grew somber. She pinched his chin and pulled it down like a lecturing mother. "I expect more of you than that, Alexander Cezanne. Don't you ever 'drink the Kool-Aid,' and especially not in my name. I specifically wanted you in The Order because I need someone like you. I have lots of worshippers, Alex. I don't need another drone. I need a soldier, an advisor, one that will tell me when I'm screwing up. Don't be a sycophant. Be a survivor. Feel free to kick my ass whenever you think my ass needs kicking."

Alex nodded. "But, what about Priest? I thought that was his job."

She released his chin and opened the door. "I fear Priest's true intentions. He's been embedded for far too long, and I question his loyalties. As well as his motivations."

Alex got out of the car and fell into line behind a defiantly marching Victoria. She slung the bag of artifacts over her shoulder, narrowly missing Alex's head.

"You don't think he'd defect, do you?"

Victoria scoffed. "Ha! You've never met Dmitri, Alex. If Priest stays with him too long, Priest doesn't stand a chance." She reached the double doors of the house and paused, her hands lingering on the handle. "Not sure I would if I was around him, either."

Alex saw the mixture of playfulness and remorse dart across her eyes despite her averted gaze. As she made to yank on the door, he put his hand over hers, keeping it closed.

"You love him," he said in realization.

Victoria only stared dead ahead, unmoving. Alex waited patiently, hoping she would break the tension first. At last, she did.

"We have a…complicated history."

"So you don't deny it?"

Victoria shook her head and turned her eyes to the ground.

"But he is the enemy."

"Yes, that is true."

Alex felt his mouth going dry, the shaky pillars of his new found faith crumbling. "But, you love him," he repeated, as though that would bring clarity.

A fleeting smile passed across Victoria's face before dissolving into darkness again. "He…" She seemed to be stumbling for the right word. "He was…and I was…At the time, it…Argh, Alex, I know my place, and I never forget the truth."

It was as though someone had just told him that Hitler and Churchill had a habit of having tea every second Sunday. "I don't understand."

She turned and leaned back against the door, and Alex knew it would be a few minutes now before they made it inside. "I'm not human, Alex, but I'm not one of them either. Not completely, anyway. I feel…isolated at times. Alone. The only one who's ever understood that isolation and shared it to some extent was Dmitri. He made me feel like he understood my pain. Keep in mind, this was all very long ago. In a moment of misjudgment, Dmitri let me know of his original intentions toward me. Then, I understood, he never loved me. He was only using me, or at best, following orders. He was just doing his job."

Victoria made to open the door again. "Alex, the ritual must begin at the prescribed time or The Order will be upset."

"Is there any real reason it *needs* to start at the prescribed time?"

Victoria smirked. "Quick learner. No, not a single one."

"Using you for what?" Alex pressed.

"Alex, please. It's ancient history. Literally."

"Using you for what?"

But this time, the door opened from within, interrupting their conversation. A shaft of soft luminescence bent out across their bodies and up the path behind them. A figure of average height, hooded in black, waited. Seeing Victoria, it fell to its knees.

"Milady." The woman bowed her head in obeisance.

Victoria rolled her eyes at Alex. "We can talk later," she mouthed to him with a wink before addressing the prostrated figured in front of her.

"Rise, priestess. Your presence is recognized and accepted. I place into your capable hands the acolyte, Alexander Cezanne. His duty being fulfilled, dress him as one of the brethren and prepare him for the ceremony."

Alex didn't know what had just happened. One moment, Victoria was trying to downplay a treasonous past, the next she was a military commander barking out orders. Moreover, he was thoroughly shocked at said order.

"Wait a second," he whispered as he leaned in toward her ear. "Priest said that it takes five years in The Order—at least—to attend the ceremony."

"Alex, there may not be an Order in five weeks let alone five years, if you catch my drift. Now, go with the priestess here. This is a great honor in The Order's eyes. Don't shun it."

The priestess rose to her feet and took Alex by the arm, leading him through the foyer and away to a separate wing of the house.

Victoria was met by the elderly house servant, Lazarus, at the base of the stairs, just beyond the entryway. She had known him for fifty-three years, all his adult life, since he had been brought into The Order as a young man. Had so little time had such a grave effect on him? She would never become accustomed to the human habit of aging.

"Your grace." He acknowledged her with a dip of his head.

Taking the sack of artifacts off her shoulder, she handed the bag to him. "Place these upon the altar. Has Priest arrived?"

"He is en route, your grace."

Of course, she internally grumbled. *Always one to demand punctuality in others while never living up to the promise himself.*

Victoria turned toward the stairs and started making her way up, the servant following her like an overly eager dog, despite his advanced age.

"Has my bath been drawn?"

"Thrice, your grace. Since you first pulled in earlier this evening. I just refreshed it ten minutes ago."

"Good, thank you. And my kalasiris?" The recreated garb of traditional Ancient Egypt seemed to appeal to The Order's members, so she made sure to always wear it at ceremonies. She was certain, as well, that a number of her male followers didn't disparage the fact the sheer, white linen was nearly transparent, giving a titillating view of her form beneath.

"On your bed, your grace."

"I trust you remembered my rose oil?"

"Next to the bath tub, milady."

Reaching the double doors to her room, she closed Lazarus out without further comment but gave him a warm smile to show her appreciation, sending him away beaming. She practically dove into the tub. If there was one thing she was going to miss if her world came to an end, it would be bubble baths.

And, if she were being honest with herself, she would miss Dmitri too.

Twenty minutes later, sprawled out over her bed and staring at the ceiling, the thin gauze of the kalasiris sticking to her rose-oil lathered skin, she heard a knock on the door and knew it was time. She opened it to find two young maidens of The Order—virgins by tradition, though what difference that made she hadn't the slightest—bowing in obeisance. Giving a hand to each as she knew they had been taught to expect, the girls led her step by measured step down the stairs, through the house, and into the basement, a painstaking replica of an Ancient Egyptian temple.

Some forty robed figures filled the room, each of them lowering to one knee as Victoria was guided down a center aisle between them. Near the rear, she spotted a very bewildered Alex, his hood off for a moment before one of his fellow brethren pulled it reproachfully over his head for him.

Candlelight bathed the room, and on the altar a fire burned low and slow in a brass plate, the offerings of lavender and basil having been thrown on only moments before and sending wafts of herbal-scented ash in spirals over the surface of the altar. Next to the fire, her acquisitions lay on display, just as requested: proof that she could outwit their adversary and steal from right under his nose that which was rightfully hers.

As she reached the front of her congregation, the maidens leaned over and kissed her hands before departing the room. They were not allowed to watch the rituals. Their innocence was to be intact, by Victoria's order. Next to the altar, a golden throne awaited her, and she sat.

A chime was struck, and the same hooded woman who had met her at the door earlier stepped forward, her arms outstretched to either side, her voice full and reverent.

"Mighty Sekhmet! Eye of Ra, Lady of the Flame, Protector of Pharaoh. Divine Hecate, Keeper of the Paths, Guardian of the Gates, Seeker of the Just. We bow before thee. Our flesh is your flesh. Our blood is your blood. Our spirits are your spirit."

"We bow before thee!" the crowd repeated as, along with the priestess, they all sank in unison to their knees.

Victoria looked down, forcing herself not to roll her eyes at the pomp and odd circumstance. The customs of The Order stretched back to ancient times. The Order itself had been intermittent through the pages of history, rising and falling, joining and ceasing, but a clear line of Priesthood remained unbroken. Little did they understand, however, that Victoria took very little from these ceremonies. It was only for the sake of the cohesiveness of her following that she allowed the silly charades to continue.

Plus, after *The Di Vinci Code,* they all thought there was actually something to this shit. Victoria swore that if she ever came face to face with Dan Brown, she was going to give him a piece of her mind and the side of her hand.

Victoria gave a graceful nod to the priestess. "I recognize the High Priestess Katherine as the speaker of The Order. Let the Voice of The Order speak."

Chancing a look at Alex in the back, Victoria smirked. She couldn't help the momentary informality; he clearly could read her expression and understood that she thought this was a bunch of poppycock. Seeing the playfulness in her eyes, he stood in danger of a chuckle himself.

"Stop it," she mouthed at him with a wink.

He only shook his head and averted his eyes.

"Milady," Katherine continued. "We see that your efforts to reclaim the artifacts were successful."

"*Almost* wholly," Victoria grumbled through gritted teeth. She stretched out and sighed, examining her nails with passing interest. "The amulet remained out of reach. Unfortunately, I fear it is the one item for which I truly have need. These pieces are tokens of the fallen proxies. We should honor them by remembering their sacrifices. But their sacrifices will be for naught if I do not possess the amulet."

"Then we must retrieve it." Katherine's words were so matter-of-fact, so logical.

"Impossible. The Guardian will not allow it. And I…cannot be near him," Victoria argued. "He is Altunai, and I am the Vessel. If I am near to him, I stand a chance that he will use me to access the human mind, and he has with him currently…one human whose mind must remain isolated."

Katherine grinned and leaned forward. "Then we must appoint a new proxy."

"A proxy?" Victoria spat back the words like a curse. Did not the high priestess know it was in the choosing of the last proxy that she felt indebted to Shep Smyth to begin with? "I think not. I will…I will find another way."

"You haven't time to find another way, your grace. It's the only logical thing to do."

Victoria mused on that for a moment, hating that Katherine's reasoning held up to scrutiny.

"Fine," she huffed, slumping back in her throne. "Whom do you suggest?"

The priestess threw off her hood and turned, examining the roomful of partially-obscured faces before her. A few fidgeted, shuffled in place. No doubt most of the ignorant following thought it a blessing to be chosen.

Taking a few steps forward, the priestess' eyes focused on the clueless expression of the acolyte.

"Him," she pronounced, pointing squarely at Alex, who in turn pointed at himself questioningly. "Yes, you, acolyte."

"No!" Victoria gasped, jumping to her feet. The teams of worshippers gawked at her, curious as to her sudden outburst. Quickly, she tried to make herself look less insane and, frankly, less human. "He was joined to The Order but a year ago. He has not pledged. He cannot be called to such duty."

"Then, let him pledge now," Katherine offered, quickly pacing through the room and taking the befuddled Alex by the arm. She pulled him roughly to the foot of the altar, as Victoria inwardly cursed herself for inviting him to the ceremony to begin with. "Pledge, acolyte."

Alex was clearly confused. He took turns looking from Katherine to Victoria and back again. He struck an awkward pose, standing up straight and crossing his hand over his heart. "I pledge allegiance to the flag of the United States—"

Katherine clicked her tongue in reproach. "Fool, no!" She slapped him over his head, making Victoria's blood boil. "Come, now, acolyte. Your *fealty.* Pledge to do the goddess' bidding, even unto death."

Alex's eyes shot to Victoria, panicked. "Death?"

"He is too young to make such a pledge, priestess." Victoria was vaguely aware that the timbre of her voice was growing rough, almost a growl at this point. "It is unfair to ask one of his tender age to submit his existence to my service."

"Unto death?" Alex repeated, his expression revealing his doubt.

Victoria rolled her eyes at his unspoken thought. "We are *not* a death cult."

Alex's eyes widened.

Katherine clapped in glee, realizing the unspoken interaction. "Ah, you are already attuned to his mind!" she exclaimed. "Surely that makes him the ideal proxy. It should make the Bonding easy. And your last proxy was nearly as young as he when you Bonded her, if I recall correctly."

This only confused Alex further. "I'm being bonded? Like, paroled?"

"Acolyte, do you know nothing of our ways? Of the abilities of our goddess?" Alex shrugged. "Priest has become lax in his duties to educate the new initiates."

"In his defense, he has been busy doing the job I originally intended for *you*, Katherine," Victoria interrupted.

Katherine continued without comment. "Yes, *Bonding*, meaning the goddess will cross-reference her soul and her body to yours. You will be able to hear her as well as talk to her with your mind."

That news seemed to perk him up a bit. "Oh, Bonding. Cool, I guess."

Victoria, however, recognized the short-sighted nature of youthful ignorance in his cheerful turnabout.

"*Not* cool," she corrected him. "The human mind and body usually are not strong enough to be able to accept the Bonding unaltered. In time, you would have terrible headaches and nightmares. You would randomly access other people's thoughts without control. Believe me, Alex, you'll regret having the ability to know what people are really thinking." She shot an accusing glance at Katherine who shrank away from the ferocity of her stare. "And to try to outsmart Dmitri? You need the cunning of a cougar to outmaneuver him and the skills of an assassin if he catches you."

"The last proxy accepted the Bonding without ill effect," Katherine chimed in.

"And the last proxy died a horrible death once Dmitri learned her identity!" Victoria snapped back.

The two women stared at each other, both equally determined. Alex's eyes darted between the two women, then he took a deep breath.

"I'll do it."

Victoria snapped her head in his direction. "You'll do what?"

Shrugging, he repeated himself. "I'll do it. I'll be your proxy."

A Cheshire cat grin spread over Katherine's face, though Victoria looked wholly disappointed. She pulled him close, and she felt every gaze in the congregation follow her questioningly. She was acting very abnormally, and they wondered why her concern for this one particular acolyte should run so deep.

"Alex, this could kill you. The Bonding *has* killed others."

He was undeterred. "I'll do it for Monique," he offered. "I'll do what helps you save the world, if it helps to save her."

The goddess gnashed her teeth, but her muscles relaxed. She was clearly relenting. "Damn it all. Damn the human heart and its obligation to love. Fine, I accept your service. Priestess, I will accept the nomination and Bond with him, but in private."

Katherine sputtered in her confusion. "In private? But the following must bear witness to the—"

"In *private,* you perverted Peeping Tom."

The shifting visage of Victoria Kent struck terror in Alex's heart. Her eyes, no longer cool jade, ran midnight black, the pupils dilating to almost swallow their frame. Her body glowed eerily, not a hot white light, but a reverent, steady shine like winter moonlight on snow. Her voice took on the timbre of her station, echoing around the room and leaving no space for argument. Victoria Kent was a shell harboring the Goddess within. With frightening fury, that inner nature was making its way to the surface. Yes, he thought, *this* was Sekhmet, an ancient deity meant to be feared. Her superhuman attributes were undeniable.

Katherine, yielding, bowed to her and turned to the congregation. "The Bonding will be done in private, just the Goddess and her proxy. Let us take our leave, then."

Misunderstanding or incredulous eyes stared back. A Bonding was a rare event, one which all of them wished to see. But for Victoria, Bonding was one of the few acts she could perform which she actually did hold as sacred. She had only allowed the privilege to a handful. Some of her following bore witness to the last proxy's Bonding only seven years before. It had been a most unusual process, even in terms of a process itself so rare.

"What are you waiting for?" Victoria hissed to them, her voice almost seeming to reverberate against the replicated temple walls. She held up her arms outstretched, a flicker of spark on each finger tip. The visual warning of her impatience hastened the congregation as they at last turned and began to file through the doorway. Only Katherine remained back.

"Lady Sekhmet, I really feel as though at least one of us should—"

"Enough!"

Katherine fell to her knees and screeched as Victoria's fingers brushed against her cheek, the zap of an electric shock crippling her body with pain. Victoria's hand lingered threateningly in midair when Katherine looked up, tears brimming the corner of her eyes.

"Tori!" Alex reached out and took her hand into his, smoothing his fingers over the back of her hand. "Victoria, don't hurt her. She doesn't mean anything by it. She's your servant."

Inch by inch, under the stroking of his hand, Victoria's tension eased. She took several deep breaths, trying to calm herself. Alex visibly relaxed as well as he saw the pitch black of her eyes brightening to their familiar blue-green hue.

"Are you injured?"

The question was clearly for Katherine, though spoken almost stoically as Victoria kept her gaze locked into Alex's. Katherine didn't speak, only shook her head as she rose, wobbling, to her feet.

"Fine, now go! And find out what the hell is taking Priest so long to get here. We're not to be disturbed until his arrival."

Katherine's footing was unsteady, but she still managed to scramble to the door, closing it forcefully behind her.

Victoria let out a long sigh, turning from Alex. "I'm sorry you had to see that. I try to keep that nature within me contained, but sometimes when I let my emotions get out of control, it just seeps through."

"What was that?" Alex's question seemed rather plain for the circumstances. Apparently he had decided to take the whole bizarre outburst in stride.

A whimsical smile crossed Victoria's face. "I'm half-Altunai, Alex, remember?"

"Yes, but what exactly does that mean? How can you—what just happened to you?"

Victoria sighed and sat on the step of the altar. Patting the space next to her, she invited Alex to sit.

"Get comfy, Alex," she suggested. "I'm about to give you a crash course in the ancient world, cross-species genetics, and alien races."

Though Anton Sluga did not know precisely the heart beats per minute of the average cottontail rabbit, he imagined it must be in the ball park of 50% to 60% of what his pulse was currently clocking.

"What are you doing with the amulet, Anton?"

Dmitri's face was full of confusion and concern. It was an odd look for him, as he was rarely taken off guard, and he wore the expression with all the comfort of a squirrel in lederhosen.

Anton threw the pair of Dmitri's Armani pants on the nearby chair. Whenever his boss did something in private—in this case, taking a shower—Anton was required to survey the room for "tasks." Sometimes this meant straightening the bed, and sometimes it meant confiscating the still-warm gun and throwing it in the Moskva River. Tonight, it meant gathering up Dmitri's peeled-off clothes and putting them in the bag that would go to the drycleaner's the next morning. Though worrying about the pleats of the pants on the dawn of the Apocalypse seemed somehow misplaced.

When the amulet had slipped out the pocket and thudded to the floor, he could hardly believe his dumb luck. There it was, resting in an indentation in the plush carpet, as though it could be a coin or a paperclip—the key to opening the gate. Just sitting on the floor of Dmitri's London flat.

"It's…beautiful," Anton choked out. And indeed it was. Barely larger than the size of half-dollar, the chunk of stone that resembled azurite was embraced in tendrils of gold thread and connected by a catch to a gold chain.

"Yes, and it's *mine*," Dmitri returned with a hard edge to his voice that sounded a warning. "Kindly set it on the bureau and take your leave, Anton."

No, he couldn't possibly let it so easily from his grip. "Sir, this seems to be real gold. Maybe I could put it in your safe at the Bank of London. I wouldn't mind running it over in the morning…"

"Anton, put…it…*down.*"

Dmitri's ire had risen to full staff in the passing of a moment. Immediately, Anton knew that short of hand-to-hand combat, in which case Anton's hand and the arm to which it was attached would probably end up separate from his torso in short order, he wasn't getting anywhere with the amulet. With caution befitting the handling of a grenade, he gently deposited the amulet atop Dmitri's bureau and stood at the ready.

"Something you want, Anton?"

"Just curious, sir, if you're done with the Mexican?"

Pure stoicism in response. "Not yet. Almost. By morning for sure. Just hope his life force is enough for me to do my part opening the gate."

"You could always feed some more, if you're in doubt," Anton suggested.

"Volunteering?"

"No, sir. I thought, maybe Smyth—"

"No! Smyth is to remain unharmed."

Curious as to the determination, Anton cocked his head.

"I need him. I think Victoria might…well, Christine's already…and I know that if Shep died too, she might feel…he lives," Dmitri suddenly declared definitively. "Besides, I'm going to tell him."

Again, Anton was confused. "Tell him *what*, sir?"

Dmitri threw his robe over the bed as he turned to his bureau, fishing out enough clothes to keep him necessarily proper.

"Everything."

As though a dagger had just gone through him, Anton stumbled back a step. He was going to…*what?* Tell him everything? Tell Shep Smyth everything? What had he done to deserve that? What sacrifice had he made? Had Smyth given up years of his life working undercover, trying to feel out the secrets of Dmitri Kronastia? The "Russian mob boss" had only taken Anton into his trust less than six months ago, finally sharing with him all that Anton secretly already knew.

Just like with Victoria and her darling Alex, Dmitri had found his token human, and again it wasn't Anton.

"You've got to be kidding! Shep Smyth?"

"He deserves to know."

"What the hell makes him more deserving than me?"

Dmitri's head cocked to the side as he looked up from the work of doing the buttons on his shirt.

"If I didn't know better, I would say you were jealous, Anton. But that wouldn't make sense, would it? You already know everything I'm going to tell him, so what would you have to be jealous over?"

The valet shifted from side to side. "Nothing, sir. It's just…how can you trust him? He's an outsider. He's a no one." Anton thought a moment. He wasn't sure if it was a good idea, but suddenly an exit seemed to open for him. "If that's your decision, sir, I wonder at what my years of service have really meant to you. And if, indeed, there's a chance the world is about to end, I'd rather spend my last few hours following my own passions and not in your employment."

"Are you…quitting, Anton?"

He couldn't believe he was saying it, and now when the end was so close. "I'm love with someone, sir. And if there's a chance I might die soon, I'd rather have her know it than not."

Dmitri looked actually sympathetic. "A secret love you've kept from me after all these years, Anton? Well you are coy. So certain she'll accept you?"

"I'm making a hopeful wager, sir."

Dmitri nodded slowly, rubbing his chin in contemplation. "Well, I can understand taking risks in the name of love, Anton."

"Then you accept my resignation?

With measured steps, Dmitri crossed the room, holding out his hand.

"I accept," he said with a heavy sigh and a handshake. "Fine, go to her. And I hope she accepts you with open arms."

As Anton turned to leave the room, he too sighed. "Me, too, sir. Me, too."

Chapter 15

"Shep, what the hell are we doing here? How the hell did we...did we—" Hector's words broke into a cacophony of coughs and gags, his body shaking with the chill that had wracked him all night.

"Just like when we were in grad school, Hector. You can't tolerate the slightest bit of cold."

Hector gave a weak smile at Shep's friendly jab. Shep searched through the cedar box at the end of the four-poster bed for another blanket. It was still all very surreal to Shep as well. When they had arrived at the converted warehouse in the Docklands after an hour's drive east from Heathrow, he was filled with more questions than answers. The presence of the alcohol in his system only served to let his mind numb for a few hours. Sobriety left him bewildered. Hector had complained of feeling even more ill, guessing that he must have picked up something while traveling, though it was as equally likely that his body was just reacting to the stress of their current situation.

Dmitri had set them up in a bedroom with two identical, queen-sized oak-framed beds. After a few hours of sleep, Shep had awoken in the middle of the night to the sound of an argument coming from the sitting room of the trendy flat overlooking the Thames. He recognized Anton and Dmitri's voices, but the words exchanged in a foreign tongue gave no hint of the nature of their dispute. At some point, it sounded as though, based on his tone, Anton had admitted defeat. Shep had heard him scramble around the residence for a few more minutes before leaving out the flat door.

That was when he had looked over at Hector and saw him paler than a ghost, shaking through a cold sweat. Shep had spent the rest of the night sitting by his bedside, talking, trying to bring comfort and distraction to his ailing friend.

As morning light was approaching, Hector finally lapsed into a light sleep. The success was almost deterred by the light rapping on the door by Dmitri Kronastia. Dmitri looked sympathetically down on the slow, rhythmic rise and fall of Hector's chest, then placed his hand on Shep's shoulder and gave him an encouraging pat.

"Looks like he's getting a little rest finally," he whispered in Shep's ear as he leaned over. Shep nodded and sighed. "Why don't you come out and get a little tea and a bite to eat, doctor? Let him sleep it off."

A cup of tea, though not his usual drink of choice, sounded refreshing at the moment. With a yawn and stretch, he followed Dmitri from the room as the latter gently closed the guest room door behind him.

The kitchen was bathed in the orange-yellow glow of early morning sunlight. It stung Shep's eyes before they adjusted a few moments later. He sat at the table as Dmitri silently fetched a tea pot, a cup, the sugar bowl, and a spoon, and set them all down on the table.

"Not much here," he commented as he opened the refrigerator and looked in. "I do have some oatmeal in the pantry that should be good, but no fresh milk I'm afraid."

"Fine." Shep's words were as short as his attention span. He could barely keep his eyes open anymore. "Did you already eat?"

Dmitri smirked as he poured hot water from the tea kettle over a bowl of oats and set it before Shep. "I had almost enough while you were sleeping."

The spoon hung in the air as Shep paused before taking his first bite. "Don't you sleep at all?"

"Occasionally, but only for recreation. I don't like to waste my time. Especially now. I take it you heard our argument?"

Shep nodded. "I wasn't going to say anything. I'm never sure what is wise to say with you, what's safe or not safe to bring up. You have quite an infamous reputation, Dmitri. But you're, um, nothing like I expected."

The smile that crossed over Dmitri's face was one of pure amusement. "Now, doctor, what did you expect? Big burly, sweaty Russian, balding, big vodka gut, and thick, sausage fingers? Someone who would shoot you as well as look at you? A hostile, hardened criminal?"

Almost shamefully, Shep confirmed that that was exactly what he had expected.

"Then, yes, I can see why you're surprised," Dmitri said with a chuckle. His smile only enhanced his youthful appearance, reminding Shep of the mismatch between his looks and his history. "Truth is, Dr. Smyth, I'm not even Russian."

"No?"

He shook his head. "The persona suits my current needs, gives me access to many resources and people that make seeing out my primary responsibility easier. Victoria does the same thing, in her own *special* way."

"Your primary purpose?" Shep's hands tried to clear the sleep from his eyes. "And that would be…?"

Shep stared into the playful expression of Dmitri's eyes, and could see plainly that he was intending to let him in on some sort of secret.

"Surely you've studied Egyptian mythology during your archaeological career?" Shep nodded. Dmitri leaned in over the table conspiratorially. "What if I told you some of the myths are true?"

Shep shrugged unceremoniously. If Dmitri was expecting to get a rise out of him with the baiting inquiry, it wasn't working. "It wouldn't surprise me that there's some level of fact behind it. Most myths are reflective of a truth that simply cannot be rationalized by the contemporary men in the period they are created."

"You are, indeed, very wise, doctor. But what if I told you that Victoria Kent's role in Egyptian mythology is only rivaled by her role in its history? What if I told you that for much of the ancient history of Egypt, Victoria was the power behind the throne, as it were?"

"Ah, now I remember!" Shep exclaimed, taking the last bite of oatmeal before folding his arms over his chest and leaning back. "Your story about how she's some sort of real life Xena, Warrior Princess. Not still trying to pull that one over on us, are you?"

Dmitri scoffed. "Hardly. What she is, doctor…Or rather, *who* she is, is something much more devastating and real. You see, Victoria is Sekhmet."

"Sekhmet?" Shep looked at him incredulously. "The lion-headed goddess?"

"Well, the lion part is more symbolic, but yes."

"The Lady of the Flame? The Eye of Ra? The Drinker of Blood?"

"Yes, yes, and no," Dmitri confirmed. "She doesn't drink blood so much as spill it. She's the most impressive warrior I've ever seen, on this planet or any other."

"'Or any other'?" Shep repeated. Dmitri Kronastia was looking crazier by the second. "And you've seen…how many, precisely?"

Dmitri shrugged. "Six."

Taking a sip of his tea, Shep decided that it was probably a good idea to humor the Russian mob boss in his lunacy. "You don't say?"

But Dmitri was all too well aware of the patronizing. He crossed his arms over his chest, echoing Shep's stance. Being in the position of having to convince someone of a truth he had spent five millennia hiding felt oddly freeing. Victoria was so much more practiced at this than him. How had she done it, so consistently gathered believers without being sent to the loony bin? Not that he was crazy, nor was she. It was just, in the modern day, there was no room for out-of-the-ordinary realities like theirs. It made him wonder how the God of the Hebrews had pulled off such showy miracles.

But he had to find a way. Dmitri had to get through to Shep, make him understand. Shep was apparently the kind of guy she wanted to be with—why else would she have fought so hard to defend his life and had hated her proxy so much for falling for him? Dmitri couldn't stand to see Victoria's heart broken anymore, even if a little evil voice in his head told him it should be him, not Shep, whom she loved. It wouldn't have been the first time another had stolen her heart away.

"Do you know you're the first person I've actually ever volunteered the truth to? Now, in five thousand years, that's saying something. I hear myself saying it, and I realize now how crazy it must sound. How Victoria has a whole contingency behind her who hang on her every word is beyond me. Guess it takes all types." He shrugged, then narrowed his eyes. "What if I could offer you some proof?"

"Have a photo album, do you? A 'gods of Karnack' yearbook?"

Dmitri didn't answer at first. He only leaned forward and reached his hands across the table, his palms open, inviting Shep to place his hands into his. Glancing warily at the expectant gaze now focused on him, Shep moved toward him but kept his hands on the edge of the table.

"Go on, Shep. Nothing to be scared of," Dmitri tried to assure him. "There's a good chance this won't work anyway. I usually can't mindspeak to most humans, and fewer still do I deign to touch to even make the attempt. But something tells me this will work with *you*."

The lilt of his voice spoke more to a mystery still concealed, but now was not the time to inquire. "Mindspeak? What's that?"

Even Dmitri's patience was getting tested now. "Just give me your damn hands, Shep. If you get scared, you just pull back. Luckily for me, you're one of the few men alive who will probably follow the conversation with no trouble."

First one finger, then another, then Shep's two hands slid over Dmitri's as the grasp tightened to a firm hold.

For a moment, nothing happened.

While Dmitri closed his eyes in concentration, Shep rolled his in disbelief.

"Am I missing something, because I'm not get—*What the fuck?*"

He was walking in long, purposeful strides up a dimly lit corridor. The walls, floor, and ceiling were a puzzle of perfectly fitted stone edifices. They were a work of pure masonry expertise, almost artful in their arrangement.

The end of the corridor opened into a chamber where, on a chaise carved of wood and laced with reeds and linen, sat Victoria. Only, it was and it wasn't Victoria. No doubt the physical appearance was the same, from the caramel-pecan tendrils of hair, arranged atop her head in an almost Hellenistic style, to the green-blue twinkle of her feline eyes. But her demeanor, her stance, her grace: they were magnified to other worldly proportions.

And she was weeping. Bitterly.

A booming voice echoed in his ears, and Shep realized that it was that of Dmitri's, though it sounded very nearby. Too nearby. In fact, it sounded like Shep himself were speaking with Dmitri's voice in perfectly accentuated Egyptian.

"Sekhmet, we must speak."

Victoria took note of the presence of another, uncurling herself from the folded position in which she had been sitting. Her clothes were a fine, sheer linen, thin enough in their weave that Shep could make out the peaks of her breasts through the material.

"Mur-sha'ht," she spoke through her sobs and tears, a title that meant master, "I am your servant. What do you wish?"

Shep continued to feel himself speak through Dmitri's voice. Indeed, he realized that he must also be seeing through his eyes. "I cannot condone your actions. I have ordered you never to attempt the Bonding. Now you see the damage you have done? Sekhmet, we must stay separate of these petty human affairs. We must rise above and let humanity make its best effort through its own struggles. We must not interfere."

"I disagree," Sekhmet-Victoria spat back. "I am as much one of them as

I am one of you. Why should I not care for the struggles of this world? Why should I not make an effort to help?"

Her voice sounded sad, reproachful.

"I did not seek her out to Bond her, Mur-sha'ht. It was not my intention to…" She looked away, ashamed. "I only sought her out to help her. If Augustus had gotten his way, she would have been dragged in chains through the streets of Rome."

Shep felt his hands—or rather, Dmitri's hands—reach out and yank Sekhmet-Victoria to her feet. He pulled her near, his lips just inches from hers. "No more. I care too much for you to punish you for this, but take your lesson from Cleopatra. Do not be the cause of another…"

He was on the floor, his head spinning and his mouth dry. A pulse, he thought his own now, was drumming in his ears. As his eyes focused, Shep made out the very concerned visage of Dmitri Kronastia hovering over him.

"Shep? Shep, are you okay?"

He nodded and accepted the hand outstretched to help him up. Dmitri braced Shep under the arm and lowered him back to sit at the table.

"Mindspeak, huh?" Shep asked through heavy breaths. "More like…mindfuck."

Dmitri slumped into the chair. Even he seemed a little out of joint. "My apologies, doctor. What I showed you was one of my personal memories. Surely, you can see the truth now?"

"Sure," Shep gasped, waving his hand dismissively. "Victoria, Sekhmet. But…what…does that…make…you?"

"Not human, Shep."

Shep looked at him confusedly. It was a preposterous statement, but the moment he heard it, he knew it was true.

"Oh, and just what are you, then?"

In the sincerest of tones, sounding like a confession, Dmitri answered. "I am Altunai."

Chapter 16

For the next half hour, Shep sat in stunned silence as Dmitri Kronastia —or whoever or whatever he really was—explained the nature of his being.

Somewhere in the universe existed a planet called Altunatus. Its inhabitants, the Altunai, were explorers and intellectuals. They often seeded a planet with human life—the formula for creation of a lower genetic version of themselves, mastered after eons of experimentation, and set up a certain level of base knowledge and advancement for the experiment group. On Earth, the initial phase of the project had ended approximately five thousand years before. The Altunai had two primary control sites on Earth: the Nile River Valley and the Yucatan Peninsula. At each location, a limited party of Altunai mentors fostered the knowledge of the native peoples, teaching them the skills they would need to develop art, government, farming, trade, and, yes, war. When the two civilizations were far enough along to fend for themselves, the period of isolation had been initiated. Thirteen baktuns long, or five thousand, one hundred twenty-five circles of Earth around its sun.

"But, how did you—the Altunai...How did they get here?"

Dmitri sighed, apparently relieved that Shep asked. Shep supposed that after his enduring silence, Dmitri was glad that he was at least attempting to take the revelation seriously and beginning to process the truth.

"We can travel through manipulations of energy, not so unlike some of your science fiction stories. But, of course, there's a catch."

"Black out period for your frequent beamer miles?" Shep joked.

Dmitri's face remained stern. "Something like that. Once we identify a planet that has the necessary elements to maintain life, we have to dock it. It's like building a bridge; once you throw the initial tie line across, you have to build another side back against the opposite shore's foundation. In short, one Altunai must stay behind, a sort of homing beacon. I was assigned to be Earth's dock."

That explained Dmitri's role, but it didn't explain Victoria's. "And Victoria?"

"Well, she's what we call 'the Vessel,'" he answered. "The Vessel has two purposes. First, she's a sort of data recorder. Victoria was born human in the Olmec Empire. When she told you she was originally from the Veracruz area, that wasn't a lie."

"How did you know that she—"

"Security camera, Shep," Dmitri interrupted. "They probably shouldn't have been in the hurricane shelters where people were sleeping, but one of my security team seems to have had an unhealthy obsession with Victoria."

"Yeah, but she also told me she was twenty-five, so I wouldn't credit her with being completely honest." Sure, women tended to low-ball their actual age, but the difference of a few thousand years was nothing to sneeze at.

"I doubt she actually lied to you," Dmitri countered. "She has a tendency to let others create their own truths, and then just plays according to the rules they make."

Thinking back, Shep realized that she hadn't actually said what age she was, only concurred with his guess. He grimaced and felt silly at the oversight.

Dmitri seemed to have read Shep's thoughts as clear as day. "Don't worry, Shep, she's gotten the better of far wiser men than you."

He sighed. "So…data recorder?"

"Yes," Dmitri continued. "Well, as part of the analysis of the experiment, one native is chosen to serve as a witness to the period of isolation. To ensure her survival, she must Bond with an Altunai. That is, we manipulate the DNA to allow the Vessels to live as long as we do and be impervious to most illnesses and injuries. The Bonding also imbues them with many of our abilities: teleportation, telekinesis, telepathy—"

"Whoa, whoa, whoa!" Shep demanded, holding his hand out in the accompanying gesture. "You mean to tell me you can read minds and move stuff around psychically?"

Dmitri gnashed his teeth in frustration. "For a man who just accused me of mindfucking him, you sound oddly surprised. But no, not now, so much. On this planet, the Altunai's abilities are severely hampered. You see, we feed off energy, transform it to be able to do all the things we can do. But Earth's energy is different than that on Altunatus. It's like traveling between countries having different standards of electric current. Victoria is, for lack of a better term, my converter plug."

"So, if you have Victoria nearby…" Shep's voice trailed off.

"Yes, Shep, you put it all together very quickly. I can see why she credited you so much; you really seem attuned to the truth when it's presented you. Most humans would just dismiss this as a bunch of rubbish and write me off as some eccentric or loony."

It was a curious thing, Shep thought. In any other situation, he was certain he'd be included among "most humans," and despite years of disciplined training and practice in not attributing relation to causation, something about this explanation just seemed logical to him. The certainty of it was almost primal. He was reminded of Occam's Razor, the philosophy which stated, all things being equal, the simplest solution was usually the right one. Still, an intern on a friend's excavation site being an international black market dealer? That same person turning out to be a possibly eons-old, human-alien hybrid creature with superpowers? The underwriter of the project being an alien masquerading as a Russian mafia kingpin whose race had seeded Earth with life as some sort of social experiment? Was this really the simplest solution?

"Okay, answer me this, though," Shep said. "You say Victoria—Sekhmet. Whatever. You say she was born in the Olmec Empire. How does an Olmec in the ancient world go from the Yucatan to Egypt and back again?"

"Getting back to the Americas was one of her finer moments. She convinced some Vikings to set out to the new world and traveled over land from where they landed in modern day Canada. The 'to Egypt' part was easy enough: she teleported. With me, no less. Our gateway to Altunatus is in Egypt, and Isis and Ra—you should understand, of course, Shep, that most of the gods of the Egyptian pantheon are, in fact, Altunai—they wanted to inspect her before departing."

"And she met their expectations, I take it?"

Again, a curious look overcame Dmitri. He seemed slightly peeved at the inquiry. "Yes, Ra's particularly."

Understanding filled Shep. He cocked his head and smiled knowingly. "That's jealousy written all over your face."

In an almost blinding show of speed, Dmitri rose from the table and began pacing nervously the length of the room. He ran his fingers through his ebony locks, pulling in frustration.

Shep gave a low whistle. "Wow, you must really love the girl to still be so upset over it after all this time."

Dmitri stopped short and eyed Shep warily. "You have no idea."

"Is that why we're chasing her?"

He shook his head again. "Unfortunately not. You see, the end of the isolation period is coming. The Altunai will be returning, and Victoria must be there to open the gate."

Shep's eyebrows slanted. "I thought you said you were the beacon. Why does she need to be there?"

"I'm just the marker, but Victoria's the key that opens the door. This," he took the amulet from his pocket and dangled it out in front of him, "this isn't just some random stone. It's a piece of Altunatus, a chip from the planet's core. It will allow the little bit more of Altunai DNA that she carries but remains dormant in her body to spark. With that power, she can harness Earth's energy and bend it to her whim, open the bridge between the worlds. Conduit, remember?"

Dmitri's eyes were full of worry and concern. Shep pondered his words.

"You said there were two roles the Vessel plays," he said. "What's the other?"

Apparently satisfied that Shep was tracking with the truth being set out before him, Dmitri continued. "When the isolation is over, the Altunai return and examine the mind of the Vessel as a sort of project oversight and review. Once the Vessel has served that task, the Altunai will use her conduit to render judgment. If they believe the experiment has been a failure, they will gather enough energy through Victoria to destroy humanity. If they believe that the experiment has succeeded in creating a civilization worthy of further study, the standard procedure is to destroy the Vessel."

"Either way, Victoria dies?" Shep asked. Dmitri confirmed it with a nod of his head. "Then why are you so set on finding her?"

"As much as I hated it, Ra's mistake could be to my advantage. You see, the Bonding that happens between human and Altunai? There are two ways for it to take place. One is by a blood transfusion. Victoria uses this method to Bond her proxies, to give them just enough power to serve on her behalf as elite members of the group of ninnies that follow her, The Order. But there's another way, a...*more intimate* way."

"You mean sex?"

"You put it so plainly."

Shep shrugged. "It is what it is."

Dmitri cleared his throat. "Yes, well, it was what it was. Victoria denied it, but the evidence of her powers is clear: Ra seduced her, Bonded her. But he was gone too soon to see the ramification of his actions. The classic one night stand, gone before the morning's light, if you will. I don't think she suspected it would happen; we had never attempted to double Bond a Vessel before. Victoria's abilities are far advanced beyond that of any of the other Vessels. Hell, she's even stronger on Earth in some ways than I would be back on Altunatus. I think once she consumes the amulet, she stands a fighting chance at not being destroyed. Or dare I say, defending humanity."

"Does...does she know all this?"

"Mostly." Dmitri sat back down across from him at the table. "She's always known about Bonding, about the Altunai, about being a conduit. What she didn't know for the longest time was my role. I am sworn to ensure the safety of the Vessel, you see, until the isolation is over. When I told her about what would happen on the day of their return, and how I would return back to Altunatus, she accused me of using her. She refused to believe my feelings for her were true. Her unbridled rage allowed me to see the full scope of her abilities, however. It is the reason I have so much faith in her now."

"Blew a gasket, did she?" Shep smiled. He had been at the receiving end of a woman scorned once or twice in his life too, and knew well the danger.

"Actually, she caused Vesuvius to erupt. I trust you've heard of that incident."

The sip of tea Shep had been taking spewed across the table. Coughing and sputtering, he grabbed a towel from the kitchen counter and began to sop up the mess.

"Okay, so it sounds like she can handle herself, if it comes down to it. When exactly does this isolation end?"

"In three days."

"You don't mean..."

"Yes, I do," Dmitri confirmed.

It was one of the oldest legends of the archaeological world, one Shep was well aware of even if Mesoamerican cultures were not his focus. The date was so well known it had even attracted a cult following. With a pang of foreboding, he recalled the lone loony in the Veracruz airport, the one Victoria had been quick to dismiss and explain away. Shit, she knew then, didn't she? She knew the crazy was probably the only one in the terminal with some vague idea of the truth.

And it explained how she could so quickly translate the modern Mayan dialect.

"The date the Mayans said the world would end?"

"Yes, Shep, though that bit of information was transferred to them by one particular Olmec. 12.21, Shep. Three days from now, could be the end of the world."

12.19.12

Chapter 17

Victoria could not stop the tears. They trickled down her face just as the blood still trickled down her wrist from where she had wounded herself, giving Alex drink from her own vein. No matter how she had prepared herself, told herself there was no other choice, she couldn't escape the guilt. Her proxies never survived long after the Bonding. The last had been the exception, holding the record for seven years.

If she removed her emotions, she reminded herself that *this* proxy didn't need to live seven years. She just needed him to render one service, and in only three days' time. If he didn't, in three days no one might survive. As Alex's eyes flinched, she felt the first wave of intense pain hit. The Bonding was under way, and there was nothing to do now but ride it out. With skin-to-skin contact, his sensations became hers. She hoped she could counteract some of the ache. Maybe sharing in it would lessen it. Or so she hoped.

She felt anxiety grip her as she remembered their conversation before he made the commitment.

"I'm half-Altunai, Alex, remember? I have many of their powers. Priest really has been woefully incomplete with your teachings. You don't know anything about all this, do you?" He shook his head. "The Altunai are not of this planet. Their abilities are immense, but the source of their power is the energy of their own planet. On this planet, their abilities fall short. In order to harvest the energy of this planet, of Earth, they needed a conduit, some being who had the DNA of both their race and the human race."

Alex had put the meaning together very quickly. "And you're the conduit? That's why Dmitri can hear and control humans only through you?"

"Yes, exactly," she confirmed. "I was engineered to be their tool. I have many of their abilities, but there's a cost. Like the laws of thermodynamics say, energy can be neither created nor destroyed, it can only be transformed. To do what I do, I need...sustenance."

He nodded. "So you siphon human life forces."

She looked ashamed. "Over the years, I've learned how to do it without killing the human, unless that's my intent. The Altunai while on Earth also feed off human energy, but they don't require touch like I do. Dmitri can absorb a human's energy slowly, discreetly. He leeches off them, like a parasite. By the time the human realizes something's wrong, it's usually too late. But let's get back to the here and now and how this relates to you. Did Priest ever discuss the Bonding?"

Rubbing his chin as he scanned through their few conversations, he only recalled one instance. "He only mentioned once that he hoped it happened to him one day."

Victoria had ground her teeth. Priest's desire for power was disturbing to her. It was no wonder he had kept so much from Alex; clearly he saw him as a potential rival to his high-ranking post in The Order. "Bonding is where the Altunai—me, for the purposes of this conversation—infects the host, you. Think of it as passing along a virus. But because I am only a hybrid, the imprint of my DNA and its effect on you won't be as strong as their effect on me. It won't stop you from aging, for example, or keep you from dying as it does with me. But you won't exactly be human anymore. Not completely."

Alex had cocked his head in suspicion. "Why do I get the feeling you're leading up to something horrible?"

"Because I am," she said plainly. "There's a transition period when the virus first takes hold of the body. It's short-lived, a day at most based on my few tries at this, usually less. After that, you'll resume a familiar sense of normality. But while you're under the fever, your body will crave. Crave everything: water, food, sex, pleasure, pain. Your senses will go mad. With keen determination, you can overcome this. But there's one thing I can guarantee."

He swallowed. Hard. Her tone was too ominous and her eyes too dark to expect anything less than tragedy. "Go on, what is it?"

Victoria's eyes studied the floor. She shamefully added, "You'll crave a life force, and for the virus to manifest in your body, you'll need to take one. It took me eons to learn how to just tap off the surface of a life. We don't have that kind of time. Alex, you're going to have to feed, and in our current circumstances, that means killing one of the members of The Order."

Alex had shuddered, the weight of what he had agreed to crashing down on him. Victoria could read his thoughts as clearly as if he'd spoken them out loud. Could he agree to this now? The Order's ways were archaic, and he knew that if they ever could find a way to help Victoria, it was a worthy goal. But could he do this? Could he commit to a fate that would see the end of an innocent's life? Was doing his part to help save the world, help save Monique, worth the burden of knowing he had stolen someone's existence?

He looked into Victoria's compassionate gaze, to the woman who for the last three years had been a mentor, a friend, a confidant, even a mother in some ways, and Victoria saw it the moment he knew his answer.

"Yeah, I'll still do it. I mean, if we fuck up, everyone could die, right?" She nodded, wide-eyed. "Just, tell me how."

"Simple," and there was an air of both relief and disappointment in her tone, "all it takes is drinking a little bit of my blood."

He had drunk with much trepidation, but drunk nonetheless.

Now, with his mouth on her skin, she opened her eyes and looked at him as he drank, immediately wishing she hadn't. Alex's face was screwed up, the pain pulsing through his body intensifying with every passing second. She could feel it through their connection, through their touch. Her blood was infecting him more and more by the moment, twisting his composition to its whim.

She leaned over and closed the space between them, whispering comfortingly, "Hold on, Alex. It's going to get rough. Just stay focused on Monique. Remember, you're doing this for her."

Alex's eyes shot open, focusing with vehemence and determination on Victoria. She could see in his mind, see the images of Monique calling out his name in the throes of passion. His body was beginning to flex the muscle of its new gifts already. He was casting out of his consciousness the mask of his true desires. In that moment, Alex looked at Victoria…and saw Monique.

She was on her back before she realized what had happened, Alex's mouth covering her own as he pushed longingly against her. Through the rough denim, she could feel the stirrings of his passion, working desperately to contain her own. She didn't love Alex Cezanne, not in *that* way, but she wouldn't deny the temptation to claim him, mark him as her own. It was simply in her nature, her *Altunai* nature, to dominate the lower species.

But her human side called to her, told her if she allowed this to happen, Alex would never forgive her when he came through the fever. He loved Monique, and he'd despise her. Maybe even refuse to take on the mantle of the proxy and see to his mission. More than that, though, Victoria would never forgive herself.

As he pulled back, she locked her gaze with his. "Fight it, Alex. Trust your own eyes. Look at me. Who am I?"

His voice was gravely, lust-filled. "*Ma chère, mon ange,*" he purred in French. "*Ma Monique, mon coeur.*"

He moved to kiss her again, his hand traveling up her side, enveloping her breast through the thin gauze of the kalasiris. Despite her determination, Victoria moaned, feeling her own resolve weakening.

"Alex," she breathed. "We mustn't..."

In his trance, he began to push against her harder. The effects of the Bonding on his psyche were spreading into her through his touch. His delusion was becoming hers, Victoria's own object of desire filling her mind's eye. As Alex pulled himself back, his eyes focused on the licentious gaze of the goddess. Victoria's visions shifted, seeing Dmitri's face looking down at her.

She stroked the side of his face. "My love. Oh, how I've missed you. Take me. Take me now."

Betrayal wracked through their bodies as Victoria moved her hands downward, beginning to fish for the zipper of Alex's pants. She needed him, needed him now. He lifted his hips, aiding her efforts. The stiff fabric slid downward, taking his boxers along, revealing his readiness to her.

"Oh, please, don't allow me to interrupt."

The distraction hit them both simultaneously, and the delusional state of their minds sharpened with an aching clarity. Victoria saw Alex, Alex saw Victoria, and Anton, the Priest, saw them both on the edge of a ritual consummation.

Their bodies parted in an instant, Alex desperately trying to hide his nudity from his mentor.

"Priest!" Victoria shouted, sitting up and catching her breath. She would feel no shame; she was not accountable to anybody, least of all Priest. Rubbing her temples with her hands, trying to maintain her air of authority, she barked at him, "What's taken you so long?"

"My apologies, milady, but I see my haphazard timing proved to be...perfectly timed."

His eyes shot to Alex who was shimmying his jeans back over his hips.

"It's the Bonding, Anton. It's a very consuming process," she explained. Realizing, however, the closeness of the ill-advised action, she stared at the floor and added sheepishly and under her breath, "but thank Ra for your arriving when you did."

Looking up, she saw devastation on Anton's face. "You...Bonded?" he said with disbelief. "You...you Bonded with...*him?*"

"Am I not at liberty to Bond with whom I will?"

Anton's lips curled in disgust. Alex looked now to his mentor, his breath raging. The delusion subsiding, the pain was beginning to wrack him again, as well as the understanding of how he almost betrayed his own heart. Grasping his head, he sat down at the base of the altar, silent tears beginning to streak down his cheeks.

Anton decided to remain resolute in his role. Fine, he thought, let Alex be a proxy. Proxies were likely to die sooner rather than later. When Alex met his fate, Anton would still be at the ready, prepared to convince Victoria of his rightful place at her side.

Priest motioned to Alex with a wary glare. "What is his mission?"

"To retrieve the amulet, as your efforts have resulted only in failure. Have you succeeded in determining where it is?"

"Yes, Dmitri keeps it with him. He is in London now; he followed you here."

Victoria looked into Anton's thoughts. She did not like what she saw. "Why are Smyth and Gonzalez still with him?"

Anton shrugged. "He's seems to be consuming Gonzalez. I fear he's not much longer for this world. As to Smyth, I don't know. But, milady, I must say, Dmitri's acting very...uncharacteristically."

Victoria's eyebrow slanted. "Meaning?"

"He intends to reveal himself to Smyth."

Surely, Anton was mistaken. "Wh-why?" She shook her head in disbelief. "No, it can't be. That goes against every one of his motives for the last five thousand years. Why would he do that, so close to the end?"

"I don't know, milady. When he shared his intent with me, I used it as an opportunity to voice my disapproval. I was able to convince him to release me from his service, pretending that I was too insulted by his betrayal of his core mission to keep working for him."

Confusion consumed her more. "Well played, but he accepted that? Something about that doesn't seem right."

"I've learned not to question serendipity."

"Oh, God! Make it stop." Alex crumpled in a ball to the floor, the pain extending to every cell in his body. For a moment, Anton wondered if indeed it was fortunate that he had not been selected as the proxy. The current state of the acolyte was evidence that he had romanticized the process.

"How much longer will he…" Anton swallowed despite the dryness of his mouth, "…suffer?"

"A few more hours. I will stay with him. I'll comfort him as much as I can. By daybreak, he will have gone through the worst. Anton, he needs the…the…"

"The sacrifice, milady?" he asked.

She nodded, her eyes closing in shame. "He's manifesting very quickly. Getting the life force now will speed the process."

"Who shall serve, milady?"

She turned to Anton with a saddened expression. "Inquire after Lazarus."

The confused man, roused from his slumber in the middle of the night, stood before Victoria's altar, eying the shaking figure of the acolyte, agape. He looked tenderly at Alex, the way a father would look at a son suffering some ill. Victoria had always reveled in Lazarus' compassion. She regretted having his life end this way.

"Lazarus, fifty-three years have passed since you pledged your fealty to me and to The Order which serves in my name. Do you wish to withdraw that pledge?"

The old man shook his head, confused. "Every moment I have lived in your service, your grace. I would not reclaim a minute."

Tenderly, Victoria reached out and cupped his cheek, speaking again in a much gentler tone. "And if this fealty demanded your life, would you grant me that wish?"

"In a heartbeat, your grace."

Trying to remain aloof, she reached out to the fetal ball that was her proxy on the ground. "Come, Alex."

Alex's eyes filled with need and distrust, the conflict brimming in his psyche as well as in his expression.

"Do not you feel the pull of his life force, love?" Victoria asked, the perfect actress playing the part of the co-conspirator. "Don't you taste his soul on your lips?"

"It tastes…" Alex paused, looking for the right words. The sensation was so alien to him, the sting in his throat—though the hunger he felt was more mental than physical—tempting yet foreign. "I taste…heat?"

"Yes, Alex," Victoria confirmed, "the taste of a soul is more temporal than tactile. Come, Alex. Place your hands on him. You must have physical contact. I promise, this is the only time you must do this. Just…touch him. Allow that heat to become your own. Draw his warmth into you."

"He will die," Alex muttered.

Lazarus shuddered, the strength of his pledge waning in this shadow of his demise.

Victoria bent over, whispering in Alex's ear. "If you do not take his life, you cannot serve as proxy. If you do not serve as proxy, Monique will die. Do you want Monique to die, Alex, dear?"

She hated herself in that moment, and hated knowing just how to manipulate him to commit murder. Victoria took both his hands in hers, guiding them toward the sacrifice.

Shaking his head slowly from side to side, Alex wept. "No, of course not. I love her."

She lowered his hands to Lazarus' face. The poor man quivered but remained speechless.

Alex, on the other hand, jolted and withdrew. "He's burning up."

"That's his life force, Alex. And he offers it up in the name of his Goddess. His soul is mine to do with as I please, Alex. It pleases me to have you take it from him." Gingerly, she again positioned Alex's fingers onto Lazarus' temples. "Drink…him…in."

Priest wasn't sure what happened next. He knew only that when his eyes opened following the flash, he beheld three things: Lazarus dead, Victoria's eyes dark as midnight, and Alexander Cezanne transformed.

Chapter 18

" So, why me?"

They hadn't moved from the kitchen, but chose instead to linger there in impervious silence for the better part a half hour. It was quite amazing when Shep looked at it; Kronastia had said just enough to make his story known, then waited patiently for Shep to process it all. For someone who thought the world might end in three days, he had the patience of a saint.

Shep, at the same time, had been playing, replaying and re-replaying the events of the last seventy-two hours in his head. Truth be told, he was analyzing things back to the beginning of time.

He had never been a particularly religious man. Following Christine's death, he had tried to develop an understanding of God, if for no other reason to assuage his own anxieties over the fate of Christine's soul. Before, if asked, he would have claimed that he held no belief of something as far-fetched as Heaven. After Christine died, however, he had felt the need to prove himself wrong, or at least allow for the possibility. As it turned out, proving to one's self the possibility of something that most people vehemently denied or unconditionally endorsed was harder than it sounded. One thing he had decided for certain: the caring, compassionate soul of the woman he loved had not ceased to exist solely because her corporeal shell had been crushed under the earth. And somehow, he always felt like she was with him, as though on the outside of a door where he stood with his hand on the handle, only to find it locked.

But here sat a man claiming to be millennia old, telling Shep that his existence, as well as the existence of every human on Earth, was no more than a philosophical enquiry by a technologically and spiritually advanced race. The irony of humanity seeking out the divine when the divine was studying humanity in turn was not lost on him.

"Why you *what?*" Dmitri asked to clarify.

Shep tapped two fingers to his temples. "You said your kind can't do all that hocus pocus without Victoria nearby. Yet you said, 'I'm pretty sure this will work with you.' There's something different about me. Something that told you I was an exception to your rule."

Dmitri Kronastia leaned back in his chair, an amused grin spreading across his face. "You miss nothing."

Shep shrugged. "I'm a college professor. Being able to detect partial truths and bullshit is part of my profession. I list it on my resume right after languages spoken."

Dmitri nodded. "Indeed. Well, let's just say you've had certain…exposures in the past that sort of primed your mind for me. But I'm more curious, Shep, why you're so willing to believe me? You'll forgive my curiosity, but I've spent so long keeping our existence under wraps that I'm surprised you accept everything I say at face value. What if it's all a trick? What if I put something in your tea—a hallucinogen, for example—so you'd see things that aren't there?"

"Did you?"

His eyes sparkled. "Of course not."

"Occam's razor."

"Interesting, Dr. Smyth. Elaborate?"

Shep rubbed his eyes. He was getting tired again, and wouldn't mind a nap soon. Actually, he should probably check on Hector; maybe he needed another blanket. But he'd play along with Kronastia a few more minutes.

"All else being equal, the simplest solution is usually the right one," Shep began. "First, Victoria Kent manages to sneak her way into the most secure excavation site I've ever seen and leave same site in the middle of a hurricane with a cache of ancient objects in tow. Secondly, she flies across the Atlantic on board a commercial airliner which she manages to make a getaway from midflight, all while killing someone without a single witness despite the fact that she did it in plain sight. Third, you present me with this," Shep took from his pocket the picture of Kronastia had given him on the plane of his wife and Victoria, "and tell me Christine knew Victoria a dozen years ago even though, by all accounts, someone looking Victoria's age should have been a child at the time. And finally, you embed yourself in my mind and show me something that happened between you and Victoria two thousand years ago. You and Victoria are aliens, what other simpler solution could there be?"

"Well, if you're so certain I did not drug you, then I guess none."

"Funny, I've spent years arguing with wack-a-doos that there was no evidence that the pyramids were built by aliens, and if they were, they used primitive tools."

"And you were right, Shep." Curious eyes met him, a sparkle of humor at the comment. "We did. Use primitive tools, that is. Teach by example, no?"

"I don't get it, though." Shep shrugged. "What do you need us for, Hector and me? You could have just as easily left us in Mexico, or even killed us. Why have you dragged *us* into this?"

"Because, Dr. Smyth, I need your help."

"My help?" Shep scoffed. He jammed the photo back into his pocket. "To do what?"

Sheepishly, Dmitri explained. "I don't want Victoria to die."

Shep leaned back in his chair, folding his arms over his chest and studying the emotions flowing over Dmitri's face. At the same moment, he remembered the look of nostalgia that the faux-Russian had held when he saw Victoria's face on the security tape back in Mexico. Shep knew that look—it was how he always looked when remembering Christine.

"Oh, I see. You *love* her." Dmitri proved unable to deny it. "And I can stop her dying…how?"

"I already know what she's willing to die for, Shep. Yes, I love her, but I know she loves another. I'm just hoping that you remind her of what she's willing to live for," Dmitri returned.

"And Hector's place in all this?"

Dmitri looked away ashamed. "…is finished. I regret that it was necessary. He was a good man."

…was…

Shep's blood went cold.

He leapt from the table. The tea cup shattered on the floor. The light from the window streamed in and hit his eyes, blinding him momentarily. He hit the wall, fell, then hit the wall again. The bedroom doorknob was jammed. His shoulder hit the center of the frame once. Twice.

On the third lunge, the door surrendered and opened.

Shep raced to Hector's side, pulling back the blankets piled uselessly over the cold corpse. He pressed his head to his chest. No pulse. Hector's eyes looked starkly at the ceiling.

"Hector? Hector!"

He damned his alcohol-addled memory and the fact that he had never been that good at CPR to begin with. With the echoes of lessons long ago forgotten, Shep started chest compressions.

One. *Push.* Two. *Push.* Three. *Push.* Four. Breathe!

Shep plugged Hector's nose and pushed air into his lungs. Nothing. He did it again, even as he felt the presence of Dmitri Kronastia lingering in the doorway behind him. Waiting.

After several minutes with no results, Shep collapsed over the lifeless body of his colleague.

"Shep, he went peacefully."

Shep's heated tears soaked the front of Hector's shirt. "I don't...understand. He was...fine just...a day or two ago. What...what happened?"

"It was the only way,,," Dmitri's voice trailed off

Shouting his grief, understanding hit him like a lead pipe. "You did this! What, why?"

"I need my strength, just like anyone," Dmitri said stoically, his eyes fixed on Hector's unmoving body. "You eat corn flakes, I eat chi life force. Besides, he was getting too close to the truth, and it's my job. To conceal our existence."

"Hector knew nothing about you being...Altunai, or whatever. How would he?"

"He had seen the scroll."

"The scroll? What bloody scr—"

In the calamity of the last few days, Shep had nearly forgotten about Hector's mention of the scroll found in the treasure cache.

Shep slowly raised himself and turned toward Dmitri. "What does it say?"

"It's a confession, Shep. A murder confession almost two thousand years old."

"And why would that tip off Hector?"

"Because, Shep, it's signed by the murderer."

"The murderer?" Shep turned the evidence over in her mind. "How can that possibly be any relevance to the here and now?"

Dmitri buried his hands in his pockets, his gestures oddly casual with a dead man in the room. "It's proof of a link. The scroll was written in Egyptian, but the murder's name…It's written in Olmec."

12.20.12

Chapter 19

Victoria could hardly believe her eyes. Even she, who had seen out the Bonding of the other proxies before, was surprised. The process always left a physical change in the selected. There was just something about the virility of Altunai DNA; somehow it knew the very characteristics of a person to enhance in order to make them all the more perfected to the human eye.

Like it had with her. She hadn't been particularly beautiful as a human, nor extremely special in any way that she thought important. She simply had a good memory, a memory that modern men called "photographic." Who would have thought so simple a trait would have been so desirable to the Altunai? Of course, at the time, she had no knowledge of why her memory and intelligence dwarfed the others of her people. Nor would she learn for many a year.

Yet, much more than her memory was enhanced after her Bonding. She grew all of three inches in the two day process, feeling the pain of every unnatural stretch of her body in excruciating clarity. Her skin, once the color of freshly turned ground, lightened to beach sand. Her hair thickened and changed color, streaks of ashen blond working through her chestnut locks. Her strength, both in body and mind, sharpened so that no mortal man could equal her cunning or her speed.

And her eyes. Of course there were those damned feline-eyes that had emerged from her encounter with Ra.

Jaguar eyes. The jaguar was due its own respect; they were a magnificent creature, and Victoria was proud to be compared to them by her former kinsmen. But the wrathful jaguar-god of Olmec legend? Nope, that was all the result of the odd blending of genetics that was Victoria.

The cat association had stuck, and when she showed up in Egypt, she was branded as the Lion Goddess, Sekhmet.

Likewise, Alex was left transformed. He must have grown two inches overnight. He hadn't been short by any means, but the Altunai ran a little on the tall and slender side. They still passed for human without exception, but the height difference was the first thing Victoria had noticed ages ago when she was presented to the High Council.

That, and of course, the emerald-jade flash of Ra's eyes.

"Who was that?" Alex asked, as he rolled over to look at her. The image of Ra freshly recollected seeped into his consciousness.

Reassuringly, Victoria squeezed Alex's hand in her own as they lay on her bed. "No one, Alex. Just a face from my past."

It had been some time since she had had to be wary of her thoughts, knowing someone was watching. The momentary image of the ancient in Victoria's head was sure to stir Alex's curiosity.

"He looked like one of them," Alex added, fishing for more information. "His eyes were…exactly like yours."

"Yes, he was—*is*—one of them."

"And what am I?" Alex's voice was wonder-filled and confused. He rolled unto his side, his face away from Victoria. "Am I one of them?"

His tone distressed her. "Would that be bad, Alex? They're not evil. They're just…different."

"Then why are we fighting them?"

She rolled over and caressed his back. "We're not *fighting* them, Alex. We're just trying to claim our due. The mere fact that the scientist uses the lab rat doesn't make the scientist a bad person. They created some sort of social experiment, but there is purpose beyond their design. The value of existence and anyone's right to endure is not for them to determine."

He seemed to accept this. Or else, he didn't think it was worth arguing. She could sense his weariness, and leaned closer to rub his shoulder.

"Sleep a little, Alex. You'll have to leave for London soon."

She kissed the back of his head before rolling off the mattress and throwing a nearby quilt over him. His body was too exhausted from the process it had endured to resist the pull of slumber, and by the time Victoria reached the door, she could hear the gentle purr of his sleep.

As expected, Priest was waiting impatiently outside the door for her.

Victoria shot him a menacing glare as she turned to lead them up the hall. "You're a bit of a pervert, you know that? Is this a habit of yours, lingering outside people's doors and listening in on them?"

Anton shrugged as he followed her. "More of a profession, really. Whenever Dmitri was enjoying one of his conquests, he specifically asked me to—"

The smack of her open palm reverberated through the hall. With eyes suddenly bloodshot from the force of the impact, Anton blinked. He slowly straightened, nursing the heated flesh of his face.

"I didn't mean to…It wasn't my…" he attempted to grovel.

"What *is* it with you?" she demanded in a hissing, whispered shriek. Her eyes shot daggers at him, and woefully Anton noticed how those eyes had darkened. "Dmitri would never lay with a human. *Never.* What are you getting at, trying to make me jealous?"

"It was a lie," Anton let out, his voice uncharacteristically shallow and low. "I've never seen him with another. At least, not more than needed to maintain his persona. I don't think he'd have it in him to…" His voice trailed off as her eyes and expression softened. "Anyway, I'm sorry."

Victoria took a moment to collect herself, her eyes brightening back to their emerald tone. She turned on her heel and made way to the staircase.

"None of the other proxies have been able to create delusions in me. It's…put me a little off kilter."

Anton was having a hard time keeping up, finding himself almost jogging behind her. "Is there something unique about Alex?"

"Nothing I can put my finger on," she answered as they rounded the corner of the banister and made their way to the library. "No doubt genetics play in his favor. I only hope it makes him better able to outsmart Dmitri."

"He'll do fine, I'm sure."

"No thanks to you," Victoria snapped back as they entered the library. She immediately took her place behind the large oak desk overlaid with blueprints. "The boy was basically clueless, Anton. I know you've been undercover and all, but you couldn't shoot him a quick email or something? You know, something simple like 'The mythic epic of Sekhmet' or 'How to serve your goddess'?"

"You're not a goddess," Anton remarked, a rebuking grin on his face.

"Keep that up, and you won't be a priest, either," she quipped back. Her focus turned to the details of the papers on the table top. "Okay, this is the plan of the building you said Dmitri is in."

"How did you get this so fast?" Anton asked, staring at the blueprints in disbelief.

"One of The Order works for the Metropolitan Buildings Office. Dmitri had some retrofit done a few years ago, so the plans were submitted for the permit."

"Russian mobsters apply for permits?"

Victoria groaned. "He always said you get away with more by playing with the rules than against them. Anyway, the flat you say he occupies is here —" her finger snapped down on the page "— 6в. Oddly, there are no records of sales on the other flats, and their plans were never submitted for permits. I think he has the whole building empty. Or, he's renting them out under the table for a little extra cash."

"Because he's so in need of it."

"Never hurts." Victoria shrugged. "Usually, it's best to accost Dmitri with a crowd around. He doesn't like to make scenes, which I have no problem causing if it suits me. Given the time constraints, however, I'm wondering if a ruse is the best option."

"Meaning?" Anton asked.

"I'm thinking of sending in Alex in disguise. Water works man, maybe. Delivery man? I don't know, what do you think would be best?"

Priest laughed, the full-bellied sound filling the room. "Are you sincere? You've been away from him for too long. If he is the only one in the building, he'd be suspicious that any stranger wasn't there by accident. You don't think he'd see right through that?"

She pounded her fist on the desk, and Anton jolted. Her words were terse. "If you have a better fucking idea, Anton, I'm all ears. There's no time for strategizing. The baktun ends in less than fifty hours."

A methodic rubbing of his chin, and Anton posed his query. "Just out of curiosity, you've known where the amulet was hidden for well over a thousand years. Any particular reason you didn't think to collect it before now? Maybe, I don't know, put it in a safety deposit box in Zurich or plunge it into a polar ice cap or something?"

Victoria huffed. "You'd think it'd be that easy. It was to my advantage to leave it as long as possible. I suspected Dmitri was monitoring my movements through the black market, trying to figure out where I hid it because one of us was going to have to retrieve it soon. I never thought, however, he'd figure out its location alone. I should have figured he has the same…bond with it as I do. I can't explain. The damn things *talks*."

Eyebrow crooked in a curious expression, Anton asked her to explain.

But Victoria seemed at a loss with her words. "It *whispers.* Speaks? Something or other. I...communicate with it. Not like a conversation. More like...an understanding?"

"Have other pieces of jewelry ever talked to you?" Anton inquired disbelievingly.

She ignored his indignation. "Look, the amulet isn't just jewelry. It has purpose. Dmitri gave it to me, and at the time, well, I sort of buried a lot of my past in the Yucatan. Told myself I was moving on, starting fresh. When I found out about the excavation, I was glad I decided to ask you to embed with Plaxis these last few years. If you hadn't been able to get the credentials to get me onsite, I was going to have to stage a mass murder."

"Yeah, instead you killed only the poor sap on the plane." He shrugged. "And Hector."

That snapped her resolve. "*Dmitri* killed Hector, Anton, not me. Don't you dare make that out to be my fault."

"Po-*ta*-toes, po-*tah*-toes," he returned rudely. "Look, you did what you had to do. I get it. I'm not blaming you. All I know is that I have put my faith in you since I was fourteen years old. I've never seen you—what's the term?—fly by the seat of your pants like you have on this. You told us we were going to prevent the end of the world then, and you sounded absolutely sure of that. Now, it seems like you're wavering."

The moment of doubt was so quick that, if Anton hadn't been almost searching for it, he would have missed it. It was briefly lived, however, and immediately Victoria's expression hardened into one of determination.

"I don't lack commitment, Anton. What I lack is resolve."

"What the hell is the difference?"

"I'm not backing out of my goal," she reaffirmed. "I'll deal with the Altunai, no matter what their *High Council,*" she spat the words with vehemence, "decides is best. What I question is my purpose. Am I doing it because it's what's expected of me, or for myself?"

A great hollowness consumed Anton, as though the very purpose of his existence had just been brought into question.

"What do you mean, for yourself?"

She looked away sheepishly, but spoke no more on the subject.

Chapter 20

Giggling and splashing, the twins broke loose of the reeds and squealed in delight as they cooled in the water. Their younger brother sloshed through the mud, trying to keep up. The children had been so patient in the trek across the desert, and in high summer, no less. Their older half-brother, however, wary of their gaiety in the light of recent events, sneered at them from the shade of the stout palm on the edge of the oasis.

Ethiopia hadn't been in her original plan, but neither had Cleopatra's death. She wasn't sure just what fate Augustus would deem proper for the four offspring now. It was better to take some distance from him before rushing into the lion's den and making their way toward Rome.

"The crown prince allows woe to consume him, methinks. What troubles you, Caesarian?"

The stately woman, his new regent, seemed unfazed by either the heat or the distance. He hated her, hated how resolute and immutable she was, where his mother, the queen, had been defeated. In his frustration, his venom was directed solely at her.

"My mother is slain, my father is long dead, and her new Roman, too. The breath of the Senate in Rome is bated and their throats parched, longing to taste my blood, and you do not think this should have an effect on me?"

She shrugged and sat up from her place on an isolated patch of grass. She had always appreciated the prince's frankness, though it was clearly a trait he had inherited from his father, Julius, and not his mother, who so often played both sides of the battle as she saw fit.

"True, these are heavy burdens for a boy so small in years. Yet, did you know you are only a year younger than your mother when she came to power?"

"Mother was queen at fourteen?"

"She never told you?" his protector queried, notching her head his way. Caesarian shook his head no. "Yes, she was. For a little while, anyway. I do not see how concerning yourself with Rome's wishes will benefit you, Caesarian." Her gaze grew somber and her words sincere. "You needn't worry, young prince, while you are with me. I will keep you safe. You have my word that I will not allow Rome or anyone else to take you."

He spat upon the ground, his lip curling in his disgust. His half-siblings were too consumed in their own sport to take notice.

"Your word means little, it seems. You promised my mother that you would not allow Rome to shame her, but Augustus has had her life nonetheless."

"Your mother shouldn't have allowed…" She began to snipe back vehemently, about to correct his misconceptions, before calming herself. A slow inhale and exhale of air followed as she brought her tone back into check. "The queen chose her fate. I lived up to my promise, Rome brought her no shame. Your mother died in defense of her nation. She died a most honorable death."

"And left its fate in the hands of her children?" he questioned. "You'll forgive me, Sekhmet, but I fail to see the wisdom or honor in such an act."

She could not argue with the boy's logic. It would be difficult for her to explain in a way that he would understand. Leaping to her feet, she chose to try to comfort him instead. Though he proved reluctant, she pulled him to the banks of the pool of water and beckoned his younger half-siblings near.

"Listen, I want all of you to understand this: I made a promise to your mother. As long as her blood flows through human veins, I will protect this family."

"Forever and ever?" the youngest boy asked.

She cupped his check. "Yes, Ptolemy, dear, even your children. And your children's children. And your children's children's children. And so on and so on."

Cleopatra Selene seemed doubtful, and looked so like her poor departed mother that it nearly broke Sekhmet's heart on the spot. "But, teacher, how can you? Won't you be old?"

"No, my sweet. You forget, I am a goddess. I will live forever, and I will always be here to protect and guide them."

Both the twins nearly exploded in a clamor. "Forever!"

Again, Caesarian was the dissenter. "So, you're saying nothing can kill you?"

Her timbre was solemn and carefully worded in response. "I swear upon the name of my father, there is nothing of this world that can kill me. And I never break a promise."

Had the prince noticed how her vow was made only to the younger three? His fate, however, was already sealed. Caesarian's life would not last even another day...

Victoria shook Alex gently, trying to rouse him from his slumber.

"Alex, you need to get up. You have to leave soon."

His body rolled over in what could best be categorized as a slump. His tongue tapped the dry roof of his mouth a few times, though his eyes remained closed.

"Thirsty..." he mumbled.

Victoria had had a cup of water waiting on the bedside table. He took it to his lips and drank down the tall glassful, following with a relieved grunt and rapid breaths.

"How am I getting there?" he asked as he wiped his mouth on his sleeve.

She smoothed his hair out of his face as he sat up and rubbed the sleep from his eyes. "Any car you like that's here, or we have a motorbike if you think that would be—Oh, by Ra!"

Victoria's hand flew to cover her mouth as she leapt to her feet and stared unbelieving at a now bewildered Alex.

"What?"

"Your eyes," she answered simply, as though this was the obvious response.

"My eyes?"

"They're—they're the same color as mine."

"What!"

Alexander Cezanne, like most men, didn't really care too much about his appearance. He was plenty good looking by the grace of genetics, but he didn't ever have the female-like desire to have a different hair color or a different nose. But his eyes? They were special. His eyes he had inherited from his mother: hazel irises with an odd quirk of a rim of golden hue around the edges. It was one of the last connections he had to her. His deceased older sister had had the eyes as well.

The eyes he had prayed his and Monique's children would someday inherit.

"What the fuck?" he exclaimed as he stood now in front of the mirror, gaping. "No freaking way, Victoria. Change them back!"

"What, you think I did that?"

Alex extended his index finger accusingly. "You think I ran out to get fitted for colored contacts while I was sleeping? Of course it was you. Now, change them back."

"I can't."

"Why the hell not?"

Now she was getting angry. "I didn't do anything to make them like that. It must have been the Bonding. I swear, I did not nor could not do a thing to change your eyes."

"Well, you change your own eye color!" he said, remembering the eerie way in which her eyes had darkened to pitch black when her ire had risen before. "There's got to be some connection. Now do something."

"Alexander Cezanne, I have no control over *anybody's* eye color, yours or mine!" Victoria crossed her arms over her chest and sat down on the bed with a huff. "I'm sorry that happened; I really am. But get over it." Her gaze softened as she turned toward him. "Besides, does it really matter what eye color my knight in shining armor has?"

He shrugged, realizing in the grand scheme of their current predicament, it really didn't.

"Good," she concluded. "Now, other than your ocular re-pigmentation, how do you feel?"

"A little pissed…" Her eyes narrowed at him contemptuously. "I guess I'm…fine? I mean, I don't feel any different, except that I can hear myself echoing in your thoughts."

Victoria locked gazes with him. *"And can you hear me now?"*

But her lips had not moved.

Perplexed with the sensation, his head cocked to the side like a curiosity-stricken puppy. "I can, but—"

"Ah, ah, ah!" Victoria admonished him both in words and with a wag of her finger. As she continued, again, her lips remained still. The words, though perceivable, were more like a second line of thought than an outsider's tongue. *"Think at me. Don't speak. I'm sorry we have to do a crash course like this, but we don't really have a choice."*

Alex stared at the floor. "Um, okay. How?"

"It's like the difference between whispering and yelling. You just have to project."

He smirked. Victoria was relieved that cute little trait of his had pulled through the Bonding. She was certain Monique would have hunted her down and given her an earful if she'd handed him back too changed.

"I don't have a diaphragm in my head, Vick."

"Your brain is the strongest muscle you have, Alex," she chastised. "You've been thinking your whole life. Now just push those thoughts toward me."

She was practically begging. Alex resigned himself to try. He took a deep breath, formed his thoughts and tried to…put them somewhere else.

The tiniest peep got through.

Emerald-jade eyes blazed anger. *"Try harder."*

"Excuse me, grandma, but I haven't had five thousand years of practice at this like you!"

"Yeah, and you won't have six days to perfect this if you don't get it down."

"Why the hell's it so important anyway? I mean, we do have cell phones in this modern era. We can even text, if you'd prefer."

"Cell phones don't communicate images, memories and emotions," she explained. *"And there's no need to throw my age in my face."*

Alex proved incredulous. "You've never sent a pic or video via text?"

"Look, Alex, this *thing works no matter how many bars we have. And it can work from several miles away. We don't have to worry about dropped thoughts either. Doesn't happen."* She swung her legs over the side of the bed and suddenly became concerned with the creases in the bedspread, smoothing them out with her hand. *"Of course, if you don't think you're talented enough…If you think this is above your capabilities, then…"*

"Are you saying I'm not good enough for this?"

"Well, you are only human," she thought condescendingly, before speaking aloud. "I guess I was just expecting too much of you. Oh, well."

"Listen, I'm plenty *capable of doing whatever…"* he began before his words turned mental.

In the form of a true master, she had tricked him into teaching himself. As Alex realized what he had just achieved, his grin rivaled hers. He felt now the sensation, what speaking through thought felt like. *Easy breezy.*

"Can you hear me?"

"*Yes, Alex. Loud and clear.*" She smiled wider. "*Well done.*"

"Oh, my God. This is so fucking cool. What else can I do?"

They didn't have much time to explore, but Victoria wanted to keep him distracted. It wouldn't be too much longer before the memory of the previous night doubled back on him.

She leapt from the bed. "*Well, every proxy is different, but you seem to have picked up telepathy pretty quickly. Took the last proxy almost a week. You'll be able to hear some humans' thoughts, but not everyone. Luckily for you, the Altunai seemed immune from a proxy's mind. Your thoughts will still be safe around Dmitri. Let's see. What else? Well, the best part of it is your increased strength and senses. Of course, I guess that depends on what you're looking at and who you're smelling. A blessing and a curse, you know.*"

"*Can I teleport like you?*"

"Oh, God no!" she exclaimed in a worried huff aloud. As concern overtook him, she quickly moved to reassure him. "*Alex, I can do it easily enough, but it takes tremendous amounts of life force. You're talking an entire shift in the space time continuum, and that doesn't come cheap. If I did it without proper preparation, I could all but kill myself. And, of course, I can only pull it off by taking a human…*"

Alex's face went white, and his words returned to his lips. "Oh, Lord. I killed a man, didn't I?"

The proxy's mind flooded with recollection in an instant. He saw himself as though outside his body, trembling from the way the fever of the Bond was wracking him with want and need. He saw himself looking at the shaking visage of the old man—his name was Larry or Lloyd or something like that?—and feeling the pulsations of current that ran up his arms when Alex had placed his hands on his face. He recalled hearing Victoria's voice, coaxing him to pull into himself the essence of the servant's existence. Alex remembered feeling the instant gratification, the consuming high when he heeded her words and did just that, heat spreading from tip to toe, his body incorporating the strength of the life force into every atom of his being.

Then he felt sick, as the image of the servant's body falling to the ground, lifeless, echoed in his memories.

And Victoria saw it all play out in his head clear as day.

"*Alex, you had no choice. You can't Bond without taking a life. The life was given willingly. It is a requirement of mine. The last proxy actually required two lives to make it through the Bond. Just be pleased that it only took one for you.*"

Blood rushed into his face in reflection of his disgust and anger. "Is that supposed to make me feel better?"

"It would be disrespectful of us to throw off the benefit of their sacrifice so heedlessly, Alex. The sacrifice to the proxy has always been considered a great honor in The Order, and when your sister was selected to be one of the chosen, she felt every bit as horrid as you do now."

His head whipped around at her words. "My sister was your proxy? What the hell—"

She stopped his words with a quick peck on his lips. "I promise, Alex, I will tell you everything. Right now, we don't have time. There's only forty-seven hours until the Altunai arrive. Please, Alex, I need you to focus. I need you to stay strong. Your sister died in pursuit of seeing through this mission. Please, Alex, you need to go."

A sea of confusion swept over him. *His sister?* How much more could Victoria ask of him? Of his family?

He looked at her sternly and spoke in slow, accentuated words that she might not mistake him. "You will explain why this was kept from me, as well as anything else you're hiding from me, the very *second* the Altunai are settled."

"I promise, Alex," she answered, "and I always keep my promises."

Chapter 21

Shep had had enough.

No more legends of ancient deities. No more alien civilization yarns. No more Dan Brown, history-on-its-head, now-the-universe-makes-sense, everything's-been-a-mass-cover-up-by-clandestine-authorities revelations.

No more chasing ghosts.

What he needed to get a grip on now were cold, hard facts. The first fact he needed to deal with was the cold, hard one lying in the bed in front of him. Hector, dead. But how?

He turned over Dmitri's outrageous claim to have been the cause, though he hadn't said how. Hector and Shep hadn't been separated since Kronastia's arrival in Mexico a few days before. As he thought back, however, he remembered the brief time that Dmitri had had Hector escorted away by his valet to the hurricane shelter hosting Plaxis' security operations. Perhaps Anton had slipped Hector some slow-acting poison then. But how would he have done it, and wouldn't Hector have said something?

"I don't understand," Shep repeated again, shaking his head.

"I took his life force from him," Dmitri again repeated. "His chi, his aura, however you want to understand. It's—it's what I feed on."

Yeah, he had heard it the first time. And the second. He heard every unintelligible word Dmitri uttered, but that didn't mean it made any sense.

"You're a...vampire or something?"

Though he was angry, though he was bitter, and frankly, though he was scared, Shep still understood that whatever Dmitri Kronastia actually was—man or Altunai or tuna fish—he was lethal, well-connected, and well-funded. Shep still had enough sense of self-preservation not to leap to his feet and lay into him like the well-rehearsed scenario currently playing through his head. He couldn't help that he had never been able to deal with the deaths of people he cared for well. Christine's death had nearly sliced his soul in two, but there was no target of vengeance he could pummel for that one. Except himself, and for that, alcohol had been his weapon of choice. With Hector, Dmitri seemed as good a hitting block as any.

But his need to make sense of this was taking his mind to fantastical places. Really, aliens were one thing, but soul-sucking, pyramid-building vampires?

"I don't care for the term, but Victoria's used it from time to time."

Shep shuddered. He just had to ask, didn't he?

"You drink blood?"

"Only ceremonially, and with a purpose. Not to take life away, Shep, but to transform it." Dmitri smiled, though he quickly trained his eyes to the ground as though trying to conceal some secret remembrance. Licking his lips, he continued. "At least, for my part. Victoria, however, she…went through a rough patch in the beginning, trying to adjust. She decided to drink blood for a while. I don't *think* she does it anymore, except to someone she's slain and for whom she holds particular disdain. You see, blood is sacred. To drink someone's blood by force to her is…Well, it's just about the most humiliating way to die in her eyes."

Shep heard movement behind him, but didn't have the will to look. A moment later, he caught Dmitri's form sinking down to his knees next to the bed and next to Shep. The Russian, or whatever, gave a long, languid sigh and bowed his head, speaking softly in a foreign tongue Shep didn't recognize. The tone almost sounded like a prayer.

"I regret his death," Dmitri proclaimed sincerely. "Few humans have impressed me so. His loss is a detriment to your race."

Shep's eyes turned first to meet the honest gaze and take in the confession, then, hesitantly, he made his wishes known.

"I want to leave now."

Dmitri's head cocked to the side. "I'm sorry, Shep, that just can't happen. You know too much."

"I never asked for that," he countered. "And, as far as what you've told me, I swear I'll never tell anyone."

The remorse now drifting away, Dmitri leaned in close and spoke inches from Shep's anxiety-laden expression. "You have already told everyone something you shouldn't, Shep. That's the problem."

Confused eyes searched madly for understanding, but found none. He had already been convicted of his crime before he'd realized he was a prisoner; Dmitri Kronastia had no intention of letting him leave. And that scared him. Scared him bad, because Shep knew, whatever Dmitri's plan was, it didn't likely involve his eventual freedom.

The door of the bedroom was open, however, and Shep could haul ass like a rabbit when necessary.

In one swift movement, he leapt to his feet and knocked Dmitri to the ground. He was already through the bedroom door and heading down the hall when he heard his pursuer growl—growl? Yes, growl—behind him. He didn't look back, just kept running toward the exit of the flat, determined to make it to the two flights of stairs that led down to the street and, hopefully, to freedom.

"Shep, you will not leave!" Dmitri barked behind him. His footfalls were quick and determined. He was gaining, but Shep's hands had already undone the deadbolt and were poised on the doorknob.

He grinned, turned the piece of shaped iron in his hand and...

...was met with the barrel of a Colt .45 and the sneer of a familiar face.

"*Hola, Señor*," José hissed. "*Como estas?*"

For a moment, he considered plowing into him, trying his luck against the brawn of the for-profit soldier. Behind him, however, and all the way up the hall and down the stairs at roughly five-foot intervals, were copycat paramilitary just like his old buddy José, each one with a gun trained squarely at Shep.

Instinctively, Shep's hands flew up into the air, offering his surrender. José walked him back into the flat as Dmitri caught up to the ruckus. Dmitri and José exchanged a few words in quick-fire Spanish, and with something that sounded like an *attaboy* and a pat on the shoulder, José holstered his weapon and returned to his post outside the door. Dmitri pulled Shep back by the shoulder, closed the door, and locked it.

Shep's chest heaved, his body too abused by alcohol, heartache, and lack of sleep for the efforts he had just undertaken. "For someone...only pretending to be...Russian mafia...you sure do...wear the jacket well," he gasped in quick huffs, alluding to the firepower lined up outside the door.

He felt Dmitri's arm around his shoulder as he was dragged back into the kitchen. With a light shove, he was forced into the seat where all the unsolicited knowledge had been presented to him before. Dmitri made his way to the cupboard, pulled out a cup, filled it with water, and placed it before Shep.

Shep just eyed it warily as his head spun from what had just happened.

"Jesus Christ, Shep, it's not poisoned, and you're redder than a beet."

Yeah, right, Shep thought, but then considered that maybe poison was the best way to go at this point. He pulled the glass to his panting mouth and took a sip. Dmitri said nothing further as he leaned against the counter, arms crossed over his chest, and waited for Shep to calm down. Finally, twenty minutes later, a collected Dr. Smyth looked at him.

"Jesus…" Shep mused, "did you know him too? You're old enough, right?"

"I don't show up in history too much, Shep. As I said, my job is to keep everything secret. As much as possible, anyway." He motioned vaguely toward the front door. "I apologize for all that, but it's necessary."

"A lot of effort to keep me in." Shep understood now that he served time at Dmitri's leisure, and he wouldn't be leaving the flat until Dmitri was good and ready to let him go.

Dmitri laughed, a slow chuckle at first that broadened into a full on fit in a moment. "You think that—" Dmitri heaved through the shaking. "You think that's all to keep *you* in?"

Shep was dumbfounded. What else would it be for? It wasn't as though Scotland Yard or MI-6 was going to make an offensive with that kind of firepower being garnered in a civilian area.

Dmitri calmed himself enough to speak sincerely, though the amused smile was still plastered on his face.

"Shep, if you're really determined to leave, then fine, leave. I can hunt you down after this whole ruckus is passed just as well as before it. José was only given orders not to let anyone leave without my permission."

"Then why?"

"Don't you get it, doctor?" Shep shook his head. Dmitri fished the amulet from his pocket and held it up. "This is the only bargaining chip I have. She wants this—badly—and she's going to be pissed as hell that she has to come to me to get it. Those men, Shep, are there to protect us from *her*."

"Bargaining chip for what?"

With a sigh, he again returned the amulet to his pocket. Dmitri leaned forward, looking suddenly drained.

"To get her to talk to me. To get her to understand," he sighed. "Maybe, if I'm lucky, just to get her to listen."

Blinking, Shep didn't know what to say. The pain was so evident on Kronastia's face. Shep knew that look. He had seen it on his own mug every morning in the bathroom mirror for the past few years. It was the look of a man who'd have given anything, *anything*, just to have his heart back for a moment.

With a loud sigh, Dmitri stood up and took Shep's drained glass away, placing it in the sink.

"Forgive me for a moment, Shep," he begged, fishing his cell from his pocket. "I need to make a quick phone call."

Chapter 22

Tap.

Tap. Tap.

Tap, tap, tap, tap, tap, tap, tap, tap…

"Victoria!"

"What!"

Anton could hardly believe his own gall at calling her by her given name, or her nom du jour, as the case may be. Luckily, she didn't seem to take offense. What she did seem a little peeved about, however, was Anton's swiping her hand off the center console of the Bentley. She had apparently been trying to drill a hole to China through the dashboard.

Maybe convincing her finally to accept the company on the way to Cairo hadn't been such a good idea after all. With a grunt, he threw the offending hand forcefully into her lap.

Her eyes flared as her irises darkened to black, and essence of her anger turned to heat, filling the car, all clear signs of Victoria's rage.

The way Anton saw it, he had two choices: he could cower, offer his humble apologies, and in all other measure grovel, or he could call her bluff for what it really was.

"You're too caught up in Alex." He opted for the latter. "Just admit it, and have some sympathy for the finely crafted wooden panel that is this center console."

He had read her perfectly, and the stark calling out served to make her retract her fiery veil of rage. With a sigh and huff, she sank back into her seat like a petulant child.

"If Alex fails, I'm never going to forgive myself," she admitted. Then, almost mumbling, she turned to look out the window as the South England countryside whipped past them. "He's the last one. If something happens, then I've broken my promise."

"Your promise?" Anton laughed as he bypassed a slow moving, late model Renault. "Your promise to do what?"

"I swore to Cleo's children that I would always protect their mother's bloodline."

With a jerk from the shock, Anton almost veered them into oncoming traffic. A swerve and a honk from the offended passersby prompted him to right the car.

"You don't mean to say that Alex is—"

"Alex?" The look on her face was of pure confusion. No, she hadn't meant Alex at all, she had meant...Well, it was none of Anton's concern. And, truly, protecting Alex's bloodline was part of her job duties as well. "Yeah, Alex," she lied, for once.

"Holy...And you're just telling this to me now?"

A woman her age—or a woman of any age, for that matter—always had a secret bag of hidden memories kept to herself. Females were gatherers by nature, always storing up enough warm memories for the cold times, cold memories for the heated moments, and lukewarm, water-colored memories to span the in-between. Certainly, Victoria had more than her fair share. But this was relevant. This mattered. If Alex was Cleopatra's blood, then...

"He will be Priest." Anton uttered it as a conclusion; there was no need to question what he instantly understood.

"*Would* have been Priest," Victoria confirmed. Cleopatra's blood or not, she'd had every intention of making that so.

She looked up in the rearview again, and for a second, that alone distracted Anton. She had been doing that a lot, hadn't she? "If we survive this, I'm dissolving The Order."

Anton nearly choked on his own tongue. "What? You can't...I mean...The Order is...Ah, hell!"

With a few more select curses from Anton, the Bentley made its way to the side of the road and grinded to a stop. He put the car in park and rounded on Victoria, eyes wide and nostrils flaring.

"What the hell do you mean, dissolve The Order?"

"I'm not a goddess, and I'm tired of playing the part," she admitted, her tone a mixture of shame and retaliation. "I'm tired of the ceremony and the bowing and the undeserving adoration. I'm not fucking divine, Anton. Just because I can read minds and live forever doesn't make me wise or brave. I can't take it anymore. I want out. I just want to spend the rest of my days…living. No cover-ups, no conspiracies, no secret society." Her chest rose as though she were sucking in all the air from the cabin, and she let it out in a long stream like a train whistle. Finally, she perched her head on her raised fingers, her eyes closed. "I don't want to be bigger than life anymore. Isn't it enough that I'm simply…alive?"

Anton rolled his eyes and tried, mostly unsuccessfully, to cage his anger. "And do what? Have a dog and cute little flat in Leicester? Fucking get a job and pay taxes and complain about the weather?" he croaked. "Jesus H. Christ, Victoria, you can control the weather. Think you're just going to find a nice guy and settle down, do you?"

"That thought has crossed my mind."

Anton snapped. The whole of his existence had been devoted to the service of The Order, to Victoria. "You have no right to make that kind of decision without consulting us."

She gasped, almost as shocked as if he had slapped her in the face. "Who are *you* to tell me that I can't make up my own mind?"

A tension was building inside of him, an unspoken secret danced a jig on his tongue. Victoria had always told him he had one of the rare minds that she had trouble accessing from time to time. She was ignorant of the depth of his devotion. If anything, all she could fish from Anton's mental stream were snippets, and usually only when he was woefully spent or divinely relaxed. It was one of the reasons that he had been selected to embed with Plaxis; Victoria knew that the occasional human's mind was open to Dmitri, but felt confident that Dmitri would never be able to take anything from Anton. But now, in the heat of the moment, that long-buried secret was threatening to pour forth.

Men kept their own stash of secrets as well, but ever so much closer to surface.

"You can't do it to us," he pled. "Our whole purpose is you. All our efforts are for your benefit. Our actions, our loyalty—we serve at your leisure. Yeah, maybe you aren't divine, but who's to say who and what are worthy of worship but the worshiper? You've guided humanity for so long, kept so many of us safe. We…You are our purpose. If there's no Order, then I don't know. What I mean to say is—"

Her eyes begged for him to finish, but Anton was cut off mid-sentence by the ringing of his cell. A frustrated groan ground out as he dug through his pockets to find the cursed Blackberry. Of all things, he had set his ring tone to Nick Cave's "Until the End of the World." Victoria grinned at the irony.

"Hello?" he asked as he flipped open his phone and put it to his ear, a slight edge of consternation in his voice. Whereas he had been slightly flushed from their conversation a moment ago, Victoria saw all the color drain from his face in a rush, leaving Priest a cotton façade in the seat next to her. "Hello, sir. I—I wasn't expecting your call. After our argument yesterday, I thought perhaps—"

Victoria understood without questioning who was on the other end of the line. The very servile lilt was back in Anton's voice, as it was on the day she had first had him contact Dmitri to offer himself to his service.

Victoria's face went nearly as white as Anton's. Without hesitation, she snatched the phone from his hand and pressed it to her ear.

"Alex?" she demanded.

Dmitri snickered. "Is that this one's name? You like patterns, it seems. Is there just something more intriguing about a man named Alex destined to perish at a young age?"

"Fuck you, Dmitri. Is he dead?"

Clearly realizing there was to be no small talk, he answered. "No. Or should I say, not yet? But we're preparing for his arrival. He's been canvassing the building most of the afternoon. I'm guessing he's waiting for nightfall."

Worried eyes turned toward the horizon and surveyed the sun's zenith. It rode low in the sky, sinking into the abyss of twilight and taking her hope with it.

"You're so predictable, darling," Dmitri continued in his condescending snarl. "Between the fallibility of The Order and the half-half-breeds of yours. Every time you want something from me, you throw these insignificant and doomed proxies my way. Are you that reluctant to face me, or do you detest humans so much?"

Her hand was shaking; fear mixed with despair and anger and screwed up her face into a tempest the likes of which Anton had never witnessed in his thirty years of service. Her eyes were black as night now. The Eyes of Ra, the legendary ancient plague of vengeance that was Sekhmet's calling card to those who had wronged her, the Pharaoh, or Egypt. It was likely the last thing many a poor man had seen with living eyes.

"How long?"

"Hmm…" The timbre of his voice had remained dark, tempting, despite the passage of time. He was catting with her, and what she hated most was how it reminded her of when things between them had been different. "Looking at my monitor here, I'm guessing thirty seconds, tops."

Now was no time for reminiscing. Victoria threw the phone back at Anton and was out of her door in a moment, circling behind the car. She moved with blazing speed, far beyond that of any human, as she nearly tore the driver's side door off the Bentley and picked up Anton by the lapels.

"You fucking idiot," she hissed, tossing him to the ground. "You kept the same phone you had in Dmitri's service, didn't you?"

"I didn't have time to replace it!" Anton pled, scrambling to his feet. "I didn't want to risk being out of contact if—"

"Shut it and get in! Now!"

Barely had he registered her request when the sound of a speeding, grinding engine caught his ears. Looking in the distance, they caught the remote speck of black tearing up the road. In fright, Anton froze, trailing the object with his eyes until he realized it was a civilian-styled Humvee.

Just like the kind Kronastia furnished for his goons.

"Holy—"

"Anton!"

Victoria's shout broke through his pause, and within another two blinks, he had thrown his body over the hood of the car and shimmied into the passenger seat with barely enough time to lift his feet off the ground before it was speeding beneath him.

Victoria must have mistaken their luxury car for a Lamborghini the way she gunned the gas. Her foot mashed the pedal as though it had insulted her mother's honor.

"Five thousand, one-hundred and twenty-five years!" she hissed. "I've been fucking planning, Priest, each and every one of them, and it's about to be ruined because you couldn't toss your Motorola in the Thames."

"You mean…it was traced?"

"Hell, yeah, it was traced."

Anton shook his head in denial. "He said…he said he trusted me. He didn't even have access to the thing. It was only in my name. I picked it up from the carrier. It's not even on a Plaxis phone plan."

Victoria's eyes turned skyward, fretting the dying light which would take the life of her proxy with it if she didn't get her ass to London and quick. Unlike Anton, Alex had been smart enough to leave his cell behind. She was still too far from the city to mindspeak to him, but maybe if she could just push the gas hard enough and Alex delayed his attempt long enough…

"Yeah, you're not the first one to get sucked into his deceit, Anton. But still, you're probably the most gullible."

Bentleys were built for comfort, not for military ops. She cursed that she hadn't taken at least the Jaguar from the house. At least *its* engine would respond under the block of lead that was her foot at the moment.

"Hold on," she cautioned.

"Why? What are you—holy hell!"

Anton's girlish scream split the air as Victoria plunged the brakes and spun the front wheel, inducing a momentum that caused the car to pivot. The scent of burned rubber infiltrated the cabin, but Victoria didn't hesitate. Within seconds, she had slammed fury back into the gas pedal, propelling them toward London and, unfortunately, in the direct path of the Humvee now just a half-mile away, locked on a collision course.

It was clear that whoever was driving the other vehicle was intending to take them out, head on.

"Milady?"

No response, just a steady increase in speed.

"Victoria?"

The other party wasn't slowing either, and he could almost make out now the silhouettes of two brawny occupants through the tinted glass.

"SEKHMET!"

His eyes followed his words, turning toward her.

Anton gasped.

Her blackened orbs were wild, her caramel-pecan hair fanned out like a halo. Her skin had paled, and over the surface, an odd gold-orange-red hue of luminescence spread. It almost looked as though flames had alighted her surface and were licking at her limbs.

"What the…hell?"

It was like he didn't exist in the same space or time with her. The distance was closing faster, faster. Anton knew he was going to die, either from propelling through the windshield when the Bentley's hood met the Humvee's grill, or incinerated from the heat pouring off Victoria's body.

"Take the wheel," she demanded, and Anton obeyed with all haste. Her hands free, she clapped them together in front of her chest. The light-heat that had crawled over her surface centralized and collected on her fingertips. With a forward thrust and a roar like a jet plane, her hands propelled forward, blasting out the windshield of the Bentley and forming over the hood into a ravenous fireball that flew out and hit the Humvee dead on.

Victoria snatched back the wheel and steered a wide left just as the Humvee exploded, barely missing the range of the blast.

As it charred and crackled behind them, she pulled the car to the side, gasping.

"That…wasn't…smart…" she wheezed, doing a spot-on impression of an asthmatic.

"Smart?" Priest repeated. "You—you just saved us. That was amazing. I never knew that you could…Milady? Victoria! What's wrong?"

Her head was lulling to the side, her eyes rolling widely.

"Chi throwing takes…a lot of…energy. I'm d…d…drained."

"Milady?"

She focused long enough to take in the concern on his face. "It's okay, Anton," she assured, beginning to calm her racing breath. "I just need…a few minutes. I need to…refocus my strength. Have to get to London. Have to…save Alex."

He felt a pang of guilt in his stomach. "It's because of me, isn't it? The phone was bugged, and Dmitri's henchmen found us because of me. It's all my fault."

"Yes, it is." No one ever said she was a compassionate goddess. Her head drooped forward on the steering wheel, her shoulders slumped from exhaustion. "But he would have found a way to get to me anyhow. I always knew we were going to be lucky to get to Egypt without his interference. But we have to go back to London, Anton. He knows about Alex, and it's almost dark. Looks like Alex will try to break in when the sun goes down." She moved the car back into gear and trained her eyes forward. "We don't have any time to—"

"Use me."

The car shuddered and lurched as she slammed the brakes back down. "What?"

Anton offered out his arm, peeling back the sleeve of his sweater and turning his wrist over in supplication. "Use me. Take my life force. Then port yourself there. Get there in time to save your proxy."

"You don't know what you're talking about, Priest. What you're suggesting will—"

He completed her sentence, "Kill me? Yeah, I know. So do it."

"You…" she sputtered in confusion. "You…want to die?"

Anton shook his head. "Not particularly, but for you, I'm willing."

"Why?"

"Because I love you, and I know I can never have you, Victoria." Looking away in embarrassment, he laughed wryly. "No one can. You belong to Dmitri. So, I'm already dead."

His words left her speechless. Not that she hadn't suspected that Anton had felt something, but she had always chalked it up to a sense of greed mingled with lust for power, a power that only she had the potential to provide him. She knew that his secret wish always was to be Bonded. She had just never understood why.

Damn, because he loved her. What an idiot.

If only she felt the same. Then, perhaps, she would have been strong enough to deny his sacrifice. Then, perhaps, she would have let another live instead of adding one more death to her lengthy list. If she was stronger—if she was divine and owning of the compassion and wisdom a divine being should possess—she would deny him.

But she wasn't any of those things. Powerless to do anything more than human, Anton became the simplest solution.

With an air of reverent gratitude, Victoria raised her hand to Anton's cheek and caressed it tenderly. His eyes closed as he cocked his head, leaning into her touch.

"Thank you," she whispered as she closed the distance between them and planted a gentle kiss on his lips.

His eyes remained closed. "I live but to serve, milady."

With another gracious kiss, she pulled on his bottom lip with her teeth and ran her tongue over the sensitive skin. It was a diversionary tactic. His heart may be willing, but his body was shaking from the weight of his decision. It worked, and she could sense his utter concentration shift into processing the sensations her physical actions were causing, loving her with the entirety of his being.

Victoria brought her arms forward and closed her hands around the pulse points on his wrists.

"I accept your offering, Priest," she whispered against his lips as she withdrew. He smiled and looked at her one last time. "I will not forget."

With a deep breath, she closed her eyes, pulled Anton's hands forward, and killed him.

The rush, the total consumption of a soul, fueled her. Without pause, she harnessed the strength and used it.

But when Victoria opened her eyes, she wondered if it had been all for nothing.

The walls of the alley framed perfectly her view of Dmitri's building across the way, the building appearing to be outwardly unguarded though any seasoned veteran like Victoria would know otherwise. Alex, however, was green. The entrance swung back into place as the hitch caught with an echoing click. Alex entered the front doors of Dmitri's London residence, and quickly came face to face with the barrel of a gun.

Chapter 23

The decision to take up residence in Alexandria had proven wise. Sekhmet had changed somehow, no longer herself. She was…too emotional, too sensitive. And yet, inexplicably happy. The combination, along with Rome's current occupation of the city, was a recipe for an explosion.

Another explosion, that is. He still couldn't believe she had set off Vesuvius a few decades before. Luckily, the true catalyst for that event had never been made known. In Rome, Sekhmet had no official presence and no reason to expose her nature to humans. In Egypt, however, she was intrinsically tied to the fate of the House of Ptolemy. It was just a matter of time before something set her off again, or worse. Even if she continued to refuse to talk him, he had to stay near and stay vigilant. He would need her eventually, and like the sorry, love-struck sap that he was, the Guardian would come running the moment she cried out for him. All would be forgiven no matter her fault, because that was his way. Their distance had always been her decision, not his.

Sekhmet was so damned committed to her Ptolemys. It wasn't as though they were of the same line that the Egyptian rulers of the Old Kingdoms had been. No, the Ptolemys were Hyksos, foreigner rulers who had seized the throne in the fallout of Alexander the Great's decline. Still, Sekhmet had vowed to serve the Pharaoh, and she had not shirked from that vow. In fact, the Guardian believed strongly that the whole reason Ptolemy I had succeeded in keeping his slice of Alexander's empire where the other Macedonian generals had failed was because of Sekhmet's influence and support. He knew for certain it was because of her backing that Alexander had succeeded in taking over much of the world to begin with. And when he passed… Well, hell, it was almost like she had engineered the whole thing just to get a power hold on the Nile again. Sekhmet broke every rule. To hell with not having any interaction with humanity and only being observer. Sekhmet had become the damned orchestrator of empires. Altunai law seemed irrelevant to her.

Then again, she had always been different. This Vessel wasn't like the others he had protected over the millennia. She was inherently Altunai in her genetic leanings. His Bonding with her had been the most intricate pairing of the six Vessels he had made. And, by far, the most enjoyable.

As always, the Bonding itself had been full of drama and strife. He had let the decision be hers: by blood or by bed. When she answered the latter, the thrill that had consumed him was unlike anything else he had experienced. Within minutes of their consummation's end, however, she had begun to writhe in pain. At first, he worried that she might not survive it. Her screams drew cries of anguish from her human mother when she was later permitted in the temple. Tlalli was, after all, her only child; the father's identity was unknown.

After a short time, the pain had passed and the pleasure-seeking neurons had begun to rapid fire in her brain. He tried to satiate her with food. She ate only scarcely, her body already purging the desire for excessive culinary sustenance. Likewise, he offered her drink. A few sips were all she would take. But when instead he offered her the requisite life force required to seal the Bond, she pulled it forward from the victim savagely, not even realizing her own actions. How she came to rationalize it so quickly had been a shock to him. He still wondered if it was sincere; Tlalli was remarkably gifted at keeping her thoughts to herself. Later as Sekhmet, that fact had remained true.

In the haze of Tlalli's cravings, she sought the pleasure of the Guardian's body. He wouldn't deny that Tlalli's Bonding left her lusciously enhanced. Bedding beyond the initial Bonding was against the code set down by the Altunai queen, but he let himself give into the temptation and took her again and again.

Doing so had been a mistake. He knew it the moment he awoke in her arms. Never had he shared his bed with a human beyond the call of duty. The Guardian knew why the moment their eyes locked when the Vessel awoke: he had fallen in love with her.

When he'd had ample time to train her, teach her, and mold her new gifts, they were called by the High Council to Egypt. The time of isolation was coming, and Isis wished to examine the Vessel before taking her leave. The customary examination didn't bother him. What did disturb him was Ra's keen interest in Tlalli. From the moment he lay those jade, possessive eyes on her, he was enraptured. Of course, Ra had some strange fascination with the humans, always studying their ways with a dedication and intimacy that other Altunais failed to understand. Had he not been brother of the queen, he likely would have been accused of seeking beneath his species. As it was, his position gave him leeway to do as he pleased. And it was no secret that he was often pleased by the company of the human women.

The Guardian had once been a skeptic, but now he understood. With a great sense of discomfort, he presented his Vessel to Isis and Ra, and in the night, Ra had somehow found her out and swept her away. Tlalli, of course, was ill-prepared to resist the charms of one the humans called God of the Sun.

When Tlalli was returned from Ra's chambers, she had borne the effects of Bonding with the prince: another change in her composition: Ra's jade, piercing eyes. Ra's taste for humans proved too much of a temptation for him to pass her by, the Guardian had supposed. Bonding with more than one Altunai was something that had never been tried. Never had been needed. It was clear, though, that whatever Ra had done to her, it was because he had wanted to, not needed to.

The Guardian was determined to confront Ra and call him out on breaking the code. However, to reveal Ra would have revealed himself. If Isis learned of his transgression, it was possible she would demand a new Guardian. Therefore, he silenced his tongue and took comfort in the isolation that afforded him pursuit of the object of his desire.

Despite her dual nature, the Vessel proved, in the long run, human in ways that drove him to the edge of frustration. Not that that deterred his feelings for her; his love for her proved limitless. But she often gave him cause for alarm, trying to use her abilities for forbidden purposes. The role of the Vessel was to record, not to alter, not to participate during the time of isolation. Tlalli became Sekhmet in Egypt, the first name change of hundreds she would make over time. Her interests in the nation's welfare took her inside the Pharaoh's abode. She served him as protector, as advisor, and when necessary, as the punisher of those who had wronged him. And how she excelled at punishing. Her skills were as keen as any warrior's; it oddly only intensified the Guardian's attraction to her.

The Guardian, however, knew his duties. He must protect her from that which threatened her, even if that threat was self-inflicted.

Over the years, she grew weary of hearing just what was and wasn't "her place." She didn't understand what harm helping her fellow man could do. But Cleopatra changed everything. Sekhmet took an instant and intense liking to the Queen of the Nile that he found baffling. Sekhmet had taught Cleo the art of diplomacy, language, seduction, and intrigue—all things learned from her observations as the Vessel. Cleo was a quick learner, and almost succeeded in what Sekhmet had convinced her was possible: the ability of the Egyptian throne to stay out of Rome's hands. Her confidence blinded her to the reality that the throne was already lost. Even Sekhmet could not take on Rome. The *latent understanding filled her with shame. She left for Rome, trying fruitlessly to see to Egypt's interest. By the time she returned, defeated and alone, it was too late. The wheels of the chariot were already in motion.*

Cleo's death nearly destroyed Sekhmet. And that was when it happened, when she had finally called out to him.

He came running. As always, whenever she wanted him, he came running.

"Why do I get the feeling you're waiting for something?"

Dmitri looked up from his cell with only a passing interest before training his eyes back at the iPhone's screen. Shep's present question wasn't his first. However, it was the first that had gotten any reaction from the sudden stoic. After randomly rattling off inquiries—*Where is Altunatus? What powers do the Altunai have? Which other cultures' gods were aliens?*—it was this simple interrogative statement that broke Dmitri's near-militant stare at his device.

"Not *something*, Shep, *someone*."

Shep raised the tumbler of scotch to his mouth and kicked back the last drops. One kindness Dmitri had afforded him was the friendship of the bottle.

"Anybody I know?"

Dmitri's mouth broke into a grin as he shook his head and laughed lowly in disbelief.

"Good news, Shep," he said after a few minutes' pause. "The gate opens in Egypt, so we'll be going down tomorrow afternoon. Won't it be good to be back in the field?"

The room was spinning slightly, Shep thought, but Dmitri didn't seem to notice. He sat perfectly still, his eyes firmly glued to the tiny screen.

"Back in the field?"

"Yeah, Shep. According to the information Plaxis was able to track down on you, you haven't been to Egypt for a while. For an Egyptologist at such a prestigious university, that seems rather odd."

By the grace of God, Dmitri rose and reached into a nearby pantry, pulling out a small bottle of vodka, the kind intended for gifting and sold in the duty-free shops at airports. He put it on the table, and within fifteen seconds, Shep was tasting the sympathetically numbing liquid on his tongue.

"I haven't been back since…" He nearly choked on his words as he held the glass an inch from his lips. "…since Christine died."

In a flash, the echoes of her final words reverberated in his mind, bouncing off his memory in a way that his ears could almost hear. His body relived the movement of the quake, the distortion of his equilibrium as the ground shook beneath him, the sway of his body as he tried to find his footing to run forward, the sibilance of the sand as it filled in the excavated chamber.

The calling of Christine's voice. *"Shep, it's beside us! It's beside us!"*

Shep felt a warmth on the back of his hands, equally physical and, somehow, emotional in nature. He hadn't even realized that he had closed his eyes until they opened again, taking in Dmitri's sympathetic gaze.

"Planning on sharing another memory with me, Dmitri?"

He smiled warmly. "Actually, you just shared one with me. My condolences, Shep. That was horrible to have to witness."

Pulling his hands back, he placed them in his lap. The iPhone lay flat on the table, and Shep could see the grainy black and white image. At once he understood what Dmitri had been watching; every few seconds the image shifted to the perspective of another camera. His security system was funneling images through the mobile device.

"Did you ever figure out what she meant?"

Shep cocked an eyebrow in misunderstanding.

"What Christine said right before she died," Dmitri clarified. "Did you figure it out?"

"Oh, no. Not really." Nursing his vodka, he felt the two poisons competing to get him plastered fighting in his stomach. "So, Egypt? Well, I know you'll tell me I'm free to not go, then tell me why it's in my best interest to go anyway, so I guess it is what it is. Will Anton be coming?"

"No, Shep. Anton is dead."

Shep's follow up was cut off by both men taking notice of the approach of footstep. Heavy footsteps, a certain unmistakable cadence in their quality.

Shep wasn't surprised when José's face and frame marched into the kitchen. He saluted Dmitri before making some proclamation, and Dmitri returned a quick native-sounding string of Español back, sealed with a *"gracias"* and José's *"de nada"* chaser.

José waited dutifully as Dmitri rose to his feet, sliding his phone into his pants pocket.

"Our guest is here and waiting for us," he declared. "Do come along, Shep. It would be rude of us to leave him unattended for too long."

"Victoria?"

Dmitri scoffed. "Better."

He followed without resisting, too weary from lack of sleep and administrations of booze to argue or ask anything else. The art of inquiry was highly overrated. It was like trying to eat just one potato chip; you never were satisfied.

"Your neighbors must be very understanding. Or extremely terrified."

As they passed the processional of hired soldiers in the hallway outside the flat, each stood to attention as they saluted Dmitri. For his part, Dmitri seemed to take no notice.

"No neighbors, Shep," he informed him as they began down the stairs. "My flat's on the third floor. There's a guest flat across the hall that's rarely used. The other four flats are primarily for storage."

At the second floor landing, he pitched right and opened the door marked "2B" to his right.

"Storage of wh—Holy shit."

His eyes raced from object to object to object, each one more rare and more awe-inspiring than the last: a full-sized Ramses statue, a sculpture that was likely a Michelangelo, an antique harpsichord, an Easter Island head—even an old west stage coach that had somehow been placed in the seemingly closed-in space without difficulty. How had it…

Oh, that's how. Looking across the expansive space, Shep noticed that the flat wasn't actually *flat* at all. There was a staircase at the far end of the room leading down, and where windows should have been on the outside wall, there were instead twin delivery bays, each with a roll-top security door. It had looked like a warehouse from the outside, and now Shep saw that part of the building still served that purpose.

"José, there's a corpse in my flat," Dmitri said matter-of-factly as they crossed the room to the metal-mesh staircase. "Take care of it."

"But, Señor…" Ah, so Mr. Channeling-Ché did speak English! "The prisoner…"

Shep wondered if they were talking about him, or about the hooded figure who sat in a folding chair before them with his hands tied around his back.

"…will be no danger to me, and I need you on duty ASAP," Dmitri returned. He looked around the far reaches of the room, as though suspicious someone was about to leap out. "You know it's just a matter of time before the cavalry shows up."

For lack of a better term, José seemed to blush. Was he embarrassed? "I offer again my apologies, sir, for failing to recognize and capture Jaguar when I had the chance."

"I've told you, José, I forgive the oversight. You never could have done it. She'd have killed you in moments if she'd wanted to. Now, go, be of *some* use to me."

José was clearly put out. With gnashing teeth, however, he turned and made his way back upstairs; his feet pounding on the metal steps sounded like fat raindrops falling on a tin roof.

Shep felt his knees buckle as he fell backward into a folding chair across from the prisoner. For a second, he worried that his world would go dark if he too was hooded and bound. The relief set in, however, when he noticed Dmitri's position next to the captive.

"You'll forgive an old man his fancies, doctor," Dmitri teased, causing Shep to smirk ruefully as he took in the youthful features of a male appearing to be no more than twenty-five, "but I do so enjoy seeing the look on a human's face when his worldview is irrevocably altered."

A clap of thunder shook the building. Shep jerked from the sound, then leaned forward and put his hands on his knees, curling his back and rolling his shoulders for comfort. "What, do you have Jimmy Hoffa under that hood? Looks a little too petite to be Marilyn Monroe. Oh, wait, I know. The Lindbergh baby?"

With nary a word more, Dmitri ripped the cloth off from the prisoner's head. A set of emerald eyes blinked rapidly, adjusting to the light the fabric had denied him. When his gaze caught the sight of the person sitting across from him, the young man's face went stark white.

"Shep?"

"Alex?"

How a family reunion had come to pass under these circumstances, neither one knew. In harmony and disbelief, they stared, each at the other and uttered in perfect synchronization.

"What the hell are *you* doing here?"

Chapter 24

In the shadows, a lion lay in wait. Well, a jaguar perhaps. She was so befitting of her feline association at the moment, slowly pacing back and forth in the alley across the street from Dmitri's building, stalking the length and width of it as though she were sizing up prey. Which she was.

Alex had gone through the front doors two minutes and thirty-three seconds ago, a loaded .45 clutched in his grip. She had expected a scuffle, or even a shoot-out, but instead heard nothing. Either his death had been quick—but she would have felt it if he had died—there were no security forces, or he had been somehow sidetracked.

One thing was for certain: if Dmitri was expecting him, there wasn't a chance that Alex was going to succeed at his mission.

She wasn't sure what emotion was appropriate for the occasion. Anger? If she was upset with anyone, it was herself. She should have known far better than to send such an inexperienced proxy and, well, naïve human unto Dmitri's turf. Disappointment? Again, self-loathing to the point of guilt. Hope? Not at this particular moment.

Frustration? Yeah, that one was spot on. Unfortunately, feeling frustrated was the worst possible emotion for her at the moment. To be frustrated was to be overwhelmed with one's lack of control or options. Lack of control and Victoria were a toxic combination. Terrible, terrible things could happen when she got frustrated. The power she intentionally pulled from humans allowed her sustenance, provided her energy to function on a daily basis. But there was a higher form of energy with which she sometimes made contact, and she had no better name for that than Gaia. The planet was alive; it pulsed with power. It wasn't a power she could beckon and wield like she could with what she ripped from men. The only times she had ever channeled it had been when her emotions had raged out of control, when her consciousness was overridden by instincts nearly primal in nature. In those times, it wasn't unusual for the earth to begin to tremble, or for a nearby volcano to suddenly decide to erupt.

Or, as she heard the clap of thunder overhead and sensed the pressure building in the air, arcing toward rain, the weather to get all crazy.

Victoria tip-toed closer, thankful for the fall of night. The street lights, however, were sure to reveal her on Dmitri's security feed. No more had the thought crossed her mind than the electric luminescence up and down the street began to flicker. In a few more blinks, all the street lights—as well as the light pouring out from the few other occupied buildings up and down the lane—were extinguished.

Damn, Gaia was some powerful mojo.

She took advantage of the black cloak, knowing the city's power grid would soon enough detect the outage and reroute electricity to the neighborhood. With feather light and fierce footfalls, she darted across the lane and pressed her back into the exterior brick of Dmitri's building. Further up the alley, she noticed the dock-bay doors: two-story steel blankets that secured the loading/unloading area. Behind it, she heard voices.

There was an instant buzzing in her brain as the images of her mind's eye went all fuzzy. Alex. She was close enough to Alex to access his thoughts. Only problem with that was, if *he* was close enough, Dmitri may be as well. Though Victoria's mind was secure from the Altunai unless she intentionally let him in, she couldn't say the same for all the humans in the vicinity. Hector Gonzalez would be dead by now. She knew from Anton's intel that Dmitri had been feeding off him. But it was more than likely that Sheppard Smyth was still alive and being kept close by Dmitri.

Damn, if there was one person that Victoria didn't want Dmitri's head getting the green light for, it was Smyth. The thieving bastard who stole Christine from her had been too smart for his own good. She knew that the moment she had saw him at the Veracruz airport. It seemed eons ago that she had panicked at the coincidence of the Mayan trying to warn the masses of the danger they were in. Thank God Smyth hadn't been into Mesoamerican cultures, or he might have put the pieces together. Maybe he had. After all this, maybe he had figured out that he was...

No, highly unlikely. Hell, even Christine hadn't figured out that one. In a panic, her breath quickened. Christine may have been able to piece clues together about why she was being assigned to protect Sheppard Smyth if she had been privy to just a few more pieces of the puzzle. Pieces of the puzzle which Dmitri had.

Fuck. Had Shep been smart enough to hold his tongue around Dmitri? That was the question.

Looking through Alex's eyes in her mind, she saw only black. He had likely been blindfolded. From the smell, taste, and sounds he was sensing, she concluded that this was a Plaxis warehouse. Dmitri had many where he put anything and everything he thought might suggest evidence of the Altunais' existence. At least, until he could sell it on the black market. He had no problem with the objects existing but staying private. No problem breaking Altunai law when it suited *him*. The types willing to pay his exuberant fees for such treasures were rarely after the pieces for their cultural or historic value. They were just spoils of their fortunes, obtained to evidence their importance, bill folds or account for their…shortcomings. But Lord help any collector who decided to go legit and cast the objects into the public domain. They usually didn't live too long after that.

"*Alex!*" She called to him mentally. The way his head began to dart about fruitlessly told her she had heard him. "*Don't talk. And for Ra's sake, stop jerking around.*"

Obediently, he stilled. "*Where are you?*"

"*I'm outside the building. Have you seen the amulet?*"

"*No.*"

"*Dmitri?*"

"*Not yet, but I think he's coming. The alpha goon who seems to be running this show just left.*"

"*Are you hurt?*"

Damn, what was she doing? Alex had just told her that Dmitri was likely on his way. No time for chit-chat. So what if he *was* hurt? She could drag him bloodied and bruised from the building *after* she broke in and kicked Dmitri's ass.

"*No,*" he finally replied, in a tone heavy with qualification. "*I feel…tingly.*"

She gave a sigh of relief. "*That's the amulet. It connects with us somehow. That's good, it means it's close.*"

"*But why does it make me tingly?*"

Yeah, hard to explain that one. "*It's just trying to get our attention. Alex, I'm going to get you out. Just try to avoid saying anything. I'll be here waiting for the right moment. I won't let anything happen to you.*"

"I'm sorry, I screwed up."

Victoria bit her lip, the tears brimming in the corners of her eyes. *"It's my fault, Alex. This is my battle, not yours. I shouldn't have… I should be able to stand up to…"* She sighed, mentally as well as physically. *"You tried your best. Now just hold tight."*

No sooner had the thought crossed her mind than Alex's head swung to the side again. A procession was making its way down toward poor Alex bound to the chair, likely a guard at each side. The sounds of footfalls on a set of metal stairs told her there were three, probably male by the heavy sound of their steps.

As the voices filled Alex's ears, Victoria listened in and cautiously took a few more steps back. She could keep Dmitri out of her head, but she was powerless to block the flow of consciousness through her from all the humans in the room as soon as he realized that channel was open to him. It wouldn't take but a few seconds to scan through Shep Smyth's mind and see *everything*, if he knew what to look for.

Oh, damn, Victoria thought, what if Smyth was one of the men who just entered the room? What if Shep saw Alex? What if Alex…

Oh, this was *not* good.

Her skin itched, she was so determined to get into the room and have it out with Dmitri. And to get the amulet. And to get Alex. And possibly, now that she knew he was so intimately involved, Smyth? Holy hell, though, how much of this could she really pull off with a room full of trained paramilitary and the one man who had ever been able to crawl under skin inside? She had to get her priorities straight and now.

Problem was, she needed to do it all.

Problem also was, she simply couldn't.

The sense of frustration swelled within her, and she felt the surge of power flowing through her as lightning flashed across the sky. Damn, she had to get that in check now. Causing a hurricane to suddenly appear over London was not going to help her. Worse, if her subconscious energy grab went too far, she was going to start rending the earth beneath her into pieces.

Or blow England off the face of the planet. No, not another Krakatau. Her heart simply couldn't take it again.

With measured steps, she inched toward the set of double doors and stretched out her mind, trying to stay just close enough to hear and see through Alex's senses.

What she saw made all hell break loose: Shep Smyth and Alex Cezanne, eyes wide, adrenaline pumping, shouting in unison, "What the hell are *you* doing here?"

Frustration skyrocketed to damned pissed and ready to do something about it. She felt a growl building in her throat, a very primal, animalistic roar, as the heavens opened up, reflecting her fury, bringing forth a rain born of rage.

Using the compass of her powers, she pushed with her mind against the door closest to her. Damn, if this sort of action wasn't going to leave her starved of energy like a son of a bitch. But at the moment, that was the last thing about which she was concerned. She kept her focus on getting Alex as far away from Dmitri as possible.

As the aluminum began to bend under her mental strong hand, she felt the familiar rush of multiple consciousnesses passing through her. Dmitri was channeling the minds of those around him through her. Including Shep's.

And Shep's very, very clear memory of Christine.

Which matched perfectly Alex's very clear memory of…Christine.

"Open up!" she bellowed at the door, as though saying it out loud would be its breaking point. And, lucky her, it was.

As the metal shield split in two, rolling inward, she dived through the opening barely wide enough to allow her passage just in time to catch the flashes of lightning beginning to swarm the sky.

Of course, Dmitri wasn't surprised to see her.

"Darling."

Three of Dmitri's henchman rushed her, guns poised for attack. *Perfect,* she thought, *bring it on.* She knew soldiers preferred taking down an enemy through coordinated hand-to-hand combat. At least the sick stock that Dmitri tended to employ were all about the slap downs. No sooner had they thrown punches than Victoria responded, trading blow for blow. They were so weak compared to her, mere children in her eyes and in conflict. Their life forces, on the other hand, were delicious, and after having shattered the skull of two, she placed her hands on the skull of the third and pulled all his strength from him, ripping his life from him instantly.

"Didn't I tell you, doctor?" she heard Dmitri say in the background with a demented sense of pride. "Such an efficient warrior."

But Shep's mind was too focused on Alex to respond. Even over the hum of all the thoughts passing through her from others, she could hear distinctly his confusion, the repeated *whys* and *hows* of his wife's one sibling being held prisoner by Dmitri Kronastia. The *whys* of Alex being bound as though he were a threat to anybody. He couldn't understand. Sweet little Alex?

Though, on a second look, there was nothing *little* about him. The guy had grown both up and out since last he had seen him. He must have put on a good thirty pounds of muscle, and his eyes…holiest of cows, they were just like Victoria Kent's.

"Well, this is just too much fun to resist joining in." Dmitri turned his face to Alex, then Shep, giving each a quick nod. "Gentlemen, if you'll excuse me."

As Kronastia made way toward Victoria, she threw another two men dead to the floor. Shep's mind was in full meltdown mode; he couldn't make heads or tails of this. Alex, taking advantage of the moment of Dmitri's distraction, jerked his body, forcing the chair to gain the distance between them.

"Shep, we don't have time for the hows or the whys," Alex said determinedly, as though he were reading Shep's mind. "We need to get out of here. Now, if not sooner."

"What are you—"

"Untie me," Alex interjected.

"I don't understand how—"

Another body flew through the air, landing dead in the space between them. The head was nearly twisted off the neck, a display of physical domination he had never before witnessed.

"Shep, we are both going to end up like this guy if you don't untie me right fucking *now*."

Uncomprehending but prepared to take his brother-in-law's word for it, Shep shook himself from his confusion and went to work on unbinding Alex. His wrists were bound in cuffs—there would be no getting those off—but he was able with some effort to undo the ropes that tied his arms and ankles to the chair, allowing Alex to rise to his feet.

"Shep, I know you're confused right now, but I need you to tell me this. Have you seen a green amulet?"

"What? Yes, Dmitri…Dmitri has it."

It was at this moment that both Shep and Alex noticed the eerie silence and the echo of their words around them. Looking across the way, their eyes landed just in time on Victoria, the last henchmen's body slumping to the ground lifeless. Her wild eyes were fixed on Dmitri as they began a balanced circling.

"Been a while, Guardian," she hissed, her frame poised as though she might have to throw him down at any moment. "Interesting company you keep these days."

His face came into view as he arced their path. "I could say the same of you. But I'm not really surprised."

"I don't know why you'd be surprised. What I want to know is, how the hell did you find—"

Her body froze when Dmitri pulled the amulet from his pocket and held it aloft, dangling it in front of her. Her eyes glazed over. Victoria looked like a starving man being offered bread.

Or a seven course meal.

"Do you hear it, my love?" Dmitri demanded, his tone a little curt. "It wants you. It wants to be claimed."

She lunged forward, trying to seize it. "Give it to me, then."

Dmitri raised the amulet high over his head, causing Victoria to stumble forward into his embrace. He caught her under the arm and pulled her close. The gravity between them was nearly tangible, and both Alex and Shep were at a loss as Victoria and Dmitri's lips met each other's.

Victoria threw her arms around Dmitri and pulled herself to him. Dmitri responded by circling his arms behind her and closing whatever distance remained.

As they pulled back from their kiss, they began to exchange words in a tongue that Shep couldn't understand. Even with their familiar voices, he couldn't believe the change in their tone. Dmitri's words were soft, almost pleading. His hand smoothed over Victoria's hair, pushing a lock behind her ear. Victoria, just moments ago the dealer of death, melted into him, her replies weighed heavy with conflict.

Dmitri leaned over to kiss her again, but this time Victoria turned away and prevented him. He exhaled, disappointed by the move, and tried to bring her lips back to his. She distanced herself, breaking free of his hold. Apparently, Dmitri didn't like that. Both his face and his words were heated. When he tried to pivot her around, however, his face met her flying fist.

In a flash of light, Dmitri disappeared and reformed directly behind Alex. The proxy was too surprised by the occurrence and had no time to defend himself before Dmitri had him in a headlock.

"God *damned,* it feels good to be able to do that again." Peals of laughter issued from Dmitri's mouth as he further secured Alex in a bear hug with one arm while holding the amulet out with the other, tempting Victoria. "Fine, we'll keep up this game a little longer, sweet. I know the amulet is screaming at you. You won't be able to deny it—or me—much longer."

Then Dmitri spoke directly into Alex's ear. "You hear it too, don't you, pretty boy? You can hear it singing you home. Of course, you can. She Bonded you, didn't she? And gave you that set of peepers in the process. I wonder, did she take you by the blood or by the bed?"

Alex's wide eyes beseeched Shep. As his gaze narrowed, he gasped, and Shep's head pivoted in confusion.

As did Victoria's, also hearing Alex's thoughts loud and clear.

And then it all happened too fast for anyone to know for sure what transpired.

There was a flash. Victoria disappeared. Shep took advantage of Dmitri's distraction to grab the amulet. That made Dmitri decide to throw Alex forward into Shep as a weapon to knock them off balance. Shep and Alex landed on the floor as Dmitri jumped forward. Victoria reappeared just in time to throw her body over the pair.

Dmitri froze.

"By the blood," she gasped, her eyes filled with tenderness and regret. "There's never been another man I've taken by the bed, Guardian. There's no other man for me but you. José, help me?"

Kissing the pavement, Dmitri was stunned by the weight of his security officer atop him. What the hell? He hadn't heard him reenter over the calamity, but the last thing he had expected was for him to turn traitor.

With a groan, Dmitri threw José off him, jumping to his feet and reaching for Victoria.

Another flash, and Dmitri was alone.

"Tlalli!" he cried, diving with an open embrace to the place her body had occupied just seconds before. But she was gone. His relished momentarily the kiss they had shared, and remembered the plea he had made to her in the Altunai tongue.

"Please, Tlalli. The baktun's over. Just…forgive me. Take me back. Guardian, Vessel…It doesn't matter anymore. Please?"

And his heart broke again in jagged shards recalling her reply.

"I cannot. This is my duty, my path. You must understand; I must see this through, for Ra."

"To hell with Ra, Tlalli. He left you behind. I stayed. I stayed."

Her eyes had looked up at his, cresting with tears. *"But only because you had to."*

They had escaped. His chance to persuade her…had escaped.

"What happened in here?"

Dmitri's teeth gnashed as he spun around, nostrils and hair flaring, to see José looking confused and stunned. So, Victoria had charmed him, hmm? Didn't matter. Dmitri was pissed, and ready to lash out.

Perfect. An object for his frustration. Dmitri drove forward and pushed the unprepared man into the wall. With a roar, he pulled back his fist and flung it forward.

Shep instinctively kicked for dear life, pushing his body beyond anything it had ever endured. He wasn't certain what had happened to get him where he was: swimming in cold, churning waters, the taste of metal in his mouth. As his arms flailed, he broke the surface with a gasp. His eyes itched but he tried to focus, to make sense of what was going on.

"Shep!"

Alex's voice was nearby, but where? He thrashed about, turning left and right, trying desperately to bob out of the water with enough leverage to gain sight through the dark. Finally, he spotted a roundness in the waves about twenty feet away, a set of luminescent eyes sparkling against the ambient light drifting out from the nearby shoreline.

He began to swim, trying frantically to remember whether or not Alex also possessed that ability. He hadn't been very close to Christine's younger brother, but that was simply because of the age difference. There was a nearly fifteen year gap between Alex and Christine Cezanne, and Alex had never really taken to Shep the few times they had met.

No reason to let the guy drown, however.

As Shep reached Alex, he was relieved to see that he was perfectly capable of swimming. Yet, he was losing buoyancy in his struggle to keep the unconscious form of Victoria Kent above the surface. What had happened to his handcuffs?

"Victoria managed to burn them off. Don't know when, but she can do things that…Yeah, you know," Alex answered. *How was he answering his thoughts?* "Help me, I can't keep her up."

Shep snaked his arm under Victoria's armpit while Alex took her other side. Now that they were turned toward the shore and making good progress, Shep tried to gauge where they were. Had they somehow fallen out of the warehouse windows? Yes, that must have been it. He remembered a flash. There had probably been an explosion, and the force of the blast had blown them into the Thames.

Only, Kronastia's flat had been in South London, nowhere near Big Ben. Shep's sight was fuzzy, but he was pretty certain there was a tower rising from the profile of buildings before them. And when had it gotten so warm? Ah, the blast. Any second now, his skin would dull from the chill of the London December night. Any second.

"Holy…" Shep's voice trailed off as his eyes finally focused. The image of the tower sharpened, and without doubt, he knew that prestigious edifice anywhere. "That's the Lotus Tower!" he shouted. "But that's in Cairo!"

Alex coughed, returning in a snappish tone, "Yeah, I figured she'd pull us here. Why fly when you can *fly*, you know?"

"In Cairo!" Shep repeated. His tone was nervous, questioning, but he continued to paddle toward the bank. "How the hell did we get to Cairo? And why in the hell did Dmitri Kronastia have you tied up in his warehouse?"

"Good to see you too," Alex muttered, taking in a mouthful of water as he said it. He coughed and sputtered, and Shep tried to relieve his burden by gathering Victoria's form closer. "Shep, we can handle details later. Right now, we need a place we can hide. I don't think he can port without Victoria near, but he sure as hell can hop on a plane."

Victoria's head rolled to the side as she momentarily came to. Her voice came out as an abrasive whisper in Shep's ear. "Anathea…Hermapolous's house."

They had reached a dock and just in the nick of time. Shep didn't think he could keep them both above water much longer.

"What?" he called to the dripping woman as he hoisted her up to safety.

"You…you know…" She coughed, water spouting from her mouth. "You know where…Anathea's house…?"

Shep reached out his hand to Alex and helped him crawl up to safety. "I know where it is, but she won't let us in. Trust me, she doesn't see anyone."

He knew from experience.

Victoria's eyes cracked open, the same jade-emerald glow as Alex's new peepers shining up.

"She will," she assured him in her meek tone.

Instinctively trying to comfort a damsel in distress, Shep pulled her into his lap. "I'm not convinced what you are or are not, but I'm pretty sure that the whole studying-under-Anathea thing was a bunch of malarkey. And you look...injured. What need to do is get you to a hospital." *And me to a shrink.*

Her chest shook as she coughed up more of the Nile. "No, Shep..." With a trembling hand, she struggled to stroke his cheek. "You don't understand; I *am* Anathea."

Horns blared as they darted from lane to alley to byway. Shep could feel the weight of the stares as they fled the streets. It was, no doubt, a curious sight to the locals: a middle-aged white man holding a passed-out, twenty-something native beauty, dripping water, in his arms as his eyes surveyed the paths ahead, a clear attempt to find his way to somewhere. Trailing behind him was an equally desperate-looking younger man, hair black and eyes inhumanly green. Something had happened to the woman, or was about to, and both these men were determined to get her out from the public eye yesterday if not before.

"How do you know where her house is?" Alex asked Shep.

Shep didn't pause to answer, only dashed to the right as he seemed to figure out their location, and spoke over his shoulder. "Before I left Egypt for the last time, I tracked down her address through some old real estate records from the 50's. I stood outside her house for two days, staring through the gate before Anathea finally got annoyed."

"So you saw her then," Alex concluded. The subtext of his comment was *you've seen her before, so it shouldn't be so surprising.*

"No, she never actually came out from the house. Her maid—at least, I think it was her maid—asked me several times to leave. The police finally showed up in the end."

He still couldn't believe he had made so desperate an attempt. Christine had been buried in Cairo. Oddly enough, when Shep had received the fax of her will from her family's lawyer, that had been one of her dying wishes. It perplexed him; Christine had never seemed particularly fond of the country. He wanted her to be buried...he didn't know. Her home town in Maine, maybe, or in the same graveyard as his own mother and father in Oklahoma. Not in Egypt, not so very far from him. As much as the thought grieved him, he was angry at her for it. How could she deny him so simple a comfort as having her resting place nearby to him?

But then, Shep thought, if her grave were far from him, he would never have to visit it. In that way, he could better face her death. It would be a reality removed. If he kept himself from Egypt, that is. So, making up his mind in his traditionally stubborn way, he swore he would never return to Cairo again until it was time for his bones to rest in a grave next to Christine. It seemed a crazy decision for an Egyptologist, akin to a surgeon vowing never to scrub in again. One thing he had to do before he left Cairo, however, was to see Anathea Hermapolous. There was no one he knew who would be more capable of proving his theory about Cleopatra's murder right. And if he was right, then Christine had not died in vain. He had been determined to come face to face with Anathea at least once.

Or, as he learned now, Victoria Kent. Shep was beyond the surprise anymore. At this point, someone could tell him that Stalin and Roosevelt took turns cross-dressing and calling themselves Golda Meir and he'd believe it with no less or greater sense of awe than what he currently felt. His emotions and his world view had been so shaken the last few days, his body had simply gone numb as a defense.

They continued through the streets for another thirty minutes without much talk. Shep had asked at one point about getting a cab, but as neither one of them had any money or identification, and as they were carrying an unconscious woman that could raise suspicion, they didn't see that as an option.

Finally, they reached the gates. Anathea's home was one of a few old English-styled mansions in Cairo, set behind heavy bars that rose ten feet high. The house itself was nothing too impressive. In London, it would have been yet another Victorian two-story. Here, however, in a city so crowded some made homes from converted cemeteries, the spacious lot was a luxury. There was a security keypad embedded in the stone column to the right of the entrance, and Shep wondered how in the hell they were going to figure out the code to get in.

He looked down at the woman in his arm and trembled. The color had drained from her face, and if he didn't know better, he would say she was deathly sick, maybe even dying.

"She is," Alex said.

Shep looked at him curiously. "Is what?"

"Sick," he returned matter-of-factly. Shep's mouth dropped as Alex continued. "Yes, I can hear your thoughts. Most of them, anyway. You're thinking really loudly right now. And don't worry; she told me the code before she passed out."

"Shouldn't we take her to a hospital?"

"Nothing the doctors could do for her. I know what she needs, but it will take me a little time to find it." Alex punched a series of numbers into the keypad, and the locks disengaged as the door swung open. "Take her inside and get her out of the wet clothes. You too, of course. I'm not sure what you're going to find to wear, but she wanted us to just stay here and lie low until morning."

"And you know all this because…"

Alex smirked and tapped two fingers to his forehead indicatively. "Lots to catch up on, Shep. Go inside now, and I'll be back soon."

The front door, oddly enough, was unlocked. As Shep walked into the foyer, he found a room full of sheet-covered furniture. On the wall above the fireplace was a portrait of Victoria, ala the Italian Renaissance. Passing through the sitting room, he found the stairs, at the top of which was a bedroom straight out of *Howard's End*.

The wet clothes fell with a slosh onto the floor of the tiled bath of the master suite. Shep tried his best not to ogle her in just her undergarments, and forced himself to throw a heavy blanket over her instead. As for himself, he walked about in boxers. The air wasn't so cold, but combined with the chill, he heard his teeth chattering.

Victoria's chest slowly rose and fell, and Shep breathed a sigh of relief that she seemed to be at ease for the moment. Cautiously, he decided to slip under the blanket on the queen bed as well. He was determined to stay awake until Alex returned, but his body had different ideas. It had endured too much. It needed to re-coup.

As the blanket began to reflect his own heat back at him, the comfort enveloped him, and his eyes slowly shut.

Chapter 25

"What do you mean, you stayed only because you were required? Would not you have stayed only for me?"

The Guardian turned, the shame evident in his repose. He hadn't meant to tell her the truth. In fact, sharing such knowledge with the Vessel was forbidden. Then again, so were a lot of the things he did with her. Her knowing stood to contaminate the findings of the study. But he couldn't help it. He loved her, wanted to share his whole heart and his whole mind with her. Moreover, he wanted her to do the same. But the Vessel was hesitant, untrusting. While he would occasionally get little insights into her head, for the most part, she kept her mind cordoned off from him. She was as much an enigma to him today as the day he first Bonded her eons before.

That was why he had broken protocol and shared with her the truth of her purpose. At the end of the period of isolation, her mind would be the record which served as evidence of humanity's right to survive. Every crop of civilization had been tweaked slightly. The Guardian knew that if Isis and Ra decided civilization had not advanced sufficiently, it would be destroyed.

He didn't want the Vessel destroyed. Surely if she knew, if she could understand how much he wanted this world to succeed so that she might, in turn, live. Then maybe she'd finally trust him. Maybe she'd finally let him in.

Maybe their Bond could be complete. He would be one with her in both body and mind. He knew he would do anything for her, anything at all. Even the ultimate sacrifice: give up his own life force to her if it proved necessary. It was the only way for an Altunai to die in this world, the ultimate act of devotion. Albeit, one that would leave their relationship terribly one-sided.

Much to his dismay, the revelation had the opposite effect. It drove them farther apart. She spurned him, accused him of loving her falsely, of only keeping her close because it was his job. Then she became his adversary. She *established her Order, an elite collection of followers who helped her to gather evidence of what she saw as mankind's accomplishments. She would be ready when the time of isolation ended to make the arguments she needed to make. She would stand among them, a representative of humanity to the Altunai when she truly belonged to neither species.*

All he could do was watch from afar and hope.

Anathea Hermapolous? Why the hell not? In the one week since he'd met her, Shep had already discovered that Victoria Kent had a history that included being an ancient world tourist, an Egyptian goddess, an Israeli special forces officer, an international black market antiques dealer, a college friend of his wife's, and a half-alien. That she was also a prominent luminary in the area of Near Eastern archaeology? It was no more a shock than finding out your straight-laced best friend led a secret life as a *Rocky Horror Picture Show* fan.

Alex had been gone for what seemed like hours. The scant amount of sleep Shep had gotten came to an abrupt end when Victoria's shaking had woken him. The seizure only lasted a few moments. As soon as he covered her with another blanket and stroked her hair in comfort, she stilled. He felt a twinge of anxiety as he looked at her and pressed the palm of his hand against her cheek. Victoria's color was really off, her breathing shallow. No matter what he did, she didn't wake. It was like she was in a coma.

In silence, he got up and found his clothes, now dried out, and dressed.

Down the stairs and into her foyer, he meandered, ripping dusty sheets off of everything. Every surface was covered in relics; not just archaeologically treasures great and small, but photographs. Ever so many photographs. Among them, there was one face that he recognized: Christine, probably about seventeen years old, posing with her parents, a child who looked barely more than a toddler, and there between them all, Victoria.

Shep picked up the picture and eyed it more closely.

"What you got there?"

Alex's voice nearly made him drop the heavy-metal gilded frame. "What? Um…just a picture."

Alex wasn't alone. Under his arm, an obviously fake-blond haired woman stood silent and expectant. When Shep's stare settled on the c-cups before him, Alex mouthed, "For Vick."

Shep wondered what Victoria would need with an Egyptian prostitute, but for the moment, his attention stayed fixed on the picture. He extended a finger and pointed to the toddler in the photo as he held it up for Alex to see.

"This you?"

Alex dragged the whore under his arm and leaned in closer, studying the photo. "I guess so. I don't remember it being taken, but looks like I was really young. Jesus, is that…?"

"Sure looks like her," Shep agreed. Even if the circumstances were beyond belief, Shep held on to his smile at having found a little memento of his wife in the collection. He replaced the photo on the table where it had stood. Turning now to Alex, he could no longer withhold his inquiries, even with present company. "Alex, what the hell is going on? How are you involved with all this? How was Christine? And what happened to your eyes?"

To the surprise of both men, the call girl spoke up in fractured English. "We make the sex now. I have no time for the chitty chatty."

Alex blushed as Shep eyed him curiously. "Actually, you're not for me. My friend, Vick, is waiting for you upstairs. That pair of double doors right at the top; just go on in. If she's asleep, don't feel badly about trying to wake her. She really needs your company."

The call girl's head whipped to the left, looking at the stairs. "You did not say woman. Costs more. I only gay for pay."

Beginning to push her upstairs, Alex gave her a warm smile. "Of course. Whatever you wish. When she wakes up, tell her that Alex sent you…to quench her thirst."

Hesitantly, she began to climb each step nervously, as though she suspected all she might get from this deal was screwed. Taking a quick survey of all the treasures on the walls and tables must have assured her of Alex's ability to deliver, however, and with a quickened step she took the last few stairs spritely and disappeared into Victoria's room. When she was gone, Alex turned back to Shep.

"I am a member of The Order," he said matter-of-factly when they were alone. "We serve the goddess."

"And by the goddess you mean…Victoria."

Alex nodded. "We know her as Sekhmet. Some call her Hecate. But, yes, Victoria."

"So, you *worship* Victoria," Shep attempted to confirm.

Alex gave a wry laugh. "No, Shep. I'm Catholic, as you know. I don't *worship* her. I serve her."

"In what capacity?"

Alex's hand ran nervously through his hair as he sat on the arm of the nearby sofa.

"Um, just as another one of The Order until a few days ago. She had me on retrieval and recovery. You see, Victoria's been on a mission for years. The time of isolation…that's the period in which the Altunai…Well, the Altunai are this group of…And humans were…Wow, Shep, I just don't know where to start with you."

Yasmin had a bad feeling about this trick. First, the guy had no cash. All he did have was some fancy clothes and a good address he said he would take her to. She didn't understand why she had agreed, but when he looked at her with those milky emerald eyes, she found herself powerless not to take up his call. But now? It was getting odder by the minute. It wasn't that a guy hadn't contracted her services before on behalf of someone else. It wasn't even that the intended receiver of her service was female—it happened from time to time. This was the first time the two things had happened together, however.

She pushed open the doors at the top of the stairs, quickly passed through, and closed them again behind. The woman—Vick, was it?—was lying on her side under a heavy blanket. She couldn't really make out more than a cascade of chestnut hair streaked with golden highlights and a lone, olive-skinned arm hanging off the side. Quietly, she approached.

"Halo?" Yasmin whispered as her hand reached up to take the blanket down. There was no answer, no movement. Unhurriedly, she began to pull at the wool, inch by inch revealing quite possibly the most beautiful woman she had ever seen, dressed in nothing but a pair of silk panties and a lacy bra.

Yasmin gasped. Sex was routine for her, even the few times it had been with women, but with the beauty in front of her? Well, even Yasmin wouldn't deny a little tug of lust playing at her insides.

She reached down and tried to shake the woman awake gently. She didn't stir. Nor did she wake when instead Yasmin tapped her shoulder. Well, there was always the princess routine. It rarely failed, and as Yasmin leaned over and lowered her lips to this woman's, she doubted it would with her either.

The moment the kiss landed, a fire blazed through her. To hell with it, even if there was no pot of gold at the end of this rainbow, she was going to enjoy the slide down. She deepened the kiss, her fingers of her free hand tracing a line up the woman's side. To her delight, she felt the muscles of the body beneath her begin to shift under the smooth flesh.

A flush of heat spread over her when she realized the woman was kissing her back. Her hand came to rest upon Yasmin's face, her thumb rubbing over her cheek bone. The other hand was soon planted on her hip, pulling her body down, closer, flush.

"*Tai-iki en kwa?*" the vixen asked in a raspy voice as Yasmin pulled back for air. It was an odd tongue she didn't understand. After a moment, she asked in English, "Who are you?"

Yasmin couldn't find words as the beauty opened her eyes, revealing bright pools of jade that seemed to twinkle in the darkness. The same as the man's. Ah, Yasmin thought, now she understood. The guy who had picked her up in the club was this woman's brother, and he knew his sister was gay. Only, in Cairo, it was hard for a woman with those particular tastes to find company.

Find a need, fill a need...

Fill your pockets, too.

Jade eyes were blazing in molten desire that played across her face. Her eyes rolled, her breaths growing airy and rapid. In a voice cracking with need, she repeated, "Who are you?"

Yasmin leaned over, licking her earlobe and soliciting a moan before she spoke. "Alex sent me to...quench your thirst."

When she pulled back, the woman was wearing a fifty-yard grin.

"God, I was really hoping you'd say that."

Chapter 26

The lack of sleep was aching in Shep's bones, and suddenly the nearby armchairs looked like the Promised Land. Plopping himself down on one of the wingbacks, he sighed deeply and rubbed his eyes. "Kronastia already gave me a Cliff Notes version on the history of Altunai-human relations. I get the whole thing. Well, not *get it,* necessarily, but understand it. What I don't get is why you're wrapped up in this?"

Alex's back straightened, and as he spoke, he looked like a soldier making a report to his superior. "I am her proxy. I carry her blood in my veins. I'm like her...I don't know, Shep. Like her minion, I guess, but totally voluntarily. She gave me a little of her abilities, and I'm using them to serve her cause."

A low chuckle was too hard to suppress. "Why in the hell would you care about Victoria Kent's cause? What does it mean to you?"

"It means I can avenge the death of my sister, Shep," Alex answered in complete monotone. "You know? Your wife."

"What are you..." He shook his head vigorously in denial. "No, Alex. I get it. Believe me, I do. When Christine died, I wanted to blame someone too. Truth is, sometimes shit just happens. Sometimes, *accidents* just happen."

"No, Shep. Christine was murdered."

"Murdered?" The thought was preposterous. "Look, Alex—"

"Well, fancy that," Alex sighed sarcastically. "The very man who's ruined his professional career trying to prove a two-thousand year old murder happened can't see the one that happened right in front of his eyes three years ago."

"Alex, really? Believe me, in some ways I'd actually be relieved to find out Christine was murdered." At least then there'd be a reason behind it, no matter how heinous. "But why, and by whom?"

Alex looked incredulous. "No fucking way. You can't figure it out?" Shep's eyes were blank.

Both their head snapped when they heard Victoria's voice at the top of the stairs.

"Alex, that's enough," she rebuked. "Shep doesn't need to be burdened with our internal politics."

A double take wasn't sufficient. Shep had to take in the view three times to be convinced he wasn't dreaming. More than refreshed, Victoria was completely renewed. Her youthful vitality was restored, her eyes and smile again bright and playful.

"I trust Yasmin showed you a good time?"

Alex's inquiry was a thinly veiled attempt to inquire if Victoria had fed. Shep was many things, but slow just wasn't one of them. It didn't take long for him to figure out that if Dmitri as an Altunai had to feed off human life force, it was likely Victoria as a partial-Altunai did the same.

Her reply only served to confirm that hypothesis. "Indeed. She's sleeping it off. She'll be fine in a day or two. Dr. Smyth, good to see you again."

"And weird to see you, Victoria," he returned as she made her way down the stairs. In the intervening time, she had redressed into fresh clothes. "So, you're Sekhmet, huh?"

She smiled. "Sounds uneventful when you say it that way. But, yes." Her expression shifted, becoming sincere. "Shep, I'm sorry I got you involved in all this. I hadn't planned to subject you to Dmitri's company. If he's hurt you in any way—"

"Treated me rather nicely, actually," Shep interrupted. "Except for the taking me prisoner and killing my friend part, he was a perfect host."

She hung her head shamefully. "I'm sorry about Hector. He was a good man. Unfortunately, Dmitri's never developed my ability to skim life rather than chug it." She was silent for a moment, before she shifted again, now sounding all professional. "What else did he tell you?"

"Enough for me to know that humanity is screwed."

Wide-eyed, she appeared to be shocked at his statement. "Why would you say that? We stand a good chance of—"

"Oh, really? Well, let's just see..."

Not knowing if his crazy idea was going to work, he proceeded with it anyway. Shep reached out and took Victoria's hand, bringing her palm to rest on his face. It happened with Dmitri, hadn't it? When Shep had been having a particularly strong memory, Dmitri had said he paid witness to it through his touch. Now, he wanted Victoria to see. See what just a few days of being mixed up in her world had forced him to endure: Hector's dead eyes; the news about the body from the airplane—the MI-6 agent had been a father to two, another on the way; a room full of slaughtered soldiers; Alex tied to a chair and held captive; Shep downing drink after drink, trying to make it all make sense.

"Is this the humanity you're meant to defend?" Shep barked at her. Victoria shuddered and leapt back as she withdrew her hand. "You and Dmitri are supposedly the superior beings, yet death and destruction follow you wherever you go. And this is what the Altunai will use to judge humanity? You'll forgive me, *goddess,* but I'd rather be judged by the goodness of true men than by the sins of false gods."

"Sheppard!"

It really shouldn't have come as a surprise that Alex rebuked him. He had made his allegiances known, and they rested with Victoria.

The proxy turned to her now, offering words of dismissal and comfort. "Vick, he doesn't know the whole truth. He doesn't understand what you've done for humanity, for everyone."

"No, Alex, on the contrary. He's right." Alex shrank back, disbelieving her consent to Shep's assessment. "I am…an animal. How will the Altunai judge us worthy of life when they see the example I've set?"

"Vick?"

A high-pitched huff came from her mouth. "What the fuck does it matter? We don't have the amulet. I can't open the gate. If the gate doesn't open, humanity gets destroyed by default. Shep's right, Alex. We are so seriously screwed."

Shep fished through his pockets until he felt the smooth surface of the stone tied onto the golden chain. As he turned and held it out, he suddenly felt like he was a hypnotist from the way Alex and Victoria's eyes tracked the object. With a grunt, he threw it toward Victoria who caught it without blinking.

"There. Your damned amulet. Do whatever the hell you want with it. I hope it was worth killing so many innocent people for."

"What is it—"

"Shh!" Victoria's hand slapped over Alex's mouth. "I can't hear it when you talk."

Alex pulled Victoria's hand off his mouth. "I can hear every word, just don't know what the hell it means."

Shep said nothing. Nothing, because he was too busy listening. He didn't understand how or why, but he could hear the whispers coming from the cursed thing, too.

Victoria drew in a deep breath and closed her eyes, straightening her frame. When she opened her eyes again, Shep took a step back. Gone were the jade discs that were simultaneously intriguing and frightening, replaced with pools of black that seemed to suck all warmth from his body. She began to chant in some foreign tongue that he recognized as the same she and Dmitri had used in London.

"Dohm merka'at faknai inbrutu. Signahm-Sekmant, Yikayutu-Osru Ankh Tawy in gerikorbutum. It's time. It's telling us, it's time."

"Us?" Alex asked, clearly wondering if he were a party to that pronoun.

"Osi...Dmitri and I," Victoria clarified as she slipped on some shoes she'd removed from a cedar chest at the edge of the room. "And Shep."

"Me?"

Alex was just a flabbergasted. "Shep?"

"Yes, Shep." Striding forward, she slipped the amulet into her pocket and grinned at the good doctor. "My poor, poor, Sheppard Smyth. I've wanted to tell you since I first saw you in Veracruz. I want to tell you now, but I'm bound by my vow. I know this is asking a lot, but please...trust me. Come with me now, and everything will make sense soon."

"Fuck you" was his witty reply. "I've had enough of this hocus pocus, apocalypse cultist, speaking in tongues hoo-haa. I'm going home, and, Alex, if you had any sense, you'd do the same. I'm going back to Boston and just—"

"Christine died in your place, Shep."

Well, that stopped him cold. "What?"

"Christine died in your place," she repeated. "Now, mind you, I never would have allowed Dmitri to kill you, but he didn't know that. Neither did Christine. She gave her life in protection of you."

"But Alex just said..." he mumbled. Oh, here came the darn headache again. "Alex said she was murdered."

"Yes, so that you would be safe," she conferred. Again, she held out her hand. "Please, Shep, come with me. I'd consider it a great favor and an honor. And if you do this for me, if you trust me now, I'll…" Her brow furrowed, as though she were in the midst of arriving at conclusion or giving into an unwise impulse. "Do this for me, and I'll give you the proof you need to know that your theory about Cleopatra was right."

"Proof?"

"Yes, undeniable proof."

Shep shifted, lurching to the right, studying the sincerity of her face. "Is it here?"

"Yes, it's here. Payable immediately."

It seemed too convenient, and he was more than a little incredulous. "I want it in advance. Then I'll agree to go with you."

Victoria bit her lip in frustration. After a pause, she turned back to Shep and palmed his face in her hands, beginning to tunnel into his mind and share with him her memory of that horrid night. "Okay, Shep. I just hope your grasp of Latin is as good as your Egyptian."

08.12.30

BCE

Chapter 27

Shep's brain was in overload. The images were so clear, the smells so stinging he shrank back slightly from the taste of incense on his tongue. He was seeing through Victoria's eyes; he knew this from having the same experience with Dmitri. Still, there was a sort of removal of self, almost like he was in her head as she spoke, interacting with her thoughts, rather than just reliving the echo of her memories.

Sekhmet sat in silence, a goblet of wine clutched in her hand. An amused grin had stretched across Octavian's face as his eyes studied her every feature.

"Do you think I've had it poisoned?" he asked with a snicker.

Sekhmet leaned forward and smirked. In one fell swoop, she raised the goblet to her lips and downed the entirety of its contents.

"I know you did, Octavian," she returned as she lowered the goblet, smacking her palette. "Cyanide, I would wager. Enough to kill a man. Luckily for me, I am no man."

She let the goblet fall, the metal clang on the floor alerting the guards standing right outside the doorway. They ran in, their pila at the ready. With a wave of his hand, Octavian dismissed them.

"She will not harm me," he assured them. With reluctance, the soldiers eased and exited. "You would find no fault in my efforts," he added to Sekhmet.

"Indeed, Caesar, I would be insulted if you had attempted anything less."

Octavian understood; if it were to be a battle of wits, they were too equally matched. Whatever tolerance the woman's body had to the poison, it meant likely that any measure of pain short of death would have no influence on her. All that was left was to hear her out.

"Your name, Lady?"

"I have many, sire. Your father by law called me as do the people of this land: Sekhmet."

Octavian chuckled, sitting back in his chair and raising his own goblet to his mouth. "Yes, he spoke of you. Consort of the queen, he said. Quite the scandal, if word of this ever reached Rome. Tell me, is it not heretical to take on the name of a goddess?"

"No more so than to take on the title of Caesar," she replied stoically.

Impulsively, he reached for the knife tied at his waist. "I am Caesar, by right and creed."

"As I am the goddess." Sekhmet rose to her feet, holding herself in sanctity before him. "For time immemorial, I have protected the house of Pharaoh, as was I appointed by the gods of the Ancients to do. I am the Eye of Ra, the Lady of the Flame, the Protector of the Nile. One who declares the house of Ptolemy an enemy will have me to contend with as well. But take leisure in this, Caesar. I desire not to be thine enemy. I would ask only that the terms of defeat be amiable to my interests."

"You assume much, but as you are clearly lacking of your faculties, I will not take my hand and slay you down."

Sekhmet stared him down, almost making him cower. "You would find my blade twice as deadly and thrice as swift, Caesar." With gallant step, she advanced, and Octavian Caesar, fearing that indeed she may be of divine influence, fell back into his seat. "Now, speak me the truth and think me not the fool. I see your mind's intents, Caesar. I see your very soul. What are your intentions with the queen?"

A few moments passed in silence, in which Sekhmet's eyes never wavered from Octavian's. For his part, Octavian did not flinch, but neither could he garner strength to rise against her.

"Ah, you intend to present her in chains to Rome, do you?" She snickered at last. The look of surprise on Octavian's face, the incredulous confusion when he realized that she had correctly intercepted his thoughts, was almost amusing. "Surely, Caesar will know that a woman of her beauty, loved not only by Mark Antony, but also treasured by your father, and bearer of children of both stocks, would turn a tender heart if rendered like a dog unto the Senate. Yes, I see your conflict as well. It is also not in your interest to kill her, but that risks an injury of its own. Strike down a woman of such regal repose who has already acquiesced her power to you, and you'll be seen as a ruthless barbarian. Worse than a Scythian, really. And that is what you fear, is it not? You wish to be

seen as an iron-handed ruler, with actions deemed worthy of praise by their inherent intelligence."

"How do you come to know this?" Octavian gasped. "Even my generals know not—"

Sekhmet extended one, lovely, ring-bearing finger and tapped it to Octavian's temple. He flinched, but remained otherwise motionless.

"It's all here," she answered. "You really are quite an interesting mortal, Octavian. In another life, I might have wished to have been your ally."

She turned and meandered through the room, taking note of its fineries. This had once been Cleopatra's private chamber, and she detested Octavian's presence in this intimate space.

"My God…"

"Goddess," Sekhmet corrected. When she reached the mantle of the fire, she turned, resting one arm on the hearth's head. "Allow me to be forward, Octavian. Even I cannot take on the might of Rome. Your father and comrade are dead. No doubt you seek retribution. You may kill her body, Octavian, but as your own thoughts reveal, either of your choices hold in it a fault. I wish to suggest to you a third path."

His grin confirmed his interests.

"Take her to Rome, but not in chains. Let her walk among the people a citizen. Let her be humiliated in the eyes of the citizenry as no more than a common tramp, one who only maintained power by bedding the Roman seat. I will take her children away from Egypt and keep them in Rome, so that they may not be a threat to you and not be considered successors to the throne. Then, after some time passes, render her back to me. I will take her into seclusion, and she will be no more a threat to you than the blowing of the wind."

"I fail to see, goddess," he ground the title like a curse word between his teeth, "how this lies in your interest. Your country falls; your ruler is dethroned and disgraced. Your civilization dies."

"Such is the river of life." She shrugged. "I only seek to keep her and her issue on this side of the afterlife. I care not for her gallant aspirations."

Standing, Octavian crossed his arms over his chest and rolled on the balls of his feet. He mused the idea.

"We have an accord. I demand only two concessions."

She gave a slight bow of her head. The movement seemed mocking, given her general contempt evidenced in her other graces.

"Yes, Caesar?"

"You will be the appointed guardian of the children of Mark Anthony and Cleopatra. You shall care for them under the watch of my sister, Anthony's true widow, in Rome. The child known as Caesarian, however, will be rendered unto me in one week's time."

"For what purpose, Caesar?"

He nearly spat at her. "For assurance, Sekhmet. Surely you do not think the queen will agree to anything if she believes any of her children will come to harm from it."

"You will have his head?"

"Are you surprised, milady?" Octavian sneered, knowing she could not deny the need of the ruse. "Nothing comes for nothing, Sekhmet. You can have the life of your Cleopatra, if I can have the life of her Caesar. Now, if you wish to see through this accord, go now unto your queen and seek her surrender. I will await word from her."

Sekhmet bowed her head in submission, and gave one last, quick sneer to Octavian.

Shep felt as though his brain was slamming into the back of his head, or trying to pickaxe its way through his eyeballs. The scene in their joined minds shifted. Now he saw himself in an opulent burial chamber—he had been in enough of them to recognize the set up—looking at the floor. As Victoria's eyes rose, they were greeted by the misunderstanding stare of three women. Two were dressed similarly to each other, braided wigs upon their heads and the finest white, linen kalisiris around their bodies. Between them sat the third, a woman who looked as though she had just surfaced from death's door. She sat entranced, numb to the world.

Cleopatra.

She was…magnanimous. Tragically beautiful. Resplendent. Perfect. And as she met eyes with Victoria, she flew from her chair and fell into the slender arms of the goddess before her.

"You came back," she cried into Sekhmet's chest. "After everything, you came back."

Sekhmet moved to soothe her, running her hands over her hair and drawing her close to her bosom. "Now, now, sweet. I told you I would return if you ever needed me."

"I don't understand, though," Cleo wept. "How did you...Does Octavian know?"

They walked toward the dais where, oddly enough for a mausoleum, Cleopatra's throne sat. Nearby, there was her wooden-framed bed covered in gold leaf, and baskets overflowed of clothing and gold. Looking to the back of the chamber, Sekhmet saw that Cleo had thought well her plan. Everywhere one looked, gold and jewels glimmered from the shadows. Octavian was holding her prisoner, but Cleopatra was keeping her wealth imprisoned with her. It wouldn't take but a few vats of oil and a torch to melt it all into a pool of nothingness.

"Octavian knows. I have spoken with him."

The queen's face fell. "And?"

Sekhmet seemed to measure her words carefully, explaining the compromise. She mentioned nothing of the one week moratorium on Caesarian's life, of course. When she was done, the queen looked aghast.

"I cannot," she uttered. Her eyes were empty, her face, stoic.

"Cannot what?" Sekhmet asked. She held Cleopatra at arm's length, studying her.

"Everything I have done has been for Egypt. How can I now allow its legacy to be sliced at the throat and left to bleed unto death?"

Sekhmet gnashed her teeth. "You are not Egypt, Cleo. To hell with Egypt. Everything I have done has been for you, not for Egypt."

"Why?"

Sekhmet shifted uncomfortably. "Make me speak it not, my queen. You know the reason."

"I would hear it from your lips," the queen begged.

A single tear ran down Sekhmet's face as she lowered her body onto the ledge where sat Cleopatra. "I have loved twice in this world, Cleo. Once to a god, and once to the queen."

Slowly, Cleopatra sat down beside her, studying her hands on her lap. "I have known this for many a year. Yet, whenever I have come to you, you have denied me."

Sekhmet's checks reddened. "I am not mortal, my queen. Knowing my body may have had certain...ramifications. If I had taken you to my bed, you may not have survived."

A glassy-eyed queen turned to the reluctant goddess. "Sekhmet, I am not likely to survive now."

As their bodies closed the distance and their lips met, Shep's mind slipped from Victoria's grasp. The vision left him breathless, confused.

"I don't understand," he panted. "She didn't...You didn't—"

"Kill her?"

Shep looked to Victoria, his heart torn as the tears ran down her face.

"I did, Shep. I took her that night. I've seen it in your mind. Dmitri has told you the two ways in which the Bonding may take place. Either they drink our blood or they are taken by an Altunai. Did he tell you also that the second way creates a much stronger bond? Cleo was already broken in spirit. Her body was overstressed from her trials. She was not strong enough to survive the Bonding."

"But to say 'murder,' Victoria. You didn't mean for her to die."

"Didn't I?" Victoria sneered. "Shep, her one wish was to preserve the legacy of her house. I knew that if she had appeared to take her own life, it would show that Egypt died on its own terms. I took her to my bed knowing it was likely to kill her, and I allowed it to happen, as though I had planned it. I was the one who sent the suicide note Octavian. I was the one who took the lives of her servants. I was the one who bit her arm and bled her, knowing that it would weaken her further and ensure death took her quickly. I *killed* her, Shep."

"And the Cleopatra statue Hector found in Mexico..." Shep's voice trailed off. The pieces were coming together. "It was your way of remembering her, wasn't it?"

"I wanted to go home, to try to start again. My absence proved too long. The Olmec civilization had died by the time I returned. I brought with me the mementos of my Bonded. I have kept a little something to remember each of them with me, always."

An image of a man possessing of a broken heart crept into Shep's mind, and he remembered his conversation with Kronastia. "Dmitri suspected you loved another, but he supposed it was Ra."

Victoria laughed. "Ra?" The smile on her face broke the tension. "He still believes that, huh?"

"You slept with him," Shep answered rather nonchalantly. "He says you're double Bonded because of him."

Even Alex laughed at that one. "You mean to tell me after all these years, Dmitri doesn't know?" he asked Victoria.

She shrugged before raising her hand to her mouth and putting her finger between her lips. When she spoke, the sound was mottled. "No, I was instructed not to tell him. But I always had hoped he'd figure it out on his own." Focusing again on Shep, she stretched out her arms and lay a hand on each of his shoulders, squeezing gently. "Shep, Ra was not my lover. Ra is my father. Come on, we need to get to Ankh Tawy and prepare before sundown."

"Memphis?" Of course, Shep knew the name for the ancient capital of the empire. "Why there?"

"That's where the gate will open, Shep, at the temple of Apis."

"The bull god," Shep added. "Any particular reason?"

"The Guardian's temple, Shep," Victoria answered. Shep looked clueless. "*Osiris's* Temple, Shep. Surely, you've figured this out by now?"

"Like Dmitri figured out Ra was your daddy?" he teased. "Okay, throw me a bone. Why Osiris's Temple?"

"Really, Shep? Okay, fine. Well, Dr. Smyth, I hate to break this to you, but Dmitri *is* Osiris."

He nearly fell over in shock. "Holy hell. The god of the afterlife?"

Victoria nodded. "The one and only."

12.21.12

Chapter 28

Osiris paced the length of the Temple of Apis. He detested being identified as the Bull. Ra was known as the Sun, and Queen Isis was an Eagle. A bull seemed so...mundane, common. Still, the civilization was yet an agrarian one, and the people drew their knowledge from their interaction with the Earth and its nature. A bull wasn't as bad as, say, a hippo. Set was still pissed at being saddled with that iconography.

He was nervous, though he knew better. As the commander of the Western settlement, Osiris had been tasked with finding the Vessel. When Ra had brought him word of his duties in person twenty-five years before, he had understood what a great honor it was. The whole success of a crop depended on finding a suitable Vessel, so in fact it was Osiris's decision that would lead to the eventual outcome of this humanity's fate.

Tlalli had been impressive since birth. It was not common for the Olmec to allow the women of their culture to learn hunting and writing. Tlalli had mastered both by mere observation. And her memory and ability to grasp higher level knowledge were far superior compared to those of her people. She had been the natural selection. The fact that she was inhumanly beautiful didn't influence his decision at all. Or so he told himself. So certain was he with his choice that Osiris had Bonded her without awaiting approval from either Ra, his superior, or the queen.

Not that he fretted that they would disapprove of Tlalli. Isis had taken an immediate liking to her. Unfortunately, so had Ra. Osiris couldn't explain it; Ra seemed completely enamored with her at first sight. After Tlalli's presentation, Osiris had taken her back to his temple to rest. Sometime during the night, he awoke to find her missing. Ra's scent was still fresh in her chamber.

Now, he waited for her return. The Altunai were leaving; the time of isolation for thirteen baktuns to begin. Tlalli was approved as the Vessel, and Isis, perhaps suspecting of Osiris's attachment to the native, had asked him to stay as Guardian. Of course he would. Only, where was his Tlalli and what had Ra done to her?

His blood boiled when he thought of Ra doing anything to his love.

Finally, at sunset, they arrived. The gate was opened, and the Altunai were passed through. Only Isis and Ra hesitated.

"My queen?" Osiris queried, seeing the words dancing on her tongue but remaining unspoken.

She shifted about. The nervous mannerisms seemed foreign to her usually collected way.

"I want you to know, Osiris, I was not aware of Ra's intentions. He acted without my knowledge or approval. Still, a thing, once done, is done. I will miss you, and I wish you well. I hope the time passes for you in ease."

His brow furrowed in confusion. "My queen? What has happened? Tlalli... What has happened to my Vessel?"

She said nothing more, but passed through the gate.

Ra leaned over. There was a certain smugness to his speech. "Tlalli awaits you in my temple in Thebes. Well done with your choice, Osiris. I hope you will not find her too traumatized from last night. There was much I needed to...show her."

The glint in his jade eyes upset him. "What have you done?"

Ra leaned in closely, whispering into Osiris's ear. "A shame you won't be able to teleport once the gate closes unless she is near. The Bonding is setting in, and I'm certain she'll need comfort. Now, Osiris, go take care of my girl."

Dumbfounded, Osiris could bear to hear no more of what Ra might have done to his Vessel. But Bonded again? There were only two ways to bond, and Osiris knew Ra did not like to share his blood.

He didn't even wait for the gate to close. Instead, he set off immediately for Thebes. The moon was rising when he arrived. He found her on the altar of the Temple of Amen-Re; how she had gotten so far away was a mystery. The Vessel was endowed with eternal youth and protected from sickness and disease, but they could not teleport or access the higher brain functions that manipulated time and space like the Altunai.

Could they?

Perhaps so, if a Bonding was tight enough. Or, if the Vessel had been double Bonded?

He picked up the sleeping form into his arms and stroked her hair. She didn't seem different. As she smiled, her eyes opened and looked into his, her earthen brown orbs now shining discs of emerald.

That's how he knew: Ra had had her.

Over time, the evidence of the double Bond only grew. She could do almost everything the Altunai had been able to do with the gate flowing energy from Altunatus. She could even call on the energy of her own planet, though she lacked the ability to yield it at will.

Osiris could never come to terms with the way in which it had happened, but there was no denying it had.

They had actually succeeded in creating a goddess.

Dmitri landed in Cairo at 4:48 a.m. on December 21. It was funny, he thought. This day was the very one for which he had waited for over five thousand years. The time of isolation was drawing to a close. At sunset, the Vessel would consume the amulet. The fragment of Altunatus, a small sampling of its energy contained within, and his presence would provide the anchor for the gate to reopen. Isis and Ra were likely still to be in power. While five millennia had passed on Earth, only a year or so had passed on Altunatus. The moment the gate opened, Dmitri would again be able to wield the power of his home planet. And he was going to use that power to kill Ra.

It was likely that he would die, too. He knew that Isis would order him executed immediately when he did. Dmitri didn't care. Ra didn't understand the mess his little one-night rendezvous had left behind. The Bonding was hard enough for a human to endure. It usually had little effect on their lifestyles, however, after the initial DNA alteration had been endured. In many ways, they continued to function…well, humanly. The double Bonding, however, had left Victoria aching and confused. She could do nearly anything an Altunai could, and it separated her from the humans. She was too beyond them to be their equal and experience life as they did. As a Vessel, she was a complete failure. And the Bond had created another consequence which caused her much grief. Like the Altunai, her body needed not food but energy to live and prosper.

She had accepted that she must kill once for the initial Bonding. Not that it would have likely stopped her if she hadn't. Her body and soul's need for sustenance would have driven her to it eventually, or she would have died. In retrospect, he wondered if Victoria had ever figured out that that's what had killed her Cleo. Her physical and mental superiority to humans made her an exceedingly proficient hunter. Nonetheless, having to kill in perpetuity had resulted in a little of her precious humanity being lost. She eventually grew indifferent to death, and in cases of someone who had wronged her or her protected ones, thrived on it.

But not at first. For centuries, she struggled with the reality, tried to find other ways to feed. Animals' energy proved insufficient, and her one attempt to harvest strength directly and purposefully from Earth had resulted in tragedy: the destruction of Thera. Had Ra known how many tears she had wept when, denying her hunger too long, her body would default to animal instincts? Had he been there to hold her all the nights she had drawn blood as well as life force from her victims as she sucked their energy from them? And when at last she had developed a balance, an ability to pull just enough of their energy from them to feel sated but not take their lives, was he the one who had felt the pride seeing the woman he loved learn to dominate her own instincts?

And, unlike the Vessels in other crops, this one's Bond was strong enough to allow for a counter transference to other humans. Victoria constantly broke all precedents. Her Bonding didn't follow any rules. Victoria's so-called proxies were a thorn in Dmitri's side, their mere existence threatening whatever tenacity of the crop that could still be gleaned. If Isis or Ra became aware of their existence, Dmitri wouldn't have to threaten Ra's life to be sentenced to death. An oversight of that magnitude was begging for punishment.

Damn Ra. Damn him to hell.

As Dmitri stepped into the early dawn light as he left Cairo airport, a little voice told him this would be the last sunrise he would ever see. He was going to die today.

He only hoped it was for the right reasons.

Chapter 29

As they waited in the back of the hookah lounge, Victoria turned the amulet over and over in one hand, and held the pipe connected to the bubbling pot in the other. The whispers had been getting steadily louder through the day, though the message remained the same.

"Ankh Tawy," Shep said out of the blue.

"Huh?" Her concentration was wholly on the fragment of Altunatus, its words almost drowning out the existence of everything else around her.

"Ankh Tawy," Shep repeated, pointing at the object in her hands. "When you were rambling off whatever you were hearing from that thing, you mentioned Ankh Tawy as well."

"And this is important *why*?"

Alex had kept silent the last two hours. He was sleepless, and the wear on his body was beginning to show. At the moment, his chin was resting on his fist, his elbow pitched on the table. As his eyelids grew heavy—a few times he had nodded off only to snap up with a start—his willingness to hold down any conversation had diminished.

Shep leaned forward with a smile. "Ankh Tawy was one of the names given to Memphis. It means 'the place which binds two lands.' In the Egyptology community, we always explained that as the meeting of Upper and Lower Egypt. I guess that's not what it refers to after all."

Victoria had to admit to herself that she was really starting to like Sheppard Smyth. Most humans' heads would have exploded long ago from the influx of earth-shattering revelations the likes of which the last week had given him. Not Shep. He took every little insight and development with an open mind and a tempered spirit. She had always respected him professionally, even if from afar. Still, she had spent many years hating him when he, in her opinion, had stolen Christine away. Old habits died hard. Now, it was all becoming clear.

"I see why Christine loved you so much."

To say he looked surprised was an understatement. "Will you explain to me how she's connected to all this? Please?"

Taking a deep breath, Victoria decided she would. There was no point in holding back. He knew almost everything else anyhow.

"About eight years ago, I read a small mention in *Archaeology* about the discovery you made in Ethiopia. Now, of course I knew you were completely right when you put your theory forward, and I knew the evidence you found was genuine. Still, I knew that if you were successful in having it considered by the community at large, Dmitri would see you as a threat to exposing our existence. He's lashed out before, you see. Tutankhamen's tomb had some references in it to the Altunai. Nothing definitive, but something that may have been helpful to anyone who knew what to look for. You recall what became of Howard Carter and the rest of his party, right?"

Of course Shep knew. It was the stuff of legends. Every member of Carter's party who had been present when Tut's tomb had been opened was dead within a few years, usually in highly suspicious ways. Except for Anathea Hermapolous, but that part of the story had obviously proved to be a clever fabrication. The superstitious delighted in blaming it on the curse placed on burial sites by the ancient priests. Shep thought Victoria's explanation of a cover-up and conspiracy was much more realistic.

Whoever thought a conspiracy theory would become a conspiracy law?

As he nodded, she continued. "Of course, I couldn't risk exposing myself either. Christine and Alex's family have been members of The Order for centuries. I have known their ancestors even before The Order was founded."

"Why is this news to me?" Alex asked through a yawn.

"Don't worry, Alex. Christine didn't know either. I mean, if you go back far enough in almost anyone's family tree, you're bound to find someone famous. That you're descended from Hannibal's bloodline isn't as impressive as it seems on first blush."

"No, not at all." Shep's sarcastic tone made her smile. "Personally, I like to think my people had a bit more of a legacy, you know?"

Victoria choked the smoke from the pipe. Oh, if he only knew… "Yeah, well, I asked Christine if she would serve as a proxy and become one of your staff. She was *supposed* to dissuade you from pursuing proof. Three months into the assignment, however, she called me to tell me she was leaving The Order, that she was falling in love with you. God, I was so mad at her. For a long time, I wanted to track you down and hurt you. Anything, just to get her back again."

"Yeah, because Chrissie so gave in to bribery," Shep laughed. He stared blankly for a moment at the beer bottle in his grip, recalling Victoria's memories of her time with Cleo. "Sounds like you, um, *liked* her."

"Ha! Not in the way you're implying, Shep. No, she only had eyes for you, as far as I'm aware. Which was one of the reasons I found it so shocking when she told me."

He nursed his bottle of warm beer. He let the silence sit between them. The afternoon had been filled with these patches of quiet sewn over a thin gauze of meaningless conversation. At first, the leisure had seemed misplaced, with all the commotion and upheaval of the last week. Shep had forgotten that his friend had died only a short time ago. He knew there would come a time for Hector to be properly grieved and mourned. That time was not now. He also remembered other things that seemed so petty now. His mortgage payment was due in a week. He had missed the deadline for submitting grades for the Fall Semester. He'd had a dentist appointment scheduled the day before.

And he hadn't even started his Christmas shopping.

How the Boston Yuletide and academic rituals seemed so distant now. Would there ever be a way to go back to everyday life after this? After all, his apartment would be just as empty of life and filled with ghosts when he returned. And he would eventually return, wouldn't he?

"Were you thinking of killing me?"

The question had shattered the relaxed atmosphere. Victoria sat up, her eyes questioning.

"When I almost kissed you back in Mexico?" she asked. He nodded. "No, Shep. I just…I saw in your mind. You looked at me like a person, not a goddess or a thing to be feared or appeased. I looked at you, and I saw the man that Christine loved. For a moment, knowing how you loved her, I was…Well, I was jealous. I just wanted to feel that for an instant, to know what she knew. I never would have killed you, Shep. Never. And you seemed more than willing at the time," she reminded him.

The burn of embarrassment heated his cheeks. "I can't explain it. I felt instinctively…drawn to you."

She guffawed at his political correctness. "You wanted to lay me flat the second you saw me in the terminal," she returned with a wink. "Don't worry, Shep. It wasn't your fault. In fact, it only shows how much you loved your wife."

"Oh?"

She nodded. "You felt attracted to me because you recognized Christine's energy in me. Rather, part of Christine's energy was mine. It's a proxy thing. Likely your body just sensed it and longed to feel what it had missed for too long. And me, well, I guess my sympathies to comfort you were a little overwhelming as well."

Alex's snore rose up from the table, making both of them smile.

Victoria tried to shift his hands to support his head, giving him a pillow of arms. "Poor baby. He's so spent; I'm surprised he stayed awake *this* long."

"Ah, Alex is tough," Shep added, mussing his brother-in-law's hair softly so as not to wake him. "He was in a car accident about five years ago, you know? Almost died. And of course it all happened is some podunk little town in Vermont where the emergency room served both humans and puppies."

"Yeah, he told me about that." Victoria's eyes narrowed. "Wait, did he lose a lot of blood?"

Shep barked a laugh. "A lot of blood? It was like he spontaneous decided to open his own Red Cross location on the eighty-nine."

"Hmm."

"Victoria?"

"Huh?" She was roused from her passing reverie. "I was just thinking, Alex and Christine share a very uncommon blood type. If he was in such a rural facility, they weren't likely to have his type on hand."

"No, they didn't actually. They didn't even have that universal donor type. In fact, Christine and I had to run up there so—"

"Double Bonded," Victoria interrupted. "That's why he has my eyes. He's double Bonded."

By the blood, Shep recalled. But wait, that didn't make any sense. Shep was a phlebotomist's dream-come-true, a universal donor with Type O-negative blood. It had been *him* that had given the necessary donation that saved Alex's life, not Christine.

Victoria snatched the beer bottle out of Shep's hands and downed the remainder. "Well, at least if nothing else, I understand that now." She gave Alex a shove. His head fell off the table as his jade eyes snapped open. "Wakey, wakey, Alexander. The world's about to end, don't you know?"

"Already?" He yawned and stretched. "Okay, let me just pay the—"

She stopped his words with two of her fingers over his mouth. "I'll take care of it."

Her life had been a patchwork of high-stakes drama and non-sequitur calm. She had never supposed the latter to precede her march to the gallows. As she drew a few Egyptian bills from her pocket, she reflected that the afternoon had passed in perhaps the best possible manner, and had been one of the most enjoyable of her life.

It was hopelessly and utterly *human*.

Chapter 30

Was it wrong of him to mourn? It wasn't as though it would be possible to do so *after* he was dead. Knowing this, Dmitri overrode his own selfish desire to go to her, to proclaim his love to Victoria one last time, to hope that she would grace his last day on Earth—his last day *anywhere,* with her presence. Like so many of the humans before, he wanted to worship her like the goddess he thought she was. He wanted to hold her in his arms and show her the colors of the rainbow, the light of the stars. He wanted to spend his last day of life making love to her, giving her pleasure until her head spun, leaving his mark on her before his existence was no more.

But that was silly. Once, they had been lovers, but it had been wrong. The truths of her purpose always hung in the air around them. Finally, he'd had to let her know, respected her and treasured her enough not to lie by omission to her anymore. Truth lay bare what love could not overcome. She felt used, betrayed. And he couldn't blame her.

So, instead, he spent this last day roaming the streets of Cairo, paying homage to the places they had once thought their own. So many of the ancient venues were now over-laced with the façade of modernity. One of Sekhmet's prominent temples had lain on a ridge above the river's old path. The locals had not yet discovered the ruins of it buried beneath their city. Maybe they never would. If a buried past provided the best foundation for the continuance of life, plumbing its depth would only shake the foundation ardently reformed and remade.

As night began to fall, his footsteps carried him toward the site where once his icon's temple stood. Seti 1 had remade the site to beget his own legacy long after the Altunai had left. Preserving it through the centuries had been no simple task, but a necessary one. Luckily, no matter in whose hands Egypt had been held, money always spoke the native tongue.

As he sighted the ruins of Karnak, Dmitri heard the call. The amulet was speaking, and its tone was getting down right demanding. Obviously, Victoria was here and still had not consumed the fractured piece of Altunatus. Why was she hesitating? Wasn't she eager to see Ra? After all this time, was it his company she ached for in the night in lieu of Dmitri's? They'd had only one night together, but Ra's reputation as a lover was legendary back home. No doubt he had left quite an impression on her.

He felt intoxicated as he passed through what remained of the first pylon. The antique gateway was a mere shadow of its ancient glory. Many of the ram-headed statues lining the walkway no longer possessed heads. As he crossed the interior courtyard, he heard voices. Soon he realized he was hearing them not with his ears, but with his mind. The bond-gate was open to him. Sheppard Smyth and Alex Cezanne were with Victoria, conversing about what should be done.

The inquiries between them made Dmitri pick up his pace. Through Shep's mind, he could see Victoria's face, her eyes wide and fear-filled. She was looking down at her hands, and as Shep's gaze tracked hers, the view of the amulet, growing bright green, made it all too clear to him what was going on.

"Victoria!" Dmitri shouted as he passed through the second pylon and into the Hypostyle Hall.

A forest of white, etched columns surrounded them. Once these columns had been painted every color of the rainbow, their reliefs painstakingly etched by the scribes, regaling the stories of the glory of the Pharaohs. Now they seemed like prison bars, holding his love in their confines, subjecting her to a fate that might mean her death.

Neither Shep nor Alex made any attempt to dissuade Dmitri's progress. If anything, they looked relieved to see him, backing away from where Victoria stood frozen in place to give him unfettered access. He was the hero arriving to battle, the doctor striding into the emergency room.

The damned god kneeling down to the supplicant.

"What happened?" he demanded as he fell to his knees in front of her. Shaking Victoria to try to bring her out of her trance proved useless. She was unreachable.

Shep ran his hands through his thinning brown hair. "No clue. One second she was telling us it was time, next thing she's just staring at that thing, looking terrified."

Dmitri rounded on Alex. "Proxy, can you get in her mind?"

Alex shook his head woefully. "No. I mean, I keep sending her thoughts, but I'm getting nothing back."

"Damn it, she's trying to open it on her own. Why didn't she wait for me? That much energy passing through just one person is going to kill her."

Alex looked panicked. "I thought she couldn't die."

Dmitri put his thumbs on Victoria's forehead and weaved his fingers through her hair, tilting her head upward. "I assure you, she can. Anything alive can die. Even Victoria." His plan for Ra resurfaced in his mind. "Even an Altunai."

Not quite sure what he thought to achieve—he had never gotten into her head before by force or by fancy—Dmitri took a deep breath and slowly exhaled a steady stream through pursed lips. His psyche reached out to her, poking and prodding her barriers. It was like trying to punch a hole through a steel wall with a toothpick. She was impenetrable. Her eyes were blackened over, an indication that she had tapped into Earth's energy field. How the hell was he supposed to pierce through that?

As sweat started to glisten on Victoria's brow, Alex grew restless. "What the hell do we do?"

"Listen, proxy, this is no time for hysterics. I have a plan." He rose to his feet, knocking the dust off his pants with the backs of his hands. Turning to Alex, he strong-armed his shoulders and pushed him down to face Victoria. "You're connected with her. Her blood is in your veins. I need you to keep trying to find a hold on her mind. Right now, her soul is inside that piece of stone in her hands. You need to pull it back out and put her right. She'll bring its energy back into her body with it. That will open the channel up and let me help her."

"Right, and I grab her soul *how* exactly?"

Dmitri smirked. "We do something that makes her want to kick our asses. She'll need to be in her own body to do it. Your job is to push her in the right direction."

"The right direction?" Alex asked.

"Yeah, 'toward the light,'" Dmitri answered, using finger quotes.

"Why are you helping us?" Alex called out as he turned. His eyes stayed locked, waiting for desperately for an answer. "I thought...I thought you were the enemy."

Dmitri's eyes shifted to Victoria's petrified form. He had never considered that he would allow things to go so far as this. Had he slighted her so badly that her pride would have her attempt to open the gate alone? "Life's too short to have enemies, Alexander. And my love for her, too strong."

Alex nodded, though Dmitri could tell he still really didn't have a clue what he was supposed to do. Dmitri gave him a reassuring pat on the shoulder before turning to Shep.

"You've been extremely patient with all this, and I'm really sorry it comes down to this, Dr. Smyth."

"Sorry about wh—"

Shep stumbled back as Dmitri's fist made contact with his lip. The pain bit through him, the taste of blood on his tongue was instantaneous. Reaching to his injury, he pulled his hand away to find traces of the sanguineous liquid on his fingertips.

"What the fuck?" Shep rose to his feet, eying Dmitri with venom.

No sooner were the words out of his mouth than another blow landed on his chin.

Then, it was on.

Shep leapt forward, his hand reaching for Dmitri's throat. Dmitri's hands steepled as he pushed up through Shep's hold, forcing his arms to circle out. Shep, quick to rise to the occasion, cocked back his fist and drove it forward. Dmitri lunged out of the way with little trouble, and the energy of the unconnected blow took Shep to the ground.

"Scream, yell. Fricking make a sound, God damn it!"

She had to hear him, had to feel that Shep was in danger. He wasn't quite sure what Shep was to her, but as her proxy's widower, surely she cared something for him. Alex would have been the more sensible target, but he needed that boy to draw her away from the energy that was surely starting to burn her soul. Dmitri had to get her attention, get her to pull back from trying to open that gate on her own.

Dmitri's taunt only fueled Shep's fire more. He rolled over on his back, determined to make another pass. He was too late; Dmitri straddled him as he gave him a stiff uppercut.

"Fuck off!" Shep barked.

Alex was trying his best to focus on Victoria.

Dmitri landed another hit, then another. "What the hell do I have to do to get you to react, human? Rip your arm off?"

Through a mouth full of blood, voice gurgling, Shep answered, "Nothing you do to my body can ever hurt me. I died with Christine."

A glint came to Dmitri's eye as his head cocked to the side, taking in Shep's defiance. Of course, that was the solution.

"As you wish," Dmitri hissed, leaning over and placing his hands on Shep's forehead.

Shep blinked a few times as the vision born of his own eyes darkened and shifted, replaced by the illustrations filling his mind's eye. He understood what was going on immediately: he was looking through one of Dmitri's memories again.

Before him, Victoria stood shaking, her eyes terror-stricken and pleading. Her attire was modern, or at least, not too out-of-date. To his amazement, she was speaking English this time.

"Please. She's…She's not even one of mine anymore. She left The Order. She loves her husband more than life itself, and I'm sure he feels the same way about her. Please? Spare this one."

Dmitri shook his head. "You know I can't do that. It's my duty. Tlalli. Your proxy is on the verge of discovering the truth. That tomb they've excavated—it holds too many secrets."

"But, she already knows half of it!"

"True," Dmitri conceded with a slow nod, "but she doesn't have proof. I don't want to, sweet, I really don't. I tried to ignore it. It's bad enough that Smyth is already going around shouting his little alternative takes on history. Now, if you don't want him to die, I must at least destroy her."

Victoria slumped down, and from her gestures Shep could tell she was giving in. "Grant me this favor, Osiris. Let me be with her when she dies. Just let me comfort her."

He pulled her close and kissed her forehead. "Okay, my love. I'll give you that. But it must be done now."

Victoria nodded, her face wet with tears. Their embrace tightened as a flash of light enveloped them.

When the brightness faded, they were no longer alone. Across a small space in a chamber—a burial chamber, maybe—sat a brown-haired, fair-skinned young woman, staring at a sketch of the glyphs she had copied from the wall before her. The paper had folded over, and the alignment of the pictorials on the page spelled out a message that had been encoded and forgotten for nearly two millennia.

Dmitri slid back into the shadows, letting Victoria approach her alone.

"Christine."

Shep's heart seized when he saw her. He understood suddenly what he was witnessing: Christine's dying moments.

Christine looked up with a gasp, surprised to find she was not alone. When she saw who stood before her, she sneered at the forsaken goddess. "What do you want?"

"Christine, you can't let Shep see that." Victoria motioned to the paper in her hands.

"Why the hell not? I'm not betraying any secrets of The Order. It's on this wall, plain as day. Well, coded a bit, but nonetheless. Says right here: 'The line of the Pharaoh was stomped by the Sekhmet's Paw while Osiris covered her prints across the desert.' Honestly, I never would have thought it of you. You've always seemed discrete, but conspiracy doesn't seem your thing."

Christine's snide tone broke her heart.

"Chrissie, if I had known you were going to find out, I'd never have Bonded you. It was never my intention to have you fall in love—"

"But I did," she interrupted. "And you would have had me kill him, too, I bet, if he had known all this." She motioned vaguely to the hieroglyphs which told the tale of Egypt's fall to Roman hands. "I pledged my fealty blindly. All this time, you were just using me to perpetuate your cover-up. You're a murderer and a kidnapper, and I despise you."

"Please, Christine, you don't know the whole story. It's not what it seems."

"No more of your rationalization," Christine returned, folding her arms. "Shep's looked like a fool because of what he's claimed, and this will prove he's been right the whole time. I don't care if this exposes you or The Order or even the Altunai. I've watched the man I love suffer for too long. But you wouldn't understand. The only person you've ever loved is yourself."

Victoria's eyes blackened. "I have loved beyond time and space, and I have lost far more because of it than you could ever imagine." Through clenched teeth, she begged, "Please, Christine, not Shep. Tell anyone but him. He must not know about us. He must remain untainted."

"Go to hell, Victoria."

Dmitri's eyes began to dart around wildly as the earth beneath them began to shake. Sand from the desert floor above flowed into the pit, beginning to fill in the spaces around their feet.

"Shep will know everything!" Christine hissed. "Your existence, your name, your true legacy. And most of all, how you killed her. Shep!"

Christine stumbled, barely able to stand. The earthquake made it difficult to move, and she fell to her knees. A voice of desperation was calling her name in the distance, and with a bitter tear, Shep realized it was his own.

Victoria turned back, looking over her shoulder at Dmitri in the shadows. "Kill her," she spoke into his mind.

"But Smyth..." Dmitri tried to argue.

Victoria's head whipped left to right violently. "He's chasing paper tigers. Do not touch him. Only kill Christine."

Stepping out of the shadows, he nodded, squaring up the trembling woman who had just noticed him.

"Oh, my God," she mouthed, her lip quivering. Turning toward the access hole at the top of the chamber, she began screaming in despair. "It's Osiris! Shep, it's Osiris!"

She had barely gotten the last word out before the god of the afterlife leapt forward, grabbed her, and spun her around.

"I tire of doing your dirty work," he hissed to Victoria.

With a snap, Christine's head twisted, and her body fell limp to the ground. Sand was flowing from every direction. The carved wall beside them broke in two, chunks mixing in the rain of earth. Dmitri scowled at Victoria, ashamed of the emotionless expression. There was a flash. Everything went black.

Dmitri's face came into view as the vision faded.

Shep's mind said fight, but his body said cave. And his heart...his lonely, bitter, angry heart said cry. *Osiris.* She's hadn't been yelling "beside us," she had been yelling "Osiris." With her last words, Christine had told Shep the name of her murderer.

Dmitri cracked a satisfied grin when the tears fled from Shep's eyes. It was just a matter of time before he—

Never had a blow felt so good as when Shep's fist connected with Dmitri's jaw.

A deafening war cry broke from Shep's throat as his rage manifested in lashings and pelts. In a thrust of hip, Dmitri was thrown aside as Shep came after him with all the revenge of a lover wronged, of a husband denied, of a man stripped of his reason to live. Shep let him have it. The rage, the anger, the pain.

But, damn, Dmitri could move fast. In a split second, he had moved out of the way, Shep meeting the stone of the pillar behind him instead. The force of the impact spun Shep around and took him to his knees.

"What's the matter, Shep? Not man enough to avenge your own wife?"

Shep charged like a bull.

Alex looked over Victoria's shoulder at the ruckus, utterly confused as the men tossed about on the ground.

"Vick, you really need to pull out of this. These two are going to kill each other."

"Must...protect...Shep."

At first, Alex thought he had imagined it. From the corner of his eye, he saw no movement of her lips.

"What?"

Again the same statement, and this time he understood it was in his head. *Victoria's mind* was connecting with his.

"Yeah, protect Shep," Alex agreed. "But you'll need to wake up to do that."

"No!" she gasped aloud. "Can't...Must open gate...Need to...save him."

Alex leapt up and ran to the scuffle. "Shep! Dmitri, she's opening the gate. She's opening the gate."

They all fell still.

Basking in an orange glow, flames with no heat, Victoria stood wrapped in glory, the amulet held out before her though her eyes were closed. As her hand fell away, the green stone floated in front of her face. The aura of flame around her burned brighter, and the stone itself appeared to be on fire before being consumed in the flame.

Victoria's eyes opened, the blackness consuming every corner where white would have been expected. Shep forgot his rage for a moment and turned to Dmitri, a question on his lips, only to see that, just as Victoria was burning in reds and yellows, Dmitri was burning in blues and greens, his eyes having gone just as dark as hers.

"Touch him not," she demanded of Dmitri, "or my wrath will be your doom."

Shep inched toward Alex.

"What's going on?" he whispered.

Alex motioned vaguely between the two. "She's pulling the force of the Earth; he's pulling the force of Altunatus. And between them"—what

Shep could only describe as a surge of physical light formed in the space between the two so-called deities—"they can open the gate."

One moment, there was nothing, and the next, two more beings, one female and one male, apparently human though both Shep and Alex knew better, were standing amongst them.

Shep grunted as Alex forced him to kneel and pushed his head down, avoiding the celestial beings' gazes.

"What the hell, Alex?"

"Sorry, Shep," he apologized, pointing at the two perfect specimens of beauty before them, "but that's what *they* told me to do."

Chapter 31

It was, perhaps, one of the oddest conversations that Shep had ever *not* witnessed. He saw all four of the Altunai, including Victoria, in a perfect improvisation of a discussion. They evidenced every gesticulation, every motion, every small movement that one would expect. What it lacked was words.

Dmitri was scowling in the direction of the newly arrived male. His bright jade eyes, the same as Victoria's and Alex's, gave him away as Ra. It would only follow, then, that the other Altunai, the one who fit nearly every representation of a celestial being Shep had seen painted on church walls or soldered into stained glass windows, was Isis. She was tall, pale ivory-skinned, with hair so fair it could have been described as translucent. She glowed, not harshly so, but a soft, ambient radiance that somehow warmed him under his skin.

In a moment, the serenity Shep felt looking at the Queen of the Altunai was lost. Dmitri leapt forward and took Ra to the ground, pinning his shoulders under his legs and circling his hands around his adversary's throat. Oddly, Isis did not stir from the commotion, but Victoria dove in, trying to pull Dmitri away. Ra hardly needed the help. Barely moving a muscle, the same flickering of bluish light crawled over his surface, gathered over his chest, and blasted Dmitri off of him.

As Ra rose to his feet, the energy began to build up again, this time in the outstretched palm of his hand, as though he were cocking back the trigger of a loaded pistol, aiming at the offender. Dmitri rolled up unto the palms of his hands, though his body remained ground level. He turned and froze, looking death in the face.

Ra sneered, pulling back his hand, about to drive the energy forward, when Victoria threw herself over Dmitri, blocking him.

"Father, no!" she cried. "I love him!"

Both Altunai males' faces turned solid as stone.

"Father?" Dmitri asked at the same time Ra gasped, "*Love* him?"

"It is enough!" Isis suddenly snapped, and all three sank to a knee before her. "You must forgive your father's ignorance, Tlalli. Men only see that part of their daughter's heart which belongs to them, and disregard all else."

Shep rose to his feet, though Alex tried to hold him down. He didn't know what exactly had transpired, but somehow, he felt obliged to speak, as though it was expected of him. "Um… Your majesty?"

The white-headed beauty turned to the prostrate Victoria. Mental speaking must have occurred, for a moment later, Isis turned back to Shep with a look of astonishment on her face. "Really?" she queried. Victoria blushed and nodded. "*Sheppard Smyth,*" she pronounced his name like a child learning a new word, "come to me."

Not knowing a reason to do otherwise, Shep obeyed, taking six tentative steps to come face to face with her. When he was within reach, she extended her arms and ran her fingers through his hair, anchoring her hands on the side of his head.

"You are the descendant of Menes?" she asked.

Shep was thoroughly confused. "Excuse me?"

"You've always been drawn to Egypt, haven't you? It's no wonder you became an archaeologist, Shep. Their blood runs through your veins." A knowing look overcame her as she wrapped her arm around him, sending a spark of familiarity through Shep, as though he knew this embrace, knew this woman as a friend. "Your bloodline goes back many generations, more than five thousand years. Tlalli fought long and hard to keep your ancestors on Egypt's throne, thinking that would have been my preference. What a frustration it must have been to her to succeed and fail, only to succeed and fail again. But she wouldn't give up on the *heqa khasewet.* Eventually, she learned that it was best to keep them safe by keeping them hidden."

"As much as I could possibly." Victoria's humble voice rose from behind them where she still submissively knelt.

Shep's synapses were firing faster than a jack rabbit on meth, trying to piece together the fragments of the known and unknown laid before him. "What a minute… *Heqa khasewet?* The Hyksos?"

He looked back to Victoria, whose lips had curled into proud grin.

Isis exchanged a knowing glance with Victoria. "Yes, Shep. The infamous 'foreign rulers' who 'invaded' and seized control from time to time through your humans' history. The last descendent of which was your ancestor, Cleopatra."

He shook his head in denial. Finally, he hit a mental brick wall. That couldn't possibly be right. "No, that's not possible. The Hyksos—they weren't Egyptian. And the Ptolemys—they weren't even Hyksos, let alone Egyptian. Wait a minute, how do you know all this anyway? I mean, you weren't around. According to what that bunch told me," he motioned vaguely to Dmitri, who had now sunk to his knees beside Victoria and held her hand in his own, "you weren't around for the better part of the last five millennia."

"I can see all the Vessel knows," the queen informed him.

Oh, right. Victoria is the Vessel, Shep reminded himself. When Tlalli started to giggle lowly, he ignored it. His eyes were stuck on Isis.

"Tlalli was charged with protection of your ancestors. Though she faltered and her mistake led to Cleopatra's death, she saw through her mission in regard to her issue and preserved the bloodline."

Shep was quite certain lightning had just struck his brain. It wasn't real, *couldn't* be real. Him? Descended from Cleopatra? Victoria's job had been to…protect him? Why? But wasn't Dmitri supposed to be protecting *Victoria*? She was the Vessel. And Shep? He was nobody.

"Did not you feel it so?" Isis continued. "Sheppard Smyth, I can hear your thoughts, and I can read your heart. Don't you understand? You've always been attracted to Cleopatra's legend because you are of her lineage. Inherently, you sensed the connection. I admire your determination to see out justice, for you thought she had been wronged. You did not know the tragic accident that befell her."

"You know all this from reading Victoria's mind?" Shep asked.

Isis shook her head as Ra hastened to her side, falling in line just behind the queen. "Not Victoria, Shep. I said I knew everything from examining the mind of the Vessel."

"But the observation…Humanity's fate…Victoria is the Vessel; I thought you'd look through her memories."

"Oh, I have. And that's how I know that her heart was of good intent when she lay with Cleopatra. It was not her intention to kill her, but likely Octavian would have seen out such a fate for her of his own motivations.

But, Sheppard, this observation was different," Isis continued. "This time our purpose was not to observe humanity, but Osiris."

Dmitri sounded as though he was trying to gasp in all the air in Egypt. "What?"

"Yes, we were fairly certain that the humanity would prosper under your and Tlalli's guidance. But, Osiris, we Altunai are masters of so much, that I feared we had forgotten why we started this practice: to learn better of ourselves. We had come to see humans as inferior, when really they are just the uncomplicated version of us. Without all the telepathy and teleporting and telekinesis, a human's heart exists only in themselves and the impact they make on others. What we needed to see, Osiris, was if an Altunai—if *you*—could develop compassion and empathy."

"I suggested your placement myself," Ra suddenly broke in, placing a hand on the queen's shoulder. "I told Isis that if we were to make ourselves the subject of the observation, then the test subject should be one of the best of us. Osiris, you were the natural selection."

Shep noted that the Altunai were just as capable of blushing as their human progeny.

Isis continued, "We did not leave you to be a Guardian so much as we left Tlalli to be a Guardian of the line of Isis, the line that was carried down by the Ptolemy. Further, if there had been no faux Vessel for you to guard, we feared you would have suspected your presence here was under false pretenses. All your trials would have been for naught. Osiris, you have done well. In your mind, I find the proof. It took time, but you see the humans now as your equals. You've grown to regret the lives you've taken. You despise your association with death, longing once again to have the ability to restore and create life. When you suspected that Tlalli cared for Sheppard deeply, though you didn't understand why or in what capacity, you protected him, brought him to her. You put Tlalli's happiness before your own.

"We still needed to have a true understanding of civilization, nonetheless, and of course that meant one with enough of the DNA markers to ensure we could read them." She turned again to a Shep Smyth whose jaw was all but scraping the ground. "Even after so many generations, the trace of my Bond with your ancestor is in the blood of your veins. Tlalli may have opened the gate, Shep, but *you* are the Vessel."

"But, why then?" Dmitri's voice was full of misunderstanding. "Why did you lie to me? How could you keep the truth from me?"

"Tlalli was told to keep her mind from you, to conceal the secret," Ra answered. "Of course, even a Bonded human may not have been able to successfully avoid your probes, Osiris. So, I mated with one of the Olmec humans in your Empire. Tlalli is my daughter and half-Altunai."

"You mean…" Dmitri's voice trailed off as, full of smiles, he looked to Victoria. "All this time I thought Ra and you had…But you and he never…The double Bonding—"

Victoria reached out to him, cupping his cheeks with her hands. "—was because he was my father. On the night in Thebes, when you suspected he had seduced me, I was being made aware of my true lineage and purpose. To be certain my Bonding would be sufficient should anything happen to you, my father shared his blood with me, strengthening my Altunai traits. And now, having consumed the amulet, I *am* Altunai, Osiris. I'm so, so sorry. I never meant to deceive you, but I was under my vow to keep the secret from you. Oh, the lengths I had to go to keep you in the dark! The Order, the intrigues, setting up situations to try your commitment. I never meant to hurt you. I had to do it all to save you. If this task failed, not humanity, but Isis would have seen to your demise. I couldn't let that happen. Everything I've done in spite of you has only been to save you. I…" She licked her lips as her head tilted in. "I've loved you always."

"Despite her telling me otherwise the night before we left," Ra mumbled to Isis under his breath in a tone dripping with accusation.

"Would you have left her alone with him for five thousand years unattended if you knew the nature of their relationship?" she returned coyly.

Dmitri was on the edge of tears. As their lips met and their bodies pressed together, Victoria's solar flare and Dmitri's lunar glow erupted into a union of golden and silver haze.

Alex, who had been calmly observing the scene in silence, slapped his hands together and rubbed them viciously. "Well, I think my job here is—"

Ra waved a hand through the air, stilling Victoria's acolyte.

"Tell me this, daughter," Ra began as he closely observed Alex. "This one has our eyes. This was not a trait we included in the human gene pool. How has this come to pass?"

"A Bonding," Victoria answered. "A double Bonding, in fact. Unbeknownst to me, his sister, also of my Bond, shared her blood with him. And myself double Bonded, by birth of my father and by bed to Osiris, the Altunai bloodline runs strong in his veins."

Shep hated to burst her bubble, but couldn't see the harm. "Victoria?" She turned to him. "It wasn't Christine's blood that saved Alex. It was mine. I'm o-negative, universal donor. The docs tapped my blood to save Alex."

She grinned in response. "Of course, that makes perfect sense. You realize what that means, Osiris?"

The faux-Russian nodded his head in amusement. "Bonded of the line of Isis by Shep. Bonded of the line of Ra by the Blood to you. And Shep himself Shadowbonded by Christine before that." All the Altunai focused on Alex. "Alex is triple Bonded."

"So you see, my Father," Victoria continued the thought, "Altunai blood runs strong in Alex's veins." She swiveled toward Shep. "Just as it does through Shep's."

It was dizzying. Him? Bonded?

"Yes, Shep, you are a proxy. You are of Menes' line and a proxy to Isis. And through Christine, you are Shadowbonded to me and—by proxy…" *Ah, so that's what that meant,* "…to Ra." She broke into a laugh, her demeanor easing until he was reminded of the coy and cordial woman he had first met in Veracruz. "Hell, under Altunai law, you're considered a member of the freaking royal family."

Well, okay. That didn't necessarily mean much. He certainly couldn't do all the mind reading and mind speaking that they others could, after all. Or could he?

Victoria beckoned. "Just *try.* A man who has never known himself to have legs will never attempt to walk. Think of whatever you treasure most, of whatever your heart sings for. Take all the passion of that thought and just let it fill you and explode from you."

Breathing deeply, Shep concentrated so hard his teeth gnashed in the effort. One word, he would try for just *one word.* He wanted his word to be powerful, to be concise. To mean everything it possibly could.

As he let out the air from his lungs, one word made contact with the minds of the others. "*Christine.*"

"So, wait," Shep resumed in his spoken voice. "This whole end-of-the-world, 2012-global-annihilation, Mayan prophecy thing? What was that all about?"

Dmitri quirked an eyebrow. "The end of the world, Shep? Are you sure that's what the prophecy says?"

Victoria came forward, a knowing smirk on her face. "*Licu tal oxlahun bak chem, ti u cenic u tzan a ceba nacomi cha' a ba yilexe,*" she pronounced with inflection that could only come from a native speaker. "Roughly, Shep, the Mayan prophecy translates as, 'And so in the thirteenth baktun's harbor, the boons of your ancestors will be lauded upon you. Your gods shall return unto you, and open a path to you which is beyond the lives you lead.' The prophecy lent itself well to my needs, Shep, so I allowed its misinterpretation by both Osiris and humans to endure. But know this, Shep: Changes are coming now. The gate is open, and things *will* change."

Isis threw her arm around Victoria, eyes filled with pride, and pulled her close. "These civilizations, both human and Altunai, have reached their pinnacle; they have the ability to love others more than themselves. Yes, there is still progress to be made, but we will make that journey together. The exchange must begin slowly. Too much knowledge of our existence at once will throw humanity into a free-fall of confusion. We need an ambassador, one who can begin to pull in likeminded individuals and bring them through the gate. Those to whom we can disperse our knowledge. I can see from your thoughts your selection, and I must say I can agree wholly."

Both looked to Alex.

Alex, in turn, danced around on the spot. "Oh, come on. Me? I'm nobody; I'm no one. Besides," he shrugged, "I have a date for Christmas."

Victoria crossed the space between them and threw Alex into a hug. "You can take Monique with you, silly proxy o' mine."

"Wait a minute!" Shep suddenly blurted, grabbing everyone's attention. His finger stretched out accusingly at Dmitri. "This happy-happy, love-love thing is great, but let's not forget you killed my wife. And *you*—" his pointed finger switched to Victoria "—told him to do it. You took my life and my love from me. You're, you're—"

"The god of the afterlife," Dmitri interrupted.

"Huh?" Confused and bewildered, Shep turned to his brother-in-law. "Alex, what about the revenge you wanted? You told me Christine was murdered, and you were right. Dmitri showed me himself what happened. How can you just stand there and pretend that nothing happened and everything's just hunky-dory now?"

"Because they've already showed me how they're going to fix it, Shep," Alex assured him, crossing his arms over his chest and leaning to one side. "Not saying I'm cool with what happened, but if they can really pull off what they showed me in my head just a minute ago, I'll go with it."

Shep looked to Victoria with a vacant and needy expression.

Victoria simply laughed and directed her comments to Dmitri. Again, Shep had the feeling that there was more conversation going on than what was being said aloud. "Yes, now that the gate is open, you might be able to pull enough energy through it to achieve that. Her body lies in Cairo. The matter could be arranged this very night. My queen, will you give leave?"

Isis folded her arms in front of her, her tone contemplative but also playful. "I do not like to interfere with the flow of life and death. Still, in this case, given that we have both blood and bond—even two bonds, I will give leave."

Though no one had moved, a piercing pain made Shep double over. He felt like a shiv had gone through his gut. Shep stumbled backward, the world suddenly spinning, and pulled his hand to his forehead in an attempt to stop it. The effort proved fruitless.

"It will be excruciatingly painful for him," Dmitri added in a very matter-of-fact tone.

"I don't think he'll mind in the end," Victoria countered.

Shep stumbled forward this time, his insides squirming as though a squirrel was trying to hide nuts under his ribcage. In a flash, the squirm turned to heat. His tongue bore the brunt of his agony as he bit down so hard that he tasted blood in his mouth. His head sizzled like a T-bone on a Coleman.

"Alex, what's hap—" Shep stammered as he fell to the ground. "Alex?"

Just before he lost consciousness, Victoria's voice called into his mind, *"It's okay, Shep. It will all be worth it when you wake. I promise, and I never break my promises."*

Epilogue

Darth Vader was somewhere in the room. And possibly R2D2.

It sounded like someone was breathing through a straw. But unlike the polyphonic droid, Shep realized that the cadence of beeps were rhythmic, steady, normalized.

A pulse. *His* pulse.

Light scorched his irises as his eyelids fluttered open. There was a residual burn in his gut and the taste of metal on his tongue. Worms were crawling up his nose and across his cheeks. *Oxygen tubes,* he realized, as he came to and reached to his face. The heart monitor continued to measure the moments in dub-lub time.

His body was simultaneously numb and supersensitive. As his pupils adjusted, the blurry images sharpened. It was a hospital room, just as he suspected: floral print walls, plastic-curtained barriers hanging from tracks, a white loose-stitch quilt over his body. Sterile. All in all, typical.

He tried to sit up, even though his head pounded harder with the effort. When he got to the half-way point, he froze as the pain shot through him. With a hiss, he surrendered back to the bed. His hand reached down to the site of the ache, and Shep was surprised to feel bandaging over his abdomen.

Where is the call button? he thought as he glanced around his immediate vicinity. There on a utility table next to his bed, he saw it. His hand barely reached the surface of the table, but with his first little sense of triumphant I-showed-you-ness, he grabbed the device and pressed the help button.

"Yes, Dr. Smyth?"

His eyes relaxed as the pain slowly began to dull. There was an IV in his arm. Perhaps the nurse had given him an intravenous pain killer?

"Hurts," he grumbled.

Laughter wasn't the reaction he expected from the female overseeing his injures. "I should think so, Shep. You *did* have a rib removed."

"What?" His eyes flew open to take in the view of Victoria Kent, dressed in scrubs. A name badge on her lapel, though, now identified her as Selene Mursad.

"Alex sends his greetings," she continued as though they had just randomly encountered each other on the street and not the intensive care room. "He's already left for Altunatus. You've been out cold for three days."

"You mean it..." Oh, talking hurt his brain. "You mean it wasn't a dream? That all really happened?"

"As real as rain," she confirmed as she sat on the edge of his bed. "Me, you, Alex, Dmitri, Isis, Ra...all real."

"Speak of the devil..."

The sound of Dmitri Kronastia's voice made his blood boil. As the gangster impostor strode into the room, Victoria rose from the bed and fell into his arms. Like they were on autopilot, their lips met. With a sense of unfulfilled vengeance, Shep growled.

Victoria and Dmitri exchanged a look full of dialogue. Their eyes darted around as, no doubt, they spoke within the confines of their own minds. After a moment, Victoria laughed.

"He just woke up; I hadn't told him yet."

"Love, perhaps you'll allow me? Could let me get back in good standing with him, don't you think?"

She nodded. "Of course. I'll wait outside. Shep, we'll see each other again soon. I'm sure Anathea will be happy to see you now if you'd care to visit her. You're on her select list of all-access researchers."

With a wink to him and another kiss to Dmitri, she turned toward the exit.

"Victoria, wait!" Shep called. At the door, she paused and turned. "So, the world was never going to end?"

"End?" She giggled. "No, dear Sheppard. In fact, that's not what the prophecy said at all. Common misconception. What it actually said is one reality will give way to another." Victoria exchanged a playful smile with Dmitri. "Shep, you're about to have living proof of just how true that is. Don't be long, darling. We have a lot of lost time to account for."

"Of course not, love. I'll be along directly."

As they were left alone, Shep wanted to leap up, grab the IV pole next to his bed, and impale Dmitri while the getting was good. If it hadn't been a dream, then the memory of what had happened to his Christine—and who had done it to her—was as real as it was raw.

"Come on, Shep, I'd port out before you'd ever get to your feet."

Realization dawned in him. "You're reading my mind?"

"Mmm-hmm."

"Without any trouble?"

Dmitri nodded. "Gate's open now. I can feed off the energy of Altunatus."

"And Victoria?"

"Yeah, Victoria the omnivore," he joked. "No more life force quelling for her, either. We both can pull our energy through the gate. That dark part of our existence is over. But that's not why I'm here, Shep."

"You're here to kill me."

The ridiculous conclusion brought an amused smile to Dmitri's face. "No, Shep. Like I just said, not killing anyone anymore. In fact, the opposite. I'm here to save someone. But first…"

Dmitri reached inside his jacket a pulled a small, leather-bound book, placing it in Shep's weary grasp. The letters on the front cover, inked in gold, were a bit of surprise.

"The Bible?" Shep asked. Dmitri nodded. "You never struck me as the evangelist type."

Dmitri continued, "One of my favorite passages from the Bible, Shep, is Genesis 2:21. I wonder, will you read it aloud?"

Perplexed, Shep didn't know what to do but to comply. *"And the LORD God caused a deep sleep to fall upon Adam, and he slept: and he took one of his ribs, and closed up the flesh instead thereof.* Yeah, he created woman. I remember it from catechism. What does that have to do with…any—"

Dmitri's hand came to rest on Shep's midriff, running over the bandaged area. "Ribs, it turns out, are where the DNA of our Bonds is the most concentrated. I know you, Shep. You're a scientist at heart; you'll want to know why. You'll want proof. I can't explain to you how it is that we can do all the things we can do. You're not ready for that yet. But as for proof, I hope you will accept my humble offering."

The last words were drowned out by the pounding of Shep's heart. Dmitri stepped away from the bed and drew back the curtain dividing Shep's bed from the one next to it.

Christine.

She was sleeping, but she looked just a beautiful as he remembered her. Just as perfect. Just as alive.

"Oh my God," Shep uttered.

"Ah, now you believe," Dmitri returned with a wink. "She won't remember her death, Shep. Isis thought it was best if she were to forget her tragic end. The question is, can you let it go and just accept her as she is?"

Tears were streaking down his cheeks. Was he kidding? He'd give up anything to have her here. Even more ribs, if that's what was asked of him.

In the moment, seeing Christine's chest slowly rise and fall with each breath, Shep found himself saying something he never thought he'd say to Dmitri Kronastia. "Thank you."

"Merry Christmas, Shep." Dmitri's arm stretched out, and he presented a hand. Shep took it as the Lord of the Afterlife said a simple goodbye and left the room.

Shep stared at Christine for hours, waiting for her to wake. When at last, near night, she did, her eyes fluttered open and took in the sight of him.

"Hey," she said meekly.

"Hey." What else was he supposed to say?

Christine winced as her hands went to her temples. "Man, I've such a headache. Feels like I've been hit by a Mac truck. What happened?"

"You were dead," Shep answered.

Her head whipped his direction. "Dead?"

"Don't worry, Osiris brought you back."

She gasped. "You know about Osiris?"

He nodded. "And Victoria, and Alex, and The Order. And the Bonding. Christine, I know it all."

She bit her lip and looked terrified at him. "Do you know why I was sent to you?" He nodded. "Are you…angry with me?"

"No, Christine. I don't care. That you're Bonded to Victoria Kent? It's nothing, babe. The only thing that matters is your bond to me. I'm bonded to you stronger than blood, stronger than life. I'm bonded to your heart, and I'll love you till the end of the world."

ACKNOWLEDGMENTS

Special thanks to Meredith. *Je suis reconnaisante pour tout ce que vous avez fait.*

In tribute to all the goddesses whose blessings and graces I have been privileged to receive: CJ, Suzanne, Irene, Susan, Mother Ann, The Wee, Sharri, Robin, Juanita, Denise, and Patricia.

In hope for the goddesses who follow: D1, D2, and E.B.

ABOUT THE AUTHOR

Killian McRae grew up in the rural Midwest, fostering a love for eclectic music, history, and literature. Her interest in writing began when she attempted to write her first book, a memoir, at age eight, but she's been playing pupil to many muses over the years. She holds a BA in Near Eastern History and claims that the contents of her iPod serve in lieu of a Masters of Musical Anthropology, spanning everything from Aboriginal tribal songs to ZZ Top. Killian currently lives with her family in the San Francisco Bay area, but dreams of moving to the East where she would own a dog, a cat, and a small coastal cottage, and would spend lots and lots of time devoted to her passion for writing historically laced fiction.